KILLING TRAIL

KILLING TRAIL

A Timber Creek K-9 Mystery

Margaret Mizushima

CROOKED
LANE

NEW YORK

Copyright © 2015 by Margaret Mizushima

Published in the United States by Crooked Lane Books, an imprint of The Quick Brown Fox & Company LLC.

Crooked Lane Books and its logo are trademarks of The Quick Brown Fox & Company LLC.

The Library of Congress Cataloging-in-Publication Data is available upon request.

ISBN (hardcover): 978-1-62953-381-0
ISBN (paperback): 978-1-62953-486-2
ISBN (ePub): 978-1-62953-382-7
ISBN (Kindle): 978-1-62953-656-9
ISBN (ePDF): 978-1-62953-667-5

Cover design by Jennifer Canzone
Book design by Jennifer Canzone

Printed in the United States.

www.crookedlanebooks.com

Crooked Lane Books
2 Park Avenue, 10th Floor
New York, NY 10016

First Edition: December 2015

10 9 8 7 6 5 4 3 2 1

To my family,
who always believed

Chapter 1

Friday, Late August

Deputy Mattie Lu Cobb liked her new partner. In fact, she was quite taken with him. She enjoyed being with him, something she'd found lacking with previous partners, and they seemed compatible. She hoped she could learn to trust him.

She wondered what trust would feel like.

Pulling her cruiser up to a stop sign, Mattie stole a quick glance. Born in Russia, he was a handsome guy: straight black hair, intense brown eyes, and white teeth that flashed when he grinned. Large and muscular, strong and rugged, he was the only one in the department who could outrun her in a cross-country foot race.

In addition to all that, he could sniff out a missing person.

He was Timber Creek County's new police service dog, a German shepherd named Robo. Together, Mattie and Robo made up the first K-9 unit ever mobilized in the small town of Timber Creek, Colorado.

Mattie turned right onto Main Street and accelerated, heading toward the town's only high school. Timber Creek High sat at the end of the nine blocks that made up Main, its backside nestled against the edge of a hogback called Smokers' Hill by students past and present. She was supposed to meet with Sheriff McCoy and John Brennaman, the school principal, to discuss setting up a K-9 inspection program for the school.

Thinking about the meeting stirred up a swirl of dread that churned in her gut. Her meetings with Mr. Brennaman during her junior year of high school had been decidedly unpleasant. Would he remember her?

She resisted checking her appearance in the rearview mirror. Usually, she didn't care much about her looks. Her skin, hair, and eyes could be summed up with brown, brown, and brown. And usually, she didn't care that her square chin made her look stubborn and belligerent. Both were true. Today she'd taken time to style her short, wispy hair so that it softened her features somewhat, and she hoped to send a message to Mr. Brennaman that she'd grown up and was now a different person.

She looked over at Robo. He panted and yawned, his tongue forming a pink curl.

"Whatcha think about how we look?"

Deepening his yawn, Robo's throat squeaked.

"Yeah, I agree. Who cares?"

As she drove, Mattie scanned the streets and sidewalk out of habit. She cruised slowly past Crane's Market, its stucco walls the color of Pepto-Bismol.

"So Robo, you're going to school, huh?"

Facing front with his ears pricked, Robo stood on the gray-carpeted platform that replaced the back seat of the Ford Taurus. He looked much more excited than Mattie would ever be about school. But that was Robo. He was one of those dogs that K-9 officers referred to as a high-drive alpha male. It didn't take much to get him excited.

She couldn't believe how her life had changed. When drug traffic in the national forest had threatened Timber Creek, local merchants and ranchers had purchased a patrol dog for the sheriff's department. And Mattie had won the assignment of being Robo's handler by beating her colleagues in a cross-country endurance test. The twelve weeks she'd spent at K-9 Academy were among the best weeks of her life. She'd loved everything about it—learning how to work with and care for the dogs, mixing with the other handlers, learning from the trainers.

Static erupted from the cruiser's radio, followed by the dispatcher's voice: "K-9 One, copy."

Mattie noted her position. She was approaching the Water Hole Bar and Grill. She picked up the transmitter and pressed it on. "Fifth Street and Main. Go ahead."

Rainbow Anderson, the daughter of two hippies who'd settled in Timber Creek sometime during the sixties and the county's improbable dispatcher, responded. "K-9 One, we need you to respond to a ten-eighty-eight in progress. Well . . . it's not in progress this very minute, but . . . well, I guess you would call this a ten-eighty-eight that already happened. Over."

"What suspicious activity? Where? Just say it, Rainbow."

"Up Ute Canyon Road about ten miles. A forest ranger called in a request to investigate suspicious activity and a blood spill."

A blood spill? Hunting out of season? "I'm en route to Timber Creek High School to meet with Sheriff McCoy. What's my priority?"

"Oh, the meeting's canceled. Sorry I didn't call you, but I didn't know you were going, too. Sheriff McCoy is heading up the canyon now."

"Okay."

"Go, code two, up Ute Canyon Road. Ten miles from Ute Canyon turnoff, look for a two-track that veers left and leads to an old hunting cabin."

Mattie signaled a right turn so she could head for the highway. The sheriff obviously thought this could be something important.

"Copy. Show me en route to Ute Canyon. Over."

Code two meant normal response without emergency lights and siren, but she quickly brought the cruiser up to speed. Sheriff McCoy might want her to search for evidence. If so, the sooner she got there, the better, before any of her fellow deputies could unwittingly contaminate the crime scene.

The dread she'd been feeling all morning changed to excitement. This would be her first K-9 assignment since the academy, and she couldn't wait to get started.

Robo huffed a quick bark. In the rearview mirror, Mattie saw him wag his tail and shift from side to side on his front paws.

He must have caught hold of my mood.

"You know you're going to work, don't you?"

Robo whined, licked the air, and stared out the windshield. At the academy, he'd outperformed all the other dogs. The few times he'd screwed up, it had been her fault, doing things like not paying close enough attention to his body language or not trusting his instincts. It seemed like she needed training more than Robo. Nervousness tightened her shoulders. The others would be watching. That put pressure on a dog—not to mention the handler—and it could be distracting.

The cruiser ate up the miles, and they reached the turnoff to Ute Canyon Road in no time. Leaving the smooth highway behind, she turned onto a hard-packed dirt road covered with loose gravel. It led upward into a canyon that cut through the mountains. She slowed for sharp curves, holding the steering wheel steady as the cruiser rattled over rough areas ribbed with washboard.

Willow and mountain juniper gave way to forests of towering pine: ponderosa with their sweeping boughs and great stands of stately lodgepole. She rolled down the front windows so she could take in the soothing forest scent to help settle her nerves.

Robo pushed forward to sniff, thrusting his nose through the heavy wire mesh that separated his compartment from the rest of the vehicle. He bobbed his head, obviously getting a nose full. She could tell from the satisfied look on his face that Robo enjoyed the scent of the forest as much as she did.

Mattie kept checking the odometer while Ute Canyon climbed ever upward. Five miles into the canyon, huge potholes threatened to swallow a wheel entirely. She steered around them, keeping to the middle of the road when she could. Leaving the canyon floor, the road clung to the side of the mountain and rose toward the peaks. Its edge, where there was rarely any guardrail, dropped off in a fifty-foot plunge.

By the time the odometer indicated she'd driven nine miles from the turnoff, the road narrowed to little more than one lane. She started up a steep rise, keeping watch for a two-track road that would veer off to the left. She hoped she hadn't missed it.

At the top of the rise, she could see dense evergreen forest that stretched for miles and miles in an undulating mountain panorama. A hundred yards farther, she spotted the two-track winding away through the trees.

"There it is, Robo. I think we've found it."

Robo waved his tail but kept his eyes on the view outside the windshield.

Mattie slowed to creep forward as she directed the cruiser off the road and down into the ditch to access the two-track. When the roadbed scraped the bottom of the car, they lurched sideways, sending Robo skidding across his platform, though he remained on his feet.

"Sorry about that."

Again, Robo went to the window and sniffed.

After a couple minutes of rough driving, Mattie spotted the sheriff's Jeep and another cruiser parked in front of an old cabin. She'd found the right place. Slowly, she bumped over the rocks in the track and pulled up beside the Jeep.

Sheriff McCoy stepped out of the cabin onto a plank porch, followed by a woman wearing a forest ranger's uniform. Abraham McCoy was a big man, built solid as a tree trunk, with massive shoulders and a thick neck. He had skin the color of a Hershey bar, dark walnut eyes, and a bushy black mustache. He'd grown up in Timber Creek and attended the town high school, just like Mattie, but about fifteen years ahead of her.

Rumor had it that McCoy could have gone to any number of universities on a football scholarship, but he'd chosen to commute to a local junior college instead so he could help his mother care for his ailing father and younger siblings. He'd been a deputy for years before the county electorate voted him in as sheriff.

The first time Mattie met McCoy, she'd been a six-year-old kid, scared to death. Her world and family had just been shattered. He was a young deputy. She could still remember the sad look on his face as he picked her up and carried her to his patrol car. For a moment, she'd felt safe, enfolded in his arms against his solid chest. For one moment.

She switched off the cruiser's engine. Getting out of the vehicle, she told Robo, "You're going to wait here."

He protested with a short yip.

In return, Mattie gave him a look that apparently quelled any further urges to kick up a fuss. She walked toward McCoy, meeting him halfway between her car and the cabin.

He introduced the ranger. "This is Sandy Benson of the US Forest Service. She called us up here."

Benson gave Mattie a firm handshake. She was a strongly built woman, muscular, a little taller than Mattie's average height. A broad-brimmed ranger's hat sheltered her auburn hair and fair skin. Her hazel eyes held a look of concern.

"I was telling the sheriff that I saw a pickup truck and dog trailer up here last week. I stopped to talk to the guy, and he said he was doing some search and rescue training with his dogs. Seemed different, him being up here alone. Usually people train in groups. But he didn't seem to be breaking any laws, so I left him to it. When I passed by here this morning, I noticed the same rig."

McCoy added a detail. "You say that was about eight fifteen this morning."

Benson nodded. "I went up Old Flowers Trail to clear some deadfall. About an hour later, I heard a shot coming from this direction. I started down the trail to check it out. On my way, I heard another shot. By the time I got back here, the rig was gone. I decided to take a look and found a large blood stain on the porch." She shrugged, spreading a hand out front. "I had no idea what to think, but with the narcotics problems we've been having around here lately, I thought I'd better call you guys."

Coming from inside the cabin, Chief Deputy Ken Brody joined them. Tall, athletic, and built like a wedge, Brody had been Mattie's biggest challenge in the cross-country test to determine Robo's new handler. In fact, Mattie knew he could have whipped her butt if they'd been running on a track. But Brody's center of gravity had been too high to maintain his speed going downhill. Mattie was built lower to the ground with decently muscled hips and powerful legs. It gave her an edge over the other runners.

Brody took an aggressive stance, straightening his back, squaring his shoulders, and tucking his thumbs into his belt, his right hand cupping his holstered handgun. He narrowed his eyes, ice blue beneath black brows, and stared at Mattie.

She straightened her shoulders and stared back, looking away only when McCoy spoke.

"Ranger Benson recorded the license plate number on the vehicle last week. We tried to run the plate, but we can't connect to the Internet up here."

"There's nothing inside the cabin," Brody said. "Floor's been swept, no footprints. Seems strange for it to be so clean."

"Yes, that's odd. Somebody trying to hide something?" McCoy said. "Poaching deer out of season?"

Brody dipped his head in a barely perceptible nod, one of Brody's macho moves that Mattie imagined he practiced in a mirror. "Maybe."

"I thought that might be a possibility," Benson said, "but it seems strange for the blood to be up on the porch like that. I doubt if an animal would get shot and bleed out up there."

Ed Johnson, a rookie who'd joined the department while Mattie was at the academy, came from around the cabin, eyes to the ground. Still in orientation, he'd been riding patrol with Brody. Built like a runner, tall and slender, he had sandy hair and a face full of freckles.

"Find anything out back?" McCoy asked him.

Johnson walked up to join them. "No, nothing but dog tracks."

"Any trash? Items left behind?" Mattie asked.

"No."

McCoy turned to Mattie. "I want you to take your dog and see if you can detect anything we've missed."

"Do you have something in mind specifically?"

Brody spoke, his voice soft, his words slowly paced as though he were addressing someone of limited intelligence. "If we did, we wouldn't need the dog to look for it, now would we?"

Mattie didn't bother to reply. It had to have been Brody's seniority that had landed him the chief deputy position; she couldn't imagine his personality ever winning him anything.

McCoy didn't acknowledge Brody's comment either. "I'd like you to search for anything that could help me decide which direction to go with this. Do we have a crime here or not? Is there any detection of narcotics?"

"I'll get on it."

As Mattie walked back to her vehicle, she saw Robo dancing and grinning in the back. She knew how he felt, and when she reached the car door, she could show all her excitement and more. It was part of the job.

"Come on, big guy. It's time to go to work." Mattie used a higher pitched voice, something she'd been taught that would rev up his prey drive and get him ready to search. "Do you want to go to work, Robo? Do ya?"

She opened the door and Robo bailed out. He pranced around at her feet, tail waving and eyes watching her every move. He followed her to the trunk of the car.

"Let's get out your things."

Though it probably wasn't necessary, she kept up a running patter while she unpacked their equipment. Already, Robo could barely contain himself. His trainer had used techniques involving reward and play to train him, and this, combined with a shepherd's natural instinct to assist humans, made Robo love his job. Although he still received rewards to reinforce certain skills, she could tell that the work itself was probably all the reward he needed.

Mattie paused for a moment to walk Robo over to some bushes. "Take a break," she told him, her signal for him to relieve himself. Nothing slowed the momentum of a search like an unplanned potty stop.

She placed Robo's water bowl on the ground, and he slurped a few times. Moisture enhanced a dog's sense of smell. Robo stood still while she put a blue nylon tracking harness on him and exchanged his everyday collar for one that he wore specifically for evidence detection. She clipped a short, blue leash to the active ring.

His work collar in place, Robo's attitude switched from happy-go-lucky to all business. It happened every time, but the abrupt change still amazed Mattie. He stood at attention, ears forward, watching her prepare.

Typically she dressed in a khaki coverall with an arm patch bearing the county emblem. Today, for the meeting at the high school, she'd dressed in her best uniform. Not ideal, but it couldn't be helped, and she decided not to give it a second thought. She strapped on a utility belt bearing several loops and pouches, all packed with her own equipment: a whistle, water and energy food, a compass, a portable radio, a small first aid kit, short strips of blaze-orange flagging tape to mark trails or evidence, and most importantly, a tennis ball for Robo to play with at the end of a successful exercise or mission.

Mattie tied an eighteen-inch strip of orange flagging tape to her wrist. It fluttered lightly, telling her that a mild breeze came from the south, across the face of the hill they were standing on, the same direction from which they'd come. She needed to start her evidence search downwind, north of the area in front of the cabin, so she wouldn't contaminate the crime scene herself. She led Robo past the group of men who were still standing near the porch.

"Go to it, Cobb," Brody said as she passed.

His words could've been construed as encouragement, but Mattie knew him better than that. She'd worked with him for seven years, ever since she'd been a rookie herself. Brody tried to appear friendly at times, but she'd learned never to trust it. She ignored him, along with the quiver that rattled her belly.

Once she reached the spot where she wanted to start, she knelt beside Robo, forced back her stage fright, and focused on her dog. She ruffled the thick, silky fur around his neck.

"Are you ready to work, Robo? Are you ready to find something?"

He gazed into her eyes, and the world faded away. Mattie knew he wouldn't let her down. He knew what to do, and so did she.

She unhooked the leash from the active ring on his collar and transferred it to the dead ring so that she wouldn't inadvertently give him an obedience signal. Standing, she gestured toward the ground in front of him and gave the command specifically used for evidence detection: "Seek."

She expected Robo to put his nose down and start working a grid. They'd done it before in training.

But he didn't.

Robo raised his head, sniffed the breeze, and then turned to stare at her, his body rigid, his ears pricked.

Mattie's heart rose to her throat. Was Robo refusing her command? Dismay immobilized her for a few seconds.

"Good dog you got there, Cobb."

"Back off, Brody," Sheriff McCoy said. He nodded at Mattie. "Take your time, Deputy."

She started to reissue the seek command, but swallowed the word when comprehension hit her. Robo wasn't being disobedient. He was showing her a full alert.

But a full alert for what? Drugs? Something in the forest?

Should she force him to walk the grid like she'd intended, and he could indicate what he'd found when they came to it?

Robo must have known what she was thinking. He walked to the end of his leash and looked south, upwind into the forest. He turned to look at her, his posture stiff and ears forward, his eyes drilling into hers.

Now what the hell do I do? Lead or follow?

Chapter 2

During training at the academy, Mattie had experienced an exercise that taught her a valuable lesson.

She and Robo were supposed to practice finding a missing person. Robo's trainer, Jim Matson, a retired police sergeant who trained police service dogs, set up a track for Robo to follow. Jim left the area and headed east, downwind on a heavily forested slope. Mattie and Robo waited an hour for Jim to get well away and hidden.

When the time came for Mattie to start Robo on the trail, she put him in his tracking harness, gave him some water, and let him sniff the scent article. Robo immediately turned toward the west and tried to lead her in the direction opposite the one Jim had taken. Mattie corrected Robo, forcing him back to the initial track. Robo tried to go the wrong way again. They wrestled with "who's the boss?" for a few minutes until Robo gave up and took the eastward track, throwing her a disgusted "if you insist" look over his shoulder before putting his nose to the ground.

Halfway into the exercise, Mattie realized she'd made a mistake. Robo was leading her in a huge circle. After a mile and a half of tracking through rough terrain—over deadfall, through streams, around huge boulders—Robo led Mattie to Jim. She knew her face was flushed with embarrassment as well as heat from the trek.

They found Jim sitting on a boulder about one hundred yards from the starting point, shaking his head. Earlier, he'd circled around and positioned himself upwind. Through a pair of binoculars, he'd watched the entire fiasco from the start of the exercise. If Mattie had listened to Robo, who was catching Jim's scent through the air, they would have found him in only a few minutes.

Jim had said, "Now play with your dog and tell him he's a good boy. And tell him you're sorry you didn't listen to him. *Always listen to your dog.*"

Later, Mattie discovered that she'd been the only rookie handler set up with this exercise. Finally, by the end of her training, she got up the nerve to ask Jim why.

In his slow country drawl, he replied, "Deputy Cobb, you are a fine officer. But I can tell that you always want to control things. I can tell by the way you shine your boots every night, and I can tell by the way you try to manage this dog. This is one of the best dogs I ever trained. If you don't learn to trust him, you'll never be any better than a human cop can be. But if you learn to listen to him and trust that he knows what he's doing, you two can be the best damn K-9 team in the country."

Mattie vowed she would do better.

Always listen to your dog.

Mattie heard Jim Matson's words as if he were standing beside her. The back of her neck tingled. She glanced at Sheriff McCoy. "He's alerting to something in the woods."

"Probably a deer," Brody muttered.

For an instant, the comment threw her. Could it be true?

But Robo's unblinking gaze continued to bore into her, erasing her doubt. She walked up to him, leaned forward, and unsnapped the leash from his collar.

A more experienced handler might send Robo into the woods off lead, but she didn't yet trust their relationship enough for that. From a loop on her utility belt, she took a thirty-foot-long leash and attached it to the ring on Robo's tracking harness.

"Okay, Robo," she said, "we'll do it your way."

Not knowing what they were after, she decided to use the tracking command. "Search."

Robo bolted toward the edge of the woods. The thirty-foot lead whipped through her fingers, making them sting. She grabbed onto the end and followed, knowing she'd have to run like hell to keep up.

Rabbit brush and felled timber marked the edge of the clearing. Robo hit it at a dead run, coming to the end of his lead at the same time. Mattie sprinted after him, giving Robo enough slack to keep moving forward.

"Good boy. Search."

Robo darted between two pine trees, entered the forest, and headed downhill. Mattie swept through the boughs, eyes to the ground, jumping over ankle-turning stones, stepping carefully between tufts of buffalo grass and scattered granite rocks. Each footfall jarred as she charged over the rough terrain. Still, she wasn't fast enough to keep up with her dog.

Robo slowed to accommodate her pace. His ears shifted forward and back, monitoring the environment up ahead and then checking on Mattie's progress behind. As they continued downhill, weaving between trees and around boulders,

Mattie heard the crack of tree branches and the thud of some-one running behind her. At least one of her colleagues was following, but she didn't dare take her eyes off the rugged terrain to check.

Within minutes, Mattie reached that familiar physical place where her body warmed and her breath came and went in rapid cycles. She knew she could maintain this pace forever—well, at least an hour or so—if she had to. The noise behind her fell away, and she kept going.

Robo lifted his head, nose to the breeze, and she knew he was trailing the scent through the air. Whatever he'd found, they would come upon it suddenly, since there was little vis-ibility. The forest had become dense, and there were no worn pathways to speak of. Dried branches scratched her arms; pine needles pricked her face and hands. Once again, the thought of Robo chasing a wild animal began to tickle her insecurities.

She was thirty feet behind Robo now, the full length of the leash, and occasionally she lost sight of him as he charged around thickets of squaw currant bushes or prickly rose. After a few minutes, they reached the bottom of the hill and lev-eled out into a dry creek bed. Without pause, Robo surged across it and up the steep bank on the other side with a half-dozen leaps.

As Mattie scrambled up the hill behind him, her leather boot sole slipped and she fell to one knee, cracking it against a sharp rock. She sucked in a breath. "Shit!"

Robo paused and looked back at her over his shoulder. She could swear he had one eyebrow arched as if asking, "What?"

"It's okay," she said, rubbing her sore knee as she got up. "Go on. Search."

Moving on with a limp, Mattie could feel warm blood trickle down her shin. Robo slowed his pace for her, staying close as he continued. In the back of her mind, she plotted their course, realizing they had charged downhill parallel to the road she'd driven up. Now they seemed to be heading up the next slope, still parallel to the road. She began to wonder if Robo had scented something when he'd sniffed outside the vehicle's window on their way up the mountain.

Despite the pain in her knee, Mattie quickened her pace. Robo responded by moving ahead to the end of his lead. Although it felt like much farther, Mattie gauged they'd covered about a mile since leaving the cabin. Once again, they headed downhill.

Disappearing from sight, Robo entered a thick stand of juniper surrounded by scrub brush. Mattie heard a deep growl, followed by a snarling bark.

Robo's lead went slack.

He'd come to an abrupt halt inside the thicket, out of sight. Stories she'd heard about dogs tracking armed criminals and leading their handlers directly into an ambush made every hair rise on the back of her neck.

Reaching for her Glock 9mm with one hand and holding onto Robo's leash with the other, Mattie hit the ground and rolled to shelter behind the trunk of a large ponderosa. She sat with her back to the rough bark, her heart pounding.

She rose to her knees, hugging the tree trunk. She knew only one thing for certain: she wanted her dog beside her. But if he'd engaged a bad guy, she might endanger Robo's life by calling him off. He'd been trained to bite and hold an arm bearing a weapon. Releasing that arm could free up the weapon to be turned against him. Careful not to expose herself too much, she peered around the tree trunk and tried to get a visual on her dog.

He was trotting out from among the junipers, a happy grin on his face.

To her amazement, he came right up and bumped his nose against the pouch that held his tennis ball, his reward for successfully completing a find. He sat down at her feet, an expectant look on his face, tail waving, ready to play.

She grabbed Robo's harness and hauled him in close, trying to shield him with the tree trunk while keeping herself hidden. "Stay," she told him.

What the hell? She tried to size up the situation. Robo must have found something in the thicket. But what?

A dope stash, maybe, but that was unlikely. Dope was usually wrapped up tight against the elements, which impeded scent release. Not a person with a gun either. If someone was armed or threatening, Robo would have engaged him. An unarmed human, then?

She looked at Robo, wishing he could speak. He met her gaze without waver. He looked alert now, his playfulness set aside. She supposed he'd noticed that she'd drawn her weapon and had decided his work was not done after all.

Still worried about ambush, Mattie peered around the tree trunk, her handgun ready. "Police! Throw out your weapon!"

From inside the thicket came a deep, menacing growl followed by a ferocious bark.

Christ! There's another dog inside there.

Robo had trailed another dog. And if that dog was all alone, unaccompanied by a human, there'd been a serious breach in his training. He'd been trained to track humans and to ignore other dogs.

From somewhere behind her, Mattie heard the crack of rocks colliding and branches breaking. The others must have crested the hill and were now headed down toward her, probably at a distance of about half a football field. But the trees were too dense for her to see them.

She assumed the one closest would be Brody. "Brody! Hold up. Take cover."

"What've you got?"

"Unidentified party hidden in some juniper."

"We've got your back."

At least now, the person in the thicket knew he had more than one cop to deal with. But on the down side, if she and Robo had failed, they now had a witness.

She pushed on. "Throw out your weapon and show yourself, or I'll send in the dog!"

Robo stood up. With ears pricked forward, he leaned around Mattie's legs to stare at the stand of juniper.

Mattie knew the threat of a dog usually put the fear of God into the heart of a fugitive. If someone was in there hiding, that ought to bring him out.

Teeth bared, a huge black dog charged a few feet out of the thicket, uttering a deep-pitched growl. Suddenly, it whined and dropped down to a crouch. When it turned to slink back into the bush, Mattie could see its haunches were covered with dirty, matted fur. It had revealed itself for only a few seconds, but long enough for Mattie to recognize it as a Bernese mountain dog. And it appeared injured.

"Great, Cobb. Your dog found another dog."

Mattie glanced behind her and saw Brody about twenty feet back, partially shielded by another large pine. He had drawn his weapon and was holding it down beside his leg.

"I'm going in with Robo," Mattie told him. "Cover us."

She unsnapped Robo's lead. She didn't want it hampering his ability to move. "Robo, show me what you found. Show me!"

Robo sprang up and darted into the scrub oak. Staying low to the ground, Mattie crashed in close behind him, weapon pointed straight ahead. Growling and snarling filled the thicket.

In the middle of the stand was a small space, relatively clear. Once inside, she could see that the Bernese had been digging. Mounds of dark earth were piled between Mattie and the dog. Robo lay at the base of the nearest mound, teeth bare and growling. The Bernese stood in a depression on the other side, hackles raised and snarling, filtered light glinting off great white teeth. It looked as if the Bernese might attack Robo at any moment.

No humans present. Heart sinking, Mattie tried to diffuse the dogs' standoff. Robo was already in a down position, the position he used to indicate his find. She stayed motionless and spoke to the other dog, hoping to soothe it.

"It's okay. It's okay."

The Bernese stopped snarling. Anxiously, it shifted its gaze from Robo to Mattie and then back. Clearly, the dog seemed most threatened by Robo. She knew that if she called him out of his crouch, the Bernese might attack; a single move on Robo's part could start a full-blown dogfight.

"Robo, quiet."

The growl rumbling in Robo's chest ceased.

The Bernese wore a red nylon collar with tags dangling at its chest. The tag on top bore white letters with the dog's name. Mattie could just make it out: Belle.

"Belle, down."

The Bernese threw another worried glance toward Robo but hunkered down, peering over the mound of dirt to watch Mattie.

This dog was obviously guarding something. Mattie tried to see over the dirt mound.

"This is interesting," Brody said with sarcasm, making his way through the juniper.

McCoy materialized through the brush off to the side, his breath heaving in noisy gusts. "What is it?"

Johnson followed Brody, sucking air, sweat gleaming on his freckled cheeks.

"Stay still," Mattie told the others. "Let me get a leash on this dog." She knew Robo wouldn't budge until she released him. Edging up to the Bernese, Mattie spoke in a soothing tone. "It's okay, Belle. Stay. Good girl."

Belle whined once. Head lowered, she peered up at Mattie, white rims showing at the base of brown eyes.

With relief, Mattie saw that the dog had decided to submit. She holstered her weapon and reached for the short leash stored in her utility belt. With slow, deliberate movements, she approached the dog. "Good girl. Let me help you."

As she moved to the other side of the dirt mound and snapped the leash onto Belle's collar, she discovered what the dog had been guarding. It snatched her breath away.

Belle had uncovered the head, chest, and arms of a girl, her waxy face smudged with mud where the dog had licked it. Dark hair, pert nose, and a bloodstained shirt. Dead.

"What is it, Deputy?"

Mattie faced McCoy. "We've got a body."

Chapter 3

As Timber Creek's one and only veterinarian, Cole Walker had endured many a sleepless night, but none had exhausted him as thoroughly as the last. And this time, he had nothing to show for it. No recovering animal, no grateful client. All he had was a manila envelope from yesterday's mail, his final divorce papers stuffed inside. They'd haunted him throughout the night.

The struggle to change Olivia's mind was now officially over. No more mulling over what he should've done, what he should've said. It was over. She'd left for Denver three months ago, moved in with her old college roommate, and filed for divorce. Said she needed to "find herself."

Cole hadn't even known she was lost.

Now, after working the longest day of his life, Cole's limbs were heavy with fatigue. He shuffled over to the gray mare he was treating for colic. She stood quietly in the stocks, used to hold horses so they wouldn't hurt themselves or the people trying to care for them. Her eyelids drooped from the analgesic he'd administered earlier, and Cole thought she looked as worn out and dejected as he felt.

He'd already passed a tube into her stomach to inject about a half gallon of mineral oil, and he'd inserted an IV into the mare's jugular vein. Now he was pushing fluids through the IV, trying to rehydrate the colicky horse.

Feeling as if he was moving in slow motion, Cole put on his stethoscope and leaned forward to place it over the mare's heart. He rested against the side of the stocks, the metal rail cold against his face, while he listened to the rapid thump in her chest. He counted the beats. Around seventy per minute, indicating severe pain . . . but still, improvement over a half hour ago.

Tess Murphy, his assistant, stuck her head through the doorway to his clinic. She'd arrived at work that morning with some kind of goo in her red hair, making it stick out every which way. Just another of the experiments she always seemed to have going on with her hair.

"Sheriff's office called," she said. "They're sending in a dog with a gunshot wound."

Cole sighed. Would this day never end? "When?"

"Not sure, but within the next half hour."

"Get the clippers, and set up for surgery."

"Already done. But I have to leave now."

"So soon?"

"Remember, I told you this morning. I have to pick up my boys early. The sitter has a doctor's appointment."

"Oh, yes." Cole couldn't remember anything about it, but he'd be the first to admit he'd been preoccupied all day. "Forward the office phone to my cell then."

Tess turned to go back inside.

Cole stopped her. "What time is it?"

"Almost four."

"Would you do me a favor on your way out?"

"Sure."

"Leave a note at the house for my sister. She's bringing the girls home today, and I doubt I'll finish before they get there. Tell her to come here to the clinic when they get in."

"Sure, I'll tape the note to the front door."

After Tess left, Cole used the stethoscope to listen to the mare's belly. Quiet. He'd hoped to hear some bowel sounds, a gurgle indicating the mare's gut had started moving again, but there was nothing. Resting one hand on the mare's warm back, Cole leaned against the stocks and let his eyes close for a minute. A dull ache throbbed behind his eye sockets. Needing a distraction, he walked over to the counter that ran down one side of the room and turned on the radio, already set on his favorite country and western station. Kenny Rogers crooned a song about his wife Lucille leaving him.

Cole switched it off.

Turning over a bucket, he sat down on it so he could keep an eye on the mare while he waited for the wounded dog. The gray appeared comfortable at the moment, her eyes closed, her lips hanging loose from the analgesic.

Should he tell his daughters about the divorce being final when they got home? He supposed there would be no reason to get into it tonight, but he knew he'd have to tell them sometime.

It had been hard on the kids all summer. It seemed like their mother was divorcing them, too, since she didn't want to see any of them. Liv had checked out of their lives the end of May and hadn't checked back in once. Cole snorted a short derisive sound. *Try explaining that to two daughters who love their mom.*

And since his plan to bring Liv back to them had failed, what would he do with them now? Who would keep track of them while he worked? And now that school was about to start, he couldn't keep shipping them off to Denver to stay with his sister. He supposed Angela could take care of herself at fifteen, but Sophie was only eight, too young to be left alone all day. And when it came right down to it, he wasn't sure he wanted Angela left to her own means all day, either. School started next week, but that only took care of part of the day. It wasn't unusual for Cole to start work well before eight in the morning and finish up well after eight at night.

Hearing gravel crunch in front of the clinic, Cole hauled himself off the bucket and walked over to the window. He saw his sister's car parked out front, so he went back to the mare to make sure her lead rope was tied securely to the front of the metal stanchion. She was still under the effect of the drugs and wouldn't be going anywhere soon. Satisfied that all was safe for the moment, he hastened through the clinic's back door and toward the lobby.

Jessie had been a lifesaver, keeping the girls with her most of the summer. But he missed them when they were gone. He missed Liv. Hell, he missed everything about his old life.

"Dad-dy!" Sophie's girlish voice lilted. She came running into the lobby, colliding with Cole's legs as he braced himself. Sophie was built like a small halfback, short and stout.

Cole bent down and picked her up, hugging her solid body against his chest. "Sophie! You've grown a foot," he said, leaning back to look down into her face.

Sophie's amber eyes danced, a grin bunching her freckled cheeks. Her dark curls were gathered back and held with a silky red scarf, no doubt a souvenir from Jessie's wardrobe.

"Aunt Jessie said maybe we could go eat at Clucken House. Can we, Dad? Can we?" Sophie paused for a breath.

"Hold on a minute, squirt. Let me give your Aunt Jessie and your sister a hug." Cole met Jessie's hazel eyes over Sophie's shoulder. It never failed to amaze him how well his kid sister had turned out, her hair styled and highlighted and her designer clothes immaculate. Letting Sophie slide to the ground, he continued to hold her with one arm while he reached to give his sister a quick hug. "How was your trip?"

"Just fine. The girls were eager to get home." Jessie slipped an arm around Angela's waist, drawing her forward from where she'd been hanging back.

Cole swept an observant gaze over his oldest. Fifteen-year-old Angela wore her typical aloof expression, but when he smiled at her, she returned it. With her pale-blond, shoulder-length hair; smooth white skin; and eyes the color of cornflowers, Angela was the image of her mother. The resemblance struck Cole harder than usual, leaving him with an empty feeling around his solar plexus.

"Hey, Angel," Cole said, using the childhood nickname he'd given Angela years ago. "Can I have a hug?"

"Hi, Dad." She stepped forward without hesitation, reaching up to encircle Cole's neck with her arms. She even gave his cheek a quick kiss, showing that she must be in a good mood. When she'd left a week ago, she hadn't been nearly so friendly. In fact, she'd been moody all summer. Not surprising, but certainly a challenge to deal with.

Cole drew a deep breath and gazed around the group. "To answer your question, Sophie, yes, you can go to Clucken House for dinner tonight."

"Yay!" Sophie jumped in excitement. Then she sobered. "Did Mom call while we were gone?"

"No, Sophie-bug. I haven't heard from her."

Sophie's eyes filled, and her face worked to keep from crying. "Oh, okay."

Her resignation hurt Cole as much, if not more, than her tears could.

Damn it, Liv, didn't you think about your children before you decided to leave?

"I tell you what," he said. "I have to wait for a hurt dog to come into the clinic, but why don't you guys go ahead and eat?" He reached for his wallet. "Here, Angela, you take some money with you to treat your Aunt Jessie. I'll come there when I can. I just don't know how long I'll have to wait for this dog."

Angela leveled her cool, blue gaze at him, and Jessie gave him a frown. He realized he'd said something wrong.

"We just got here, Dad," Angela said.

"I'm not trying to get rid of you, Angel. I just thought you must be hungry." He turned to Sophie and drew a red bandanna from his pocket to wipe the tears that had trickled down her cheeks.

"Come on, squirt, don't be sad. If you're not too hungry, could you stay here and visit with me for a little while?"

Sophie sniffed. "Yes."

Cole sat down in one of the lobby chairs, taking Sophie onto his lap. "What did you girls do this week?"

"I took them into the office a couple times to rearrange files," Jessie said. "I needed to move the old ones out to storage. Angela took over and completely restructured my system."

Cole met his daughter's eyes. "Way to go, Ange."

A smile of satisfaction softened her face. "It was Aunt Jessie's idea."

Jessie said, "But you carried it out. I could've never done all that by myself."

"Did I help?" Sophie said, the plaintive tone coming back into her voice.

"You sure did," Jessie said.

"Yeah, right," Angela countered, spoiling everything.

"That's not nice," Sophie whined.

"The truth hurts."

A muscle tensed in Cole's jaw, leaving a sore spot.

"I'm starved," Jessie chimed in. "I could eat a whole steer, but I'll settle for a Clucken burger."

Cole threw her a grateful look.

Angela rolled her eyes. "You and Dad always eat hamburgers at Clucken House. How can you go there without eating chicken?"

"Oh, I don't know," Jessie said. "We were raised on beef, I guess."

"Beef. It's what's for dinner," Cole said, wiggling his eyebrows at his daughters.

Angela didn't miss a beat. "Beef. It's what clogs your arteries."

Cole clapped a hand over his heart. "Angel . . . say it ain't so."

Smiling now, Sophie bounced off his lap and headed toward the door. "I'm having a hamburger, too. Just like Aunt Jessie and Daddy."

Cole walked them out to the car, opening doors on the passenger side for his daughters, getting Angela settled in front and Sophie in back. When he finished, Jessie signaled to meet her by the trunk. In a hushed voice, she said, "Cole, you look like hell. What's going on?"

It was easy to tell that Jessie made her living as an attorney; it had taken her very little time to pin him down.

Cole spoke in the same low tone. "We'll have to talk later, after the girls have gone to bed. Do you think you could stay here tonight instead of going out to Mom's?"

Jessie gave him a probing look. "All right. I'll call and tell her something."

He watched Jessie and the kids drive away before going back to check on the horse. She looked about the same. He listened to her heartbeat, noting the rate had increased. Removing the stethoscope's earpieces, he straightened and observed her for a moment.

She wasn't out of the woods yet.

The mare stood as she had before, gray head resting against the front bar of the stocks, eyelids lowered, lips slack. When he pressed and released the pink membrane of her gums, it blanched and stayed white for too long, indicating poor capillary infusion. The mare was going into shock.

Apparently, his treatment had supported her for a short time, restored her fluids and diminished her pain, but it hadn't solved the problem. He'd known this was more than a simple colic and now he suspected a torsion.

He reached for the bottle of analgesic, inserted the needle, and pulled ten cc's into the syringe. Grasping the buffalo cap at the end of the IV tubing, he jabbed the needle through it to deliver the pain medication into the mare's bloodstream. He hoped he could make her more comfortable.

After rolling open the double door at the back of the room, Cole released the stocks and untied the mare. He made a clicking sound with his tongue, and she backed out, her shod hooves scraping against the concrete floor. He decided to put her in one of the runs under the shed, so that if she died, he'd be able to get a tractor in to move her body out for the knacker man to come haul away.

He needed to take a moment to call the mare's owner and give him a progress report. If he waited any longer, there might not be anything positive to say. And now that he thought about it, there weren't a whole lot of positive things he could say about his own life right now either.

Chapter 4

After calling the mare's owner, Cole began to clean up the equine treatment room. Soon he heard a car pull up in front of the clinic. Glancing out the window, he saw a silver-and-blue patrol car marked Timber Creek County Sheriff parked out front, parallel to the building, offering him full view of the driver's side.

He watched as a female deputy opened her door and stepped out, a grimace crossing her face as she straightened. When she moved to close the door, Cole could see that she must have injured her right leg. Her khaki trousers were torn and bloody at the knee, and she was walking with a limp. In general, she looked a bit worse for wear, brown hair tossed, face scratched, clothing smeared with dirt.

A black-and-tan German shepherd, mouth hanging open in a pant, rode in the back part of the vehicle. At first, Cole thought this was his patient. But the woman went around to the passenger side to open the front door, and when she came back around front, Cole could see that she was leading a Bernese mountain dog.

The deputy and the Bernese both limped toward the clinic's front door. Cole went inside to meet them.

After passing through the exam room, Cole found the deputy waiting in the lobby with the dog sitting quietly at her feet, a stoic expression on its face. The woman was bent forward, scratching the dog behind its ears.

Cole recognized the Bernese immediately. "What have we got here?"

The deputy looked up, showing Cole a set of intense brown eyes framed by dark lashes. "I'm Deputy Mattie Cobb and this is Belle. She's been shot."

"Belle belongs to my daughter's friend. I know her very well."

A strange mix of surprise followed by relief crossed the deputy's face. "I noticed your clinic name on her rabies tag. I was hoping you could tell us who her owner is."

"I can do that. It's Grace Hartman. She rarely goes anywhere without this dog." Cole extended his hand. "Pleased to meet you, by the way."

The woman's handshake was as firm as her jaw.

"Let's bring her into the exam room," he said, holding the door open.

Cole offered his hand to Belle for a sniff and then placed it on her head. He leaned down to take a look at her hip, matted with blood and dirt. "How in the world did you get yourself shot, Belle? What have you been up to?"

"Grace is how old?"

"Just turned sixteen this summer."

"And what does she look like?"

"Dark hair that's usually in a ponytail." Cole brushed the bridge of his nose. "Little ski-jump nose with a sprinkling of freckles."

The deputy wore a grim expression. "Who are Grace's parents?"

"Garrett and Leslie Hartman. They live on a ranch out west of town." Cole had a thought. "Wait a minute. Is Grace in some kind of trouble?"

"No, nothing like that. Excuse me for a minute. I need to go outside to make a phone call." She started for the door.

Cole spoke, making her pause. "My assistant had to leave, so I'll need your help holding Belle."

"I'll be right back." She removed her cell phone from her pocket as she went through the door.

Cole plugged the hair clippers into the wall socket and reached for a muzzle made from nylon straps. While he waited for the deputy to return, he stroked Belle lightly on the head. She looked up at him with woebegone eyes. "Who shot you, girl?"

He didn't have to wait long. The deputy was as good as her word and returned within a few minutes.

"I'll have to clean her up before I can tell what we've got," Cole told her.

He slipped the muzzle in place over the dog's nose and secured it while the deputy held her by the collar. Belle offered no resistance whatsoever, and he leaned down to pick her up. "Let's get you up on the table where I can take a look at you."

The deputy assisted by clasping Belle under the stomach and lifting her hips. Belle struggled for a moment, and her nails screeched against the stainless steel tabletop until she settled, her huge paws gripping the slick metal. Cobb pulled Belle in close to her chest.

Shaving away the matted hair, Cole spoke above the noise of the clipper. "Has anyone notified the Hartmans that Belle's been shot?"

Deputy Cobb looked up from the dog and stared at him with eyes that Cole thought probably didn't miss much. "The sheriff is taking care of that now."

Cole bent over Belle's furry rump and the clipper whirred as he guided it over her skin, leaving a clear path of closely cropped hair in its wake. Soon, he found the bullet's entry, a small hole where blood had coagulated, located in the meaty part of her leg between her hip and stifle. He shaved carefully around its edges and then turned off the clipper.

Gently, he examined Belle's leg, raising it to check the inner part of the thigh. Belle whimpered, and Deputy Cobb murmured something in a soothing way, rubbing the brown patch of fur at Belle's cheek.

"I can't find an exit wound," Cole said. "The bullet's still in her leg. I'll have to take an x-ray to find out where it is. She's going to need surgery. Do you know if she's had anything to eat or drink today?"

There was a furrow of worry on Deputy Cobb's forehead. "I gave her some water before I brought her in. I don't know about food."

Cole smoothed the fur on the dog's back and placed his stethoscope to listen to her heart sounds. He was reassured by the steady thump. "I'll keep her overnight and take out the bullet in the morning. I have to run some blood work to make sure she's healthy enough to handle the anesthesia, but I expect she'll do fine."

"Someone from the police department needs to be here when you take out that bullet. We'll need it for evidence."

Cole gave her a skeptical smile. "You plan to prosecute someone for shooting a dog in Timber Creek County? It's a pretty common offense around here."

"It shouldn't be. And yes, I plan to."

Cole admired her determination. "Can I call you in the morning and set up a time? I'll have to arrange for my assistant to come in, and she doesn't usually work on Saturdays."

"Yes. I'll give you my cell number before I leave. Call the station if you can't reach me. I also need to talk to you sometime about taking care of Robo, our new police dog. We just got back from training a couple weeks ago, and his vet care's up to date, so I hadn't gotten around to it yet. I have his records at home."

"Is that the shepherd in the back of your car?"

"Yes."

"Can you bring his records with you when you come in the morning?"

"Yes, sir."

Cole wished she wouldn't call him sir. Made him feel like an old man. Besides, he couldn't be much older than she was. He was only thirty-seven, for Pete's sake. Not ancient by anyone's standards.

"I'll give her something for pain and start her on antibiotics."

That done, they lifted Belle down off the table, and she sat on the floor, stoic and quiet. Cole removed the muzzle, leaned over, and patted her on the side. "I'll take her to the kennel room. Come on, Belle. Let's get you comfortable."

The deputy followed him into the kennel area and watched while he put Belle in one of the large, chain-link dog runs. He put in a cushion-type dog bed for her to use.

Belle stood inside the run, head and tail drooping. She gazed out at the deputy, her eyes pleading not to be left behind. Deputy Cobb's face took on a tortured look. Cole tried to reassure her. "She's always been strong and healthy. She'll be fine. I'll call Garrett and tell him about her condition."

She frowned slightly. "I'm sure that Sheriff McCoy will tell him that Belle's safe here with you. I imagine right now they're trying to figure out how this thing happened."

"All right. Garrett will call me when he has time. If not, I'll give him a ring in the morning. My daughters just got home from Denver, and I need to join them now for dinner anyway."

"Sounds like a good plan." Deputy Cobb reached into her pocket and extracted a business card. "I'll leave you my cell phone number on the back of my card."

"You know how to reach me, right? After hours, the office forwards to my cell phone."

She nodded, reached through the wire mesh to trace a finger along Belle's cheek. Belle licked her hand. The deputy squared her shoulders and straightened.

As Cole followed her to the door, he noticed she still favored her right leg. "Would you like an ice pack?"

She turned with a frown. "What?"

"For your knee. I can see that you hurt it."

She glanced down at her knee as if she hadn't noticed it before and shook her head. "No, thanks. It's nothing."

Cole watched her go out to the patrol car, saw the joyous greeting the shepherd gave her as she opened the door and settled behind the wheel. She turned to grasp the big dog by the scruff of the neck, giving it a playful shake. Cole wondered if there wasn't some softness beneath that tough girl exterior.

Chapter 5

After Mattie left the vet's office, she drove to the station, her mind going back to the scene at the shallow gravesite. Dark hair worn in a ponytail, little ski-jump nose with a sprinkling of freckles—matched the girl's description. She'd also worn rings on most of her fingers; only the ring finger on her left hand had been bare.

She'd called Sheriff McCoy as soon as she learned who owned Belle, and he would take care of having the parents identify the girl's body. Then someone would have to notify Dr. Walker of her death, and that was going to be hard. He'd mentioned that his daughter and the victim were friends, and he appeared to know her well. Mattie sighed, thinking about the pain this would bring to the family. But it couldn't be helped, and she planned to set up an interview with the vet's daughter as soon as possible.

When she and Robo entered the station, Brody stepped out of the chief deputy's office. Neither of them wasted time on pleasantries.

"You're running on overtime, Cobb. You need to get your paperwork done ASAP and get out of here."

"Affirmative. Have you heard from the sheriff? Has he identified the body yet?"

"Haven't heard, but I ran the plate. It's registered to Mike Chadron."

"I know Mike," Mattie said. "He has a Bernese mountain dog kennel, breeds and trains show dogs."

"Yeah. Do you know him well?"

"No. He went to high school here, but several years behind me. Has anyone talked to him yet?"

"I drove out to his place," he said. "He's not there. Truck's gone. Looks like all his dogs are gone. I poked around a little bit out back by the kennels. No barking. Maybe he went somewhere to a dog show."

"Yeah, but why would he have been up there in the mountains this morning with his dogs? That doesn't connect."

"Maybe not, but we're not gonna solve it by standing around here talking. I'll check back early tomorrow morning to see if he's come home."

"Okay."

Mattie went to the staff office and cleared her paperwork as quickly as possible.

The office wasn't air-conditioned and it had been a warm day. Robo had gone to his dog bed by the wall and was now lying on his back, belly exposed, snoring.

She smiled. "Hey, Robo, you ready to go home?"

At the sound of his name, he rolled off his back and got up on his feet in one smooth motion. Haunches raised, he lowered his shoulders, stretched, and yawned. He followed her out to the patrol car.

Nothing left to do except pick up a knucklebone at Crane's Market for Robo. Once there, she decided to pick up a few staples for the woman who'd been her foster-mother. Though Mama T was aging, she still had a houseful of foster kids, and bringing food was one way that Mattie could help.

Mama T's house had been her last foster home in a long string of placements that had started when she was six. While Mattie loaded packages of hamburger and cheese, gallons of milk, and a variety of vegetables into her cart, she remembered how Mama T introduced herself to new foster kids.

"My name is Teresa, but you can call me Mama T." She would add with a wink, "The name Mother Teresa has already been taken."

Mama T dished up love with her cooking: green chili, homemade tortillas, fry bread. While Mattie had learned to love the intense flavors of the Mexican food Mama prepared in her kitchen, she'd never picked up the knack of cooking it herself.

It was only a few blocks to Mama T's place, and the streets were quiet this time of day, when families were inside preparing for dinner. She parked in front of the house, a single-story clapboard painted smoke blue with a white trim. Mama T's yard was pristine, her grass clipped, small plaster chipmunks scattered about frozen in midscamper, pansies with their happy faces blooming in the flower beds. It was the only place Mattie had ever lived that she could think of as home.

Mattie told Robo to wait in the car before gathering up the bags of groceries and skirting around the side of the house to enter through the kitchen door. The aromas that filled the warm room were as wonderful as she'd imagined. To Mattie, chili powder, cumin, and chili peppers spelled comfort with a capital *C*.

Mama T stood at the stove stirring something that smelled delightful on the old-fashioned, wood-burning stove that she still used. Short and plump, Mama T wore her long black hair, shot with gray, pulled back in a tight bun at her nape. Wearing an old sleeveless housedress that had once been red but was now a faded pink, she turned to greet Mattie. Her smile was warm in her brown, weathered face, though it showed a couple gaps where front teeth were missing. She put down her long-handled spoon and opened her arms.

Mattie set the groceries on the table, and stooping slightly, she allowed herself to be taken in by Mama T's embrace. *Yes*, she thought, *this is home.*

"*Mijita*, you are too good to bring us food," Mama said, releasing Mattie and turning back to the stove.

The endearment, "my little daughter," made Mattie's heart swell. She smiled and started to put away the groceries. "It's nothing."

"You say that, but if you saw the way these kids eat. Only horses eat more!"

"Oh, I've seen them. I used to be one of them, remember?"

The smile Mama T gave her brought back memories of many times shared in this kitchen.

"Will you stay with us tonight for dinner?"

After finding the body of a teenage girl, Mattie craved the quiet solitude of her own place. "Sorry, I can't. It's been a long day, and I've got Robo in the car. I need to take him home and feed him."

"I'll send some green chili pork home with you, then."

The aroma coming from the pot made Mattie's mouth water. She realized she hadn't eaten since breakfast. "I'd love some."

Mama T ladled up some of the thick soup, sealed it into a plastic container, and then packed several homemade corn tortillas in aluminum foil. She placed the food in a paper bag, gave Mattie a kiss on the cheek, and sent her on her way.

Once home, Mattie showered and changed into denim shorts and a black tee. The shower refreshed her, but her knee still throbbed. A bright-red strawberry with purple bruising colored her kneecap.

She grabbed a beer out of the ancient refrigerator that sat hunched in her kitchen like a little old person with rounded shoulders. She twisted off the bottle cap and put the beer to her lips, welcoming the tang. The first swallow tasted so good that she had to keep herself from chugging it. She'd allow only one tonight. Not like before.

Gathering up her bag of food, a pen, and her training journal, Mattie stepped out onto her back porch, a concrete slab attached to the small adobe house she rented on the west edge of town. State Highway 12 divided Timber Creek into two halves. On the east side, well-manicured lawns spread in front of modern houses, each with a freshly painted fence, colorful flower beds, and a shiny car parked in the driveway. On the west, adobe houses were small, built eighty to a hundred years ago, and had barely any lawns to speak of, let alone shiny cars.

Mattie sat down on the concrete step and stretched her sore leg out in front of her. In the backyard, Robo was gnawing on the knucklebone she'd bought for him on the way home. He lay stretched out among tufts of buffalo grass and weeds that she kept whacked down with an old push mower the landlord supplied. Six-foot chain link surrounded her small backyard, provided by Timber Creek County in anticipation of Robo's arrival. A huge blue spruce towered in the corner, casting a long shadow in the early evening light. Yucca, agave, and cholla—the only plants that Mattie set out in a "flower bed"—lined the back part of the fence.

Mattie liked prickly things; they suited her.

She ate her meal, savoring the spicy chili and dipping the soft corn tortillas in its broth. She thought of Grace Hartman, her parents, and what this young girl's death would mean for the community. Was her death an accident? Had the killer panicked and tried to cover it up? Or had someone killed the girl on purpose—and if so, why?

When she finished eating, she uncapped her pen and focused on what she should record in her training journal, one of a K-9 officer's most important tools. By recording a police dog's successes and problems, as well as training methods to remedy problems, a handler enhanced the dog's credibility in court when it came to submitting evidence that the dog found.

And today Robo had certainly scored a number one success. Mattie was so proud of him that it was difficult to know what to write in her log. She knew she needed to be objective, but to her, Robo's performance was nothing short of miraculous. After all, he hadn't even been trained in cadaver work. It was amazing he'd found a body like that.

After recording some notes, she sat for a moment savoring her beer and watching Robo enjoy his bone. Their bond was growing, and today she'd crossed a bridge in her ability to trust her partner. She hoped this success would be the first among many.

Her cell phone rang and she pulled it from her pocket, noting the caller and connecting at once. "Deputy Cobb."

"It's Sheriff McCoy, Deputy. Our victim is Grace Hartman. Her parents identified the body." He paused for a moment. "This is important, and we need to handle this investigation by the book. I posted Deputy Garcia up there to guard the crime scene, and he'll stay through the night. I'm calling in a detective and a crime scene unit from Byers County. They'll arrive early tomorrow morning. I've set up a meeting at seven o'clock and I want you to be there."

"Yes, sir. The vet told me that his daughter is one of the girl's friends. We need to notify him as soon as possible and set up an interview with her."

"Agreed. Do you want me to do it, or can you handle that?"

Mattie hated even the idea of it. "I can do it."

"All right, you're authorized to tell him about the death. Give him as few details as possible, but I know Cole Walker, and he's a man who can keep things confidential. Tell him we'll call in the morning and set up an appointment for his daughter to talk with the detective. At least one of her parents should be with her for the interview."

"Yes, sir."

"You did a great job today, Deputy. If it wasn't for our K-9 unit, this girl's body might have never been found."

"Thank you, sir. I'm glad we were in place to do it."

Mattie ended the call. Glancing at the time, she decided to wait another half hour to let Dr. Walker enjoy time with his daughters before she called and destroyed his evening.

Chapter 6

Cole hurried to finish up at the clinic so he could join his family at Clucken House, but when he started to drive past his home, he saw that they'd already returned. The divorce and when to tell the kids still weighed on him, but he struggled to keep his game face on while he ate the burger they'd brought home for him. Soon, he glanced at the clock and, with more than a little relief, suggested that the girls watch television for a while before bed.

Sophie reacted to the idea of bedtime with sadness, something Cole had grown used to over the summer.

"Who's going to read me a story?" she asked, her voice quavering.

Cole looked at Jessie, who gazed back at him, saying nothing. "I have to check on two sick animals," he said.

Jessie gave him an intense *we'll-talk-later* glare and then turned to Sophie with a cheerful smile that Cole thought looked slightly forced. "I'll read you a story, honey. Just like we did at my house."

Glad to leave his children in his sister's capable hands, Cole climbed into his pickup truck and drove away from the two-story log home that he and Liv had designed together. Liv had decorated it with a western motif—heavy leather furniture,

Navaho rugs, western art—and made it a comfortable place to return to at night. Without her, it felt awfully empty. A dull ache filled his chest.

At the clinic, he turned on the lights in the shed and made his way out to check the mare. She was down. He paused outside her pen, watching her roll onto her side and grind her head against the hard-packed dirt floor. Discouraged, he opened the gate and moved toward her, murmuring softly, trying to soothe her with his voice. Sweat darkened her gray coat, and when he listened to her heart, it was racing in rapid, uneven beats.

He needed to recommend they put her down. She wasn't going to make it much longer, and it was cruel to let her suffer.

With boots dragging against the concrete pad outside the building, Cole unlocked the clinic door to let himself in. Immediately, a terrible stench assailed him. Flipping on the light switch, he went into the kennel room to find Belle lying in her run surrounded by viscous, liquid feces.

Cole was so tired that his thoughts were sluggish inside his head. Obviously, Belle was sick with diarrhea. But why? A bullet wouldn't cause this.

"Belle?"

She raised her head to look at him with dull eyes and then let her head flop back to the floor as if it were too heavy to hold up.

Approaching the kennel, he noticed several solid lumps amid the liquid mess, lumps that looked like small, white balloons. Puzzled, he turned to grab a pair of latex gloves. After putting them on, he entered the kennel and picked up one of the lumps. Sure enough, it was a balloon, and it contained something, a substance that felt solid between his fingers but shifted when he squeezed it, like sand or powder.

A possibility burst into his sluggish brain.

Stripping off one of his gloves, he reached into his pocket to pull out the deputy's business card. Then he reached for his cell phone.

★

When Mattie checked her caller ID, it read, "Wireless Caller," and gave an unfamiliar number. She answered the call anyway. "Deputy Cobb."

"This is Dr. Walker. Could you come to the clinic?"

"Is Belle all right?"

"She's pretty sick. There's something I need to show you."

"I can be there in about ten minutes."

She disconnected the call and glanced at Robo. He remained hunched over his bone.

While she put her things away, she wondered what to do with him. She'd accepted the responsibility of taking care of this valuable animal when she agreed to be his handler, and that meant keeping him safe and secure twenty-four hours each and every day. Taking him with her might expose him to Belle's illness. Much as she hated it, she was going to have to break up his bone fest and leave him locked up in the house.

She stepped out on the porch and called him.

Robo arched over his bone, pulling it close to his chest. Then he remained still, every muscle tensed, as he avoided eye contact.

Oh, Christ, now he's going to challenge me for the bone.

She stepped off the porch and approached him. "Leave it," she said in a firm voice.

Robo's eyes flicked her way, then off to the distance as he placed his chin on the bone.

"Robo, come," she commanded, pointing to a spot directly in front of her feet.

With a covetous glance at the bone, Robo forced himself away from it and slinked up to sit by her feet. Exhaling a sigh of relief, Mattie placed a hand on his collar to keep him from returning to the bone. "Good boy. Come with me."

Together they moved toward the house, Mattie proud that she'd won an important skirmish. Aggressive male dogs often challenged their handlers, and it was crucial to stay in charge.

Once inside, Mattie gave Robo one of the small Milk-Bones she kept handy in a bowl on the counter. Though he took it, he gave her a look that said he knew she'd taken him away from something better.

"You can chew your bone later. But now you're going to wait here while I go out for a little while."

Mattie checked his water bowl and, finding it full, grabbed the keys to her patrol car.

"You be good while I'm gone. I'll be back soon."

As she left, Robo watched with a hangdog expression that made her want to take him with her.

After turning onto the highway, she headed out of town. About a mile outside the city limits, she turned down the lane that led to the vet clinic.

As she drove past the log home that belonged to the vet, Mattie noticed that lights were on inside. She wondered about his family. She'd seen his wife around town, one of those gorgeous women who always looked perfect. She knew they had kids—she'd seen two girls with their mother—and she'd noticed the doctor before, too. With his walnut-colored hair and eyes and rugged good looks, he was hard to miss.

She'd also heard that the vet's wife had left him. It was amazing the things you picked up when you were having dinner at Clucken House.

She pulled up in front of the clinic, exited the patrol car, and went to the front door. Finding it unlocked, she let herself into the lobby.

"Come on in here," the vet called from the other room.

Going through the swinging door, Mattie saw Walker bending over Belle, who was prostrate upon the stainless steel exam table. Mattie's heart sank. "What's wrong with her?"

"She's had severe diarrhea, and she's dehydrated. I need to get her started on some fluids." Walker handed Mattie a green lab coat. "Wear this to protect your clothing. Could you help hold her while I put in an IV?"

"Sure." Mattie put on the lab coat and then reached to pick up Belle's foreleg. The dog's fur was matted and dirty . . . and she reeked. Seeing the beautiful animal in such a condition brought an ache to Mattie's chest. She stroked the white blaze on Belle's head with her free hand.

They worked together in silence while Walker shaved a patch of hair off the inside of Belle's leg. To Mattie, it was obvious the man was dead on his feet. His face was ashen, and circles of fatigue darkened the skin beneath his eyes as if drawn there with charcoal.

Walker circled his fingers around Belle's foreleg near the elbow joint and squeezed. "Hold it tightly," he said to Mattie. "Like this."

Taking a firm grip on Belle's leg with both hands, Mattie tried to hold it exactly like he'd shown her. When the vet poked the IV needle through Belle's skin, Mattie looked away, but her eyes drifted back in spite of herself. Blood dripped from the open end of the needle when he found the vein, and Walker quickly attached tubing and a bag of fluid.

"You can release now," he said as he taped the IV in place with long strips of white tape.

He moved over to the countertop behind him and picked up a plastic bag. Turning, he held it out for Mattie to see. "I found these in her kennel. She passed them through her bowel. They're evidently what made her so sick."

Inside the plastic bag were several items that Mattie recognized instantly. Balloons. And they were filled with something. Dope.

Feeling her jaw drop, Mattie raised her eyes to the doctor's face. "But how did someone get her to swallow it?"

"I've been thinking about that. A big, docile Bernese mountain dog like this? Someone probably choked it down her, past her tongue. Then they followed it with something good, meat or something, to make her swallow."

Mattie placed a hand on Belle's head, gazing down at the sweet dog. "Someone used you as a mule," she said, thinking aloud. The heartache she felt for Belle's plight turned quickly to anger. "Who could have done this to her?"

"Maybe the same person who shot her."

Mattie's mind raced. Taking these dope-filled balloons into consideration, the person who killed Grace had to be involved with transporting drugs. Mike Chadron? Did that explain why he and his dogs were missing?

Walker threw away the wrappers that had come off his supplies. "Thanks for helping me get the IV started. It'll take a while to drip. You're free to go if you want."

Mattie decided now was as good a time as any to give him the bad news about Grace, even though he looked too tired to handle it. "There's something I need to tell you first."

"What?"

"We found Grace Hartman's body this morning. In the same place we found Belle."

He looked dumbfounded, shook his head in denial. "That can't be. Are you sure?"

"Yes, her parents have identified her body."

His breath expelled as if he'd been punched. He looked around, found an exam stool, and sat down on it. "She just got her driver's license. Was it a car accident?"

Mattie shook her head and made a quick decision to share the manner of death. He and his daughter would need to know that much in order to set up an interview. "No, she was shot and then buried in the forest. Belle had uncovered her, and my patrol dog found them. We don't know yet if the shooting was accidental."

Walker's face blanched, and he sagged forward to place his head in his hands. "Good God," he murmured.

Mattie gave him a moment, thinking how she would phrase her next questions.

After a minute or two, he sat up and stared at her with red-rimmed eyes. "How are you going to find who killed her?"

"Do you know of anyone who might have wanted to hurt her?"

"Of course not. She's just a kid."

Mattie gestured toward the bag of dope. "Someone put these balloons inside Belle. Could it have been Grace?"

"No way! This dog was her baby. There's no way she would've force-fed Belle."

"Could Grace have been involved with the drug traffic we've been having through the national forests?"

Walker stood, his hand clenched. "No. Don't even go that way. Grace was a good kid, a smart kid. She's an honors student, for Pete's sake."

Mattie tried not to let her skepticism show. There were plenty of honors students across the nation who intellectualized themselves into trouble with the police every day.

"We'll need to talk with your daughter. The one you said was friends with Grace."

He looked startled. "But she doesn't even know yet."

"I know you'll need to tell her first, prepare her. But we still need to talk to her sometime in the morning. Maybe late morning?"

"I don't know."

"Your daughter could have information about Grace that we need to know. It's important."

He looked down at the floor, and she could see he was thinking it through. She hoped he'd get past his knee-jerk, protective response. Finally, he nodded. "We'll set something up. Call me in the morning."

"Do you happen to know if Belle came out of Mike Chadron's kennel?"

"Yes, she did. Garrett bought the dog as a pup from Mike and gave her to Grace last summer."

"What do you know about Mike? Does he take good care of his dogs?"

"Mike seems like a responsible guy. Keeps health records on his dogs, takes them to dog shows. Appears affectionate toward his animals." Walker paused. "Why do you ask? I don't think Mike has anything to do with Belle, other than being the one who sold her to the Hartmans."

The information matched what Mattie knew about Mike. Because of the dog kennel, she knew more about him than most of the guys in town. He was in his early twenties, grew up in Timber Creek, and worked as a cook at Clucken House.

Thinking aloud, she said, "I wonder if he makes much money off the dog kennel."

Walker frowned. "Mike wants to make a living off his kennel and quit his job at the restaurant. Usually, he asks me to bill him and set up monthly payments for his dogs' care. But the last couple times he's been in, he's paid his bill in cash."

One thing related to the drug trade was cash, and lots of it. "Do you think Mike would use his dogs as mules?"

Walker shook his head. "I can't imagine it, but I guess anything's possible. Maybe to help pay his kennel expenses? I don't know. But what does this have to do with Grace?"

Mattie didn't feel she could tell him her reasoning yet. She looked back down at the sick dog. "What do we do for Belle now?"

"I need to x-ray her belly, see if there are any other foreign objects in it. I might as well x-ray her leg while I'm at it."

"I can stay for a few minutes and help. I know you have a lot to do here."

"I'd appreciate it if you'd give me a hand with the x-rays. Can you stay for a half hour?"

"Sure. Then I'd better take this evidence over to the office and get it locked away for the night."

Walker fell silent and looked grim as he set up his x-ray machine. His eyes burned as he handed Mattie a lead apron and mitts. "If someone shot one of my girls, I'd kill him."

She shared similar feelings. "We'll track this person down. It's just a matter of time."

He nodded, breathed a sigh, and focused his attention on positioning the x-ray machine above Belle. Mattie watched him, a dedicated father who wanted to protect his children from harm. So different from her own upbringing.

She decided she liked this person, a feeling that, when it came to men, she rarely allowed.

Chapter 7

Cole slipped the x-rays into the clip at the top of the light box, turned on the light switch, and stepped back to view the films. Deputy Cobb stood beside him, apparently as anxious as he to see what they would show.

The view of Belle's abdomen looked clean.

"See this?" Cole said, pointing out various anatomical landmarks. "Here's her stomach, intestines, and bowel. There's nothing more inside her."

"Good."

He turned his attention to the x-ray of Belle's leg. He pointed out a white spot adjacent to her femur. "There's the bullet, right there. It looks like it's lodged against her thigh bone, toward the inside."

"Will that be a problem to take out?"

"It could be. Lots of blood vessels and nerves there. The bone doesn't appear fractured. We're lucky about that. We'll have to see how she is in the morning. I'm guessing she may not be well enough for surgery. It may have to wait until the next day."

"Would that be hard on her?"

"She'd suffer less than she would if I used anesthesia on her in this condition. Besides, we don't know yet if she'll recover."

Concern filled the deputy's face, and Cole realized he'd been too blunt. "I bet she'll pull through. She's strong and healthy. Let's move her to the floor, and you can go if you want."

Together they lifted the heavy dog off the exam table.

"Will you be staying with her tonight?" the deputy asked.

"Yes, at least until I get this bag of fluid into her. Then I'll see how she looks."

"I can take a shift watching her tonight. I couldn't help but notice that you look pretty beat."

Cole drew a hand over his face. "You're right. I'm going on forty-eight hours without sleep. But you go. You've got your own work to do."

"After I run this dope over to the department, I could come back for a few hours. You could go to your house and get some rest."

Cole looked at Belle, still stretched out on the linoleum. It would take several hours to drip this IV bag of Ringer's. After that, there'd be nothing more he could do tonight. His body craved sleep, and his eyes were starting to blur. If he could lie down for a few hours, it would make a big difference.

"I'll take you up on it," he said. "Come back when you can, but wash up real well before you go. I don't want you taking anything to your own dog if this happens to be contagious. I think the diarrhea was caused by the foreign objects in her gut, but you need to take precautions just in case."

"Sure."

When she removed her lab coat, Cole noticed the angry bruise on her knee. "Did you put some ice on that knee?"

She glanced down at it as she went to the sink to wash. "No, but it'll be fine. I've had worse."

"Suit yourself," Cole said, annoyed. He left to go spray down the floor in Belle's run. *What is it with women? They never seem to listen to good advice.*

The deputy appeared in the doorway. "I'll be back in a half hour or so."

"The door will be open."

Cole finished up and returned to check on Belle. She raised her head to look at him when he entered the room. Though she didn't try to get up, he thought she looked better. Sliding down against the wall to sit on the floor beside her, he took out his stethoscope to listen to her lungs. Her breath sounds were good. He leaned his head back against the wall and closed his eyes.

The next thing he knew, someone was nudging his shoulder. Liv?

"Dr. Walker."

Cole forced open his eyes to find Deputy Cobb bending over him. Remembering that Grace was dead hit him hard in the chest. Blinking, he rubbed his eyes to clear away the mist that filled them. "I must've fallen asleep."

"Sheriff McCoy came to the station, so I was gone for about an hour. You can go home now and get some rest."

Cole cleared a lump from his throat. Picking up his stethoscope, he hauled himself up off the floor. When he knelt beside Belle, she raised her head and licked her lips as if to greet him. Placing a hand on her side, he listened to her heart, steady and even. Her lungs remained clear.

"I think she's going to make it," he told the deputy, watching relief cross her face. He patted Belle. "You're going to get a bath first thing when you're better."

Belle's tail beat once against the floor.

Cole glanced at the deputy. She was watching him, and his eyes held hers for a moment. Again, he had the sense that she observed people and her surroundings carefully with those dark eyes of hers, wary, as if unwilling to be taken by surprise. Grateful for her help, he offered her a smile that he knew would be tinged with his sorrow.

"I'll be back in a couple hours. You can call my cell phone if you have any concerns." He wrote the number on a pad held by a magnet on the refrigerator.

Deputy Cobb had already put on her lab coat and was settling down on the floor next to Belle.

"Call if you need me," he said on his way out.

Keeping firm control of his emotions and trying not to think too much, Cole went to the utility, stripped off his clothes, and stuffed them into the washing machine. He scrubbed his hands and arms and then put on a set of clean surgical greens. Walking out to the truck, his legs felt like lead. He was almost too tired to drive the few hundred yards to the house.

At home, lights were blazing from the great room windows. With dread, he realized that Jessie, and maybe even the kids, had waited up for him. He pressed the garage door opener and parked the truck inside. Then he let himself into the kitchen.

The overhead light snapped on, pinning him against the door.

"Cole!" Jessie snapped. "It's about time."

"Good Lord, Jess. Cut me some slack here. It's been a hard night."

Jessie looked at Cole hard and apparently tried to swallow her temper. "I've been waiting for you, and I'm getting tired."

"*You're* getting tired?"

Jessie's voice softened. "I know. You are, too." She glanced around the kitchen, apparently looking for a peace offering. "Want something to eat?"

"No. What I want is to lie down and sleep for an hour or so. There's a deputy sheriff up there watching that dog. I have to relieve her later, so she can go home sometime tonight."

As he spoke, Cole moved through the kitchen and into the great room, Jessie trailing behind. He crashed onto the brown leather sofa, slid down into the cushions, and leaned his head back. He stretched his legs out in front of him.

"What's going on, Cole? I can tell something's happened."

Cole drew a deep breath, releasing it slowly. His world seemed to be slipping away. And now his original concern about the divorce paled in comparison to the loss of Grace, a girl who'd been like a part of his family. A girl who would never have the opportunity to grow up. How could he tell Angela?

"Well, Jessie, I've had some bad news."

Jessie slid down in the chair across the coffee table from him. "What?"

"First off, I got my divorce papers yesterday."

A look of sympathy crossed her face. "That's hard. But you knew it was coming, Cole. And now you need to move on. You've got to find someone to come in and help with the girls. You shouldn't keep putting it off like you've been doing all summer."

"And I just learned that Angela's friend, Grace Hartman, died this morning."

A look of profound shock took over his sister's face. "My God, Cole! What happened?"

He shrugged. "She was shot."

"Someone shot her? On purpose?"

"I don't know yet. I suppose it could've been an accident, up in the mountains, some poacher. But whoever did it tried to cover it up."

Jessie sat in stunned silence.

"And now I've got to get some sleep, so I can think well enough to figure out how I'm going to tell Angie in the morning. Right now, I can't even imagine it."

"Okay. But you also have to decide what you're going to do about the kids, Cole. You can't keep going on in this limbo. Now that school's starting up, they won't be able to stay with me in Denver for weeks at a time."

Cole searched his sluggish mind for a plan. "How long can you stay?"

"I have to leave Sunday. I need to be in the office on Monday."

"Is this still Friday?"

"Just barely."

"I'll ask Mom to look after the girls this week. Then I'll start looking for someone to help out."

Jessie made an exasperated sound. "Sorry to burst your bubble, but that won't work. Mom didn't even enjoy raising us, you know, and Angela told me she won't stay out there anymore. I guess Mom does nothing but complain about Olivia. It's not good for the girls to be exposed to that."

Cole's head pounded. He closed his eyes, leaned sideways, and slid down onto the sofa. "I'll take care of it, Jessie. I'll think of something. I'll fix it."

"I'm willing to help, but you've got to decide which way you're going to go. I think you should advertise for help."

"Um-hmm," Cole agreed as he let himself slip into oblivion. The last thing he felt before dropping off to sleep was the weight of a soft, fleece throw as Jessie placed it over him.

After some indeterminate time, he struggled to pull himself back to consciousness. Someone was shaking him.

"Dad! Da-ad!"

His tired body jumped several inches, as if hit with an electric cattle prod. "What? What is it?"

Illuminated by dim light coming from upstairs, he could make out Angela, her face white and distorted by pain.

"I'm sick." She moaned, clutching her stomach. "My stomach hurts."

"Where's your mo—" Cole cut himself off before making a terrible mistake. "Where's your Aunt Jessie?"

"Cleaning the bathroom. I didn't make it to the toi—" Angela retched, clapping her hand over her mouth.

Cole leapt into action, grasping Angela by the arm and steering her out of the great room to the kitchen sink. "Here, Ange."

She clutched the edge of the sink and heaved. The sound and smell made Cole feel nauseous himself, but he held her gently and pulled back her hair. Once the spasm passed, he led her to a chair and then filled a glass with cold water from the tap.

Kneeling down beside Angela, he handed her the water. "Do you feel any better?"

Her hand trembled as she reached for the glass. Taking a sip, she shrugged. He noticed her face had a greenish tint. *Poor girl.*

Angela's stomach gurgled. "Oh, no . . ." she moaned. "I have to get to the bathroom." She took off, heading toward the one under the stairwell.

Cole followed at a slower pace, wondering what the hell had made Angie so sick. As he waited outside the bathroom door, Jessie came down the stairs carrying a mop and bucket, looking harried and not at all as cool as she had when they'd arrived from Denver.

"Has she been exposed to flu?" Cole asked.

"Not that I know of. I suppose she could have picked up something without my knowing, but this came on all of a sudden." Jessie paused. "What about food poisoning, Cole?"

He thought back to dinner. "She's the only one of us that ate chicken. I'd better call Dr. McGinnis and see what we should do. Can you wait here and see if she needs anything?"

"Of course."

Out in the kitchen, Cole found the list of emergency numbers Olivia had typed up and pinned next to the phone. After dialing, his call was answered on the second ring. He was surprised to hear the doctor's voice on the line.

"Dr. McGinnis here."

Cole identified himself and told the doctor why he was calling.

Dr. McGinnis replied, "I've lost track of how many calls I've had tonight. Don't tell me. Angela had dinner at Clucken House, right?"

"Yes, that's right."

"And she ate chicken."

"Yes."

"I suspect we've had an outbreak of salmonella. There's not much we can do for her except watch her for dehydration. Give her water or ginger ale or whatever clear fluid she can tolerate. This should pass in four to six hours. If she's not keeping something down by morning, better give me another call. Call sooner if she appears dehydrated or if her symptoms intensify."

Hanging up the phone, Cole felt miserable. Poor Angel. She'd probably never want to eat at Clucken House again. Even if she did, he knew he was never going to let her.

And after what happened to Grace, he might not let either of the kids out of the house again anyway.

Chapter 8

Saturday

Mattie danced to the rhythm of a slow country song. Her hips moved in a languid sway, pressed against those of a dark Latino whose face—oddly enough—looked exactly like the vet's. In one hand she held a cold bottle of Dos Equis with a slice of lime, while her other hand caressed the back of the man's neck. His dark gaze deepened, and she arched into him, tilting her head back.

Leaving a trail of soft kisses, his lips traveled down her neck. She closed her eyes.

"Who are you?" she whispered.

He licked her arm, one slurp, leaving a wet track on her forearm like the footprint of a garden slug.

Her eyes popped open and met Robo's, his muzzle inches from her face. He opened his mouth in a gentle pant. A bead of saliva dripped off his black lip.

Mattie groaned. "I can see that you must be hungry."

Robo started his happy dance, weight shifting back and forth on his front paws, nails clicking on the hardwood floor.

To protect herself from Robo's wet tongue, Mattie pulled the soft quilt that Mama T had made for her high school graduation up over her head. Soft strains of a country song on the radio faded as the announcer's voice broke in.

"It's five minutes after six on a beautiful Saturday morning . . ."

With a start, she raised her head to check the time.

After six? She'd slept through the alarm. No wonder Robo was trying to wake her. She threw back the quilt and sat up on the side of the bed.

"Okay. I'm getting up."

Mattie leaned forward, propping herself against her knees. It had been a short night. The vet hadn't come back to the clinic to relieve her until three fifteen in the morning. He'd said his daughter was sick.

Rubbing her eyes, Mattie peeked at Robo from between her fingers. By this time, he was beside himself.

"Go get your leash."

He darted from the room, returning moments later with the blue nylon strap dangling from both sides of his mouth.

Mattie got up, slipped on black running shorts and a gray tee with "Timber Creek County Sheriff Department" stenciled on the front, and sank back down on the bed to put on socks and running shoes. She was tempted to lie down and pull the quilt back up, but she knew Robo wouldn't let her. She clipped on his leash, led him through her small living room, and then opened the front door so they could step outside.

Taking in a deep breath of the brisk mountain air helped clear her head, and she thought of Grace. The teen would never enjoy a Colorado morning like this again. The sun had risen to sit above the tops of the eastern peaks, its slanted rays making colors vibrant. The tan clay road out front appeared orange, and the pink plastic geraniums her neighbor had set out in pots turned a deep rose. Saddened, Mattie leaned forward against the rough adobe wall of her house to stretch out her hamstrings.

"Okay, big fella, let's go." She took to the road, setting a brisk pace.

Robo ran beside her, his coat deep black in the morning light, his tongue rosy pink against his dark muzzle. He knew their route as well as she did but stayed in heel position rather than surging out front. Though nothing new, his obedience impressed her. The signal was tied to his equipment—everyday collar and leash meant heel, tracking harness meant out in front.

They hit the foothills at the edge of town and started up T-hill on a pathway worn smooth over the years by footsteps of children, hikers, and runners like herself. On the way up, she took turns with Robo, sometimes taking the smooth path while he dodged the rocks beside it and then letting him have the trail while she handled the more challenging footing.

The pathway ended when they reached the T near the top, a letter made from piled-up rocks whitewashed each fall by incoming high school freshmen. She left the trail and struck off for the summit, her body warmed by the effort of running uphill, her breath deep and even.

At the summit, she was surprised to meet another runner coming up the backside. It was the rookie, Ed Johnson. What the hell was he doing out here?

Johnson stopped in the opening between two rocky prominences, blocking the route Mattie intended to take. He looked winded. Bending forward at the waist, he braced himself with hands against thighs and puffed.

"Hey, Johnson," Mattie said. "What are you up to? Trying to kill yourself?"

He gave her a sheepish grin, freckles standing out against his pale skin. "If I'm going to be your backup, I figure I'd better get in shape."

His words took her by surprise. "I appreciate that."

"Besides, I might want some of that action myself someday."

"What action?"

"Being a K-9 cop."

Any warmth Mattie might have been feeling toward the kid melted away.

"I was hoping you'd teach me some things," he continued.

Not in this lifetime. "You have enough to learn with this being your first job. Most handlers spend several years on the force before they work K-9."

"I figured Timber Creek might be different, it being so small." He reached to pet Robo's head.

"Don't do that," Mattie snapped.

Johnson jerked back his hand.

"Okay, rookie. Your first lesson is to never touch a police dog without asking the handler's permission."

"Sorry."

Mattie glanced at her watch. "I need to finish my run." She edged past, keeping herself between him and Robo, and then started running again, down the hill's backside.

"Catch you later," Johnson called after her.

Robo glanced back, but Mattie merely raised one hand to acknowledge she'd heard him. Halfway down, she began to feel silly. Maybe she'd overreacted. *Geez*, she told herself, *no reason to act like such a bitch.*

★

At the office, Mattie opened the patrol car door and let Robo out. "Come with me," she said, and he trotted along beside her off lead. She had five minutes to spare before the meeting about Grace.

Inside, Rainbow was sitting at the dispatcher's desk. Since she wasn't required to be in uniform, she often wore flowing costumes made from gauzy fabrics with psychedelic colors. Today was no different, and she'd added a pink scarf tied with a floppy bow to hold back her long, blond hair. On anyone else, it might've looked ridiculous, but somehow Rainbow pulled it off.

"Good morning, Deputy." Her blue eyes twinkled. You could always count on Rainbow being twinkly in the morning.

"What's up?"

"I heard about you and Robo finding that girl yesterday." Rainbow sobered for a moment. "That's terrible. I mean, it's not terrible about you finding her. It's terrible about her being dead. I mean, killed."

"Yeah, it's bad."

"I canceled my party tonight."

Mattie had forgotten about Rainbow's party, since she'd never planned to go to it in the first place. She hated parties. Seemed like someone always showed up either drunk or high, and she felt responsible for doing something about it. "Okay."

"It didn't seem right, most of the sheriff's department partying after what happened to that poor girl."

"Yeah, I guess not."

"So I have all this food," her voice rising at the end as if asking a question. "And I can freeze some of it, but I don't know if the tofu cheesecake will freeze, so I'm just inviting a few friends over, and I hoped you would come. Anya Yamamoto from the hot springs will be there, and I want you to meet her."

"Gee, Rainbow, I don't know. I've got a full shift today, and I'm a little wiped out from helping out at the vet clinic last night. I think I'll have to pass. But thanks anyway."

"If you change your mind, just come on over. I have plenty of food, and feel free to bring Robo."

"So you know those hot springs people?"

"Yeah. Haven't you gone out there yet?"

"Not yet. But I thought I might drive out there when I have time and check things out." Mattie remembered a comment Brody had made a while back that the people out at the hot springs were a bunch of idiots, some kind of health freaks. But then, Brody was an idiot, so she hated to lend him too much credibility.

Still, drug traffic had started through Timber Creek shortly after the group's arrival.

"What are they doing out there, Rainbow?"

"They're building a world-class health spa."

"Uh-huh," Mattie said, doubtful that a world-class anything would take off in Timber Creek. "You got any messages for me before I go into briefing?"

"No. But come on over tonight if you have a chance. I think it would be fun to get to know you better."

Mattie searched Rainbow's face for a hidden agenda, but she wore a smile that was completely genuine. Mattie smiled back halfheartedly and then turned to go into the briefing room, Robo at her heels.

Brody and Johnson were already there, seated at one of the Formica-topped tables. Mattie took a seat at the far end of a different table, across the room from them.

"Lie down," she said to Robo in a quiet voice, pointing to the floor. He circled once and lay down next to her feet.

"Hey," Johnson greeted her.

Mattie nodded, picked up a flier that summarized the latest regional bulletins, and started to read. Sheriff McCoy entered the room soon after, shadowed by a petite woman with highlighted hair the color of dark honey and a knockout figure. With a gallant gesture, McCoy indicated a seat up front for the woman as he stepped to the podium.

"This is Detective Stella LoSasso from Byers County." McCoy gestured toward the woman. "She'll be handling this investigation. As I believe you may all know by now, our victim's name is Grace Hartman. Detective LoSasso will interview her parents later this morning. But first, Deputy Cobb, I want you to take her up to the crime scene, and you two go over it with a fine-tooth comb. Use the dog."

"Yes, sir," Mattie said.

Detective LoSasso turned and swept her with a searching gaze. Mattie nodded in acknowledgment while the detective lifted her head slightly. Mattie felt as if she'd been given the once over but had no idea if she'd passed inspection.

"I'll summarize what we know so far," McCoy said. "The dog that we found at the crime scene had eight balloons filled with cocaine in her belly."

"Wow," Johnson muttered.

Brody gave him a look meant to squelch further comments.

"The rig that Ranger Benson spotted up there belongs to Mike Chadron, and we've put out a BOLO for it," McCoy said. "Mr. Hartman told me last night that Grace was driving a dark red Honda CR-V, and I've put out a BOLO for that vehicle as well. I believe the car could be hidden somewhere in the mountains near the crime scene. Ranger Benson will organize a search for it. Deputy Brody, tell us what you found at Mike Chadron's place."

Brody cleared his throat. "Basically nothing. I went there last night and again this morning, but he's gone. His rig and his dogs are gone, too."

McCoy nodded. "I want you to put together a warrant request to search his place. See if you can get Judge Taylor to sign off on it this morning."

"All right," Brody said.

"Deputy Cobb found out last night that the veterinarian's daughter is one of our victim's friends." McCoy looked at Mattie. "Did you arrange a meeting to interview Dr. Walker's daughter?"

"I notified Dr. Walker of the death late last night. But his daughter got sick with food poisoning from eating at Clucken House during the night, so he doesn't plan to tell her until this morning."

"I heard about the outbreak," McCoy said.

"He's agreed to let us interview the girl after he's had a chance to tell her about her friend's death. I'm supposed to call later and set it up."

"All right. You and the detective can set up an appointment after you finish at the crime scene. Deputy Brody, you get to work on that warrant. Deputy Johnson, you take patrol." McCoy straightened and swept the group with piercing eyes. "Now let's get to work and bring this child killer to justice."

Chapter 9

Carrying her briefcase, Detective LoSasso rounded the patrol car and headed toward the passenger side. Mattie noticed that the men watched the attractive woman even while they walked over to their own vehicles. She hoped one of them would trip over his tongue.

LoSasso's civilian clothing, tight black slacks and a turquoise blouse nipped in at the waist, emphasized her hourglass figure. Mattie couldn't help but feel frumpy in her khaki uniform, a feeling that surprised her. Usually, she wouldn't even notice, much less bother to care.

She secured Robo in the back area of the cruiser and then took her place in the driver's seat, reaching for her patrol log to make a notation of the time.

"Are you the only woman in the department?" LoSasso asked as she found her seatbelt and pulled it across her lap.

Mattie looked at her, noticing that in the bright sunlight, the detective looked older than she'd originally thought. Lines were etched around her eyes and the corners of her mouth. LoSasso slipped on her sunglasses, brushing back a strand of highlighted hair that had fallen forward against her cheek.

"Rainbow Anderson, our dispatcher, is the only other woman that works weekends," Mattie said. "There are others who do office work during the week."

Detective LoSasso sniffed. "That bit of fluff doesn't really qualify. I meant, are you the only female deputy?"

Mattie resisted the urge to defend Rainbow. She thought LoSasso was acting like a snob, but after all, Rainbow did appear a bit fluffy today. Hell, Rainbow looked fluffy almost every day. Mattie turned the key and the car's engine roared to life. "Yes, I'm the only female deputy in the department."

"How long have you worked K-9?"

"About three weeks on the job. I just finished training. But I've been on the force more than seven years."

LoSasso pursed her salmon-colored lips, turning her face away to gaze out the windshield.

Mattie put the cruiser in reverse, backed out of her parking space, and steered the car toward the highway. It was going to be a long drive up the mountain.

After about ten minutes on the road, LoSasso broke the silence. "You didn't turn up any evidence when you did a grid search yesterday?"

Mattie gritted her teeth. "When I started the grid search, Robo alerted to the forest. That's when I let him trail the scent, and he turned up the body."

"Didn't you go back to the search?"

"We also turned up the dog. She was injured and needed a vet. So I took her." Even to her it sounded lame, a poor reason to abandon an evidence search. Mattie felt like kicking herself. The glory of Robo's discovering a dead victim had been erased by her own inability to stay on track.

"I see," LoSasso responded. "Shoddy detective work, Deputy. By now, your canine's nose could be useless at the crime scene."

Mattie hated to admit the woman might be right. "Maybe so. But we'll do a sweep anyway. Dope could've been hidden in or near the cabin. We'll see if we can turn something up."

LoSasso nodded.

"Mike Chadron, the man we were talking about at briefing, shows and sells the same breed of dog as the one we found at the gravesite. I found out last night that he sold that dog to our victim."

"Was our victim involved in drug traffic? Did she use her dog as a mule?"

"We don't know. The vet swears she wasn't that kind of kid."

"We'll follow up on that when we talk to the daughter."

Mattie nodded. Once again, silence deepened until they reached the turnoff to Ute Canyon Road.

"How far from here?" LoSasso asked.

"About ten miles, but it's slowgoing. Pretty rough."

"I realize in the hoopla of finding a body, you might lose track of what needs to be done next, but I think Sheriff McCoy should have done a better job."

Mattie wouldn't stand for that. "Working with a K-9 team is new to Sheriff McCoy. It was my responsibility to go back to the evidence search, not his."

"If anything was left at the crime scene, the perp's been back to get it by now."

"Sheriff McCoy left a deputy there to guard it overnight, until we could get a detective up there today."

"Aha. Good thinking."

Mattie gave her a sharp look at the note of sarcasm and then directed her attention back to the road, dodging potholes and steering carefully around hairpin turns.

"Well, it is what it is," LoSasso said. "We'll just have to wait and see what we can get."

Robo paced back and forth in the back, sniffing out the windows as the car lurched up the pitted road. By the time they reached the two-track that led to the cabin, he seemed as eager as Mattie to get out of the patrol car.

"Listen, I didn't mean to come on so hard about the handling of the crime scene," LoSasso said as they pulled up next to the yellow tape around the cabin. "It's just a pet peeve of mine: cops mismanaging the scene before I get a chance to do my work."

Switching off the car engine, Mattie turned to face LoSasso directly. "We agree on that. And I admit I may have bungled things, but I'm learning. I don't usually make the same mistake twice."

"Let's start over," LoSasso said, offering her hand. "I'm Detective Stella LoSasso. Call me Stella."

Mattie extended her hand as well, and the two women clasped hands firmly. "You can call me Mattie."

Stella removed her sunglasses and gave Mattie one of her measuring looks. "Let's go get a better look at the cabin."

Mattie opened her car door and got out, noticing that Robo was dancing side to side on his front feet, eager to follow. "You wait here," she told him.

Robo's perked ears fell, and his body slumped.

As Stella exited the vehicle, she wore a smile that transformed her face, and their eyes met over the roof of the car. "I didn't know dogs were so capable of pouting."

"He's full of it every time I put the kibosh on something he wants to do."

"How do you resist it?"

"It's easy. If I give in to him once, he'll test me for days. It's just better to be consistent with him."

"Must be challenging."

"The rewards are worth it."

They had come up next to the taped-off area, and Deputy Cy Garcia stepped out of his cruiser to meet them, moving stiffly as though he'd been sitting for a long time. He was of Hispanic descent and built like a fireplug. He usually worked the night shift.

"Things were quiet last night?" Mattie asked by way of greeting.

"Yeah, not a thing happened." He gave Stella a once-over.

She extended her hand. "Detective LoSasso."

"Cy Garcia." They shook hands, and he turned back to Mattie. "Are you here to relieve me?"

"Not exactly, but Sheriff McCoy said to tell you to go on home. We'll be here a while, and he'll come up later to determine if we can let the scene go."

"Okay then, I'll leave it to ya." He got back into his vehicle and left.

Stella turned to Mattie. "Do you want your dog to work this area before I go in?"

"Yes. I'd like to do a sweep of the cabin first. Then I'll have Robo do a grid search out here."

"Sounds like a plan. Maybe I'll just take a look around back while you're at it."

Robo was delighted to see Mattie coming back to the vehicle and greeted her with his usual exuberance. She prepared

for the search as she had the day before and led him around
the perimeter, ducking under the tape when she came to the
cabin. He stayed close to her left side as they stepped up onto
the plank porch and went inside the rough log building.

Mattie paused at the threshold to allow her eyes to adjust
to the dim light. "Sit," she told Robo quietly.

He sat at her left heel.

She looked around the cabin, taking in log walls smattered
with cobwebs, a plank table and chairs in the center of the
room, and a bare metal frame with wire support for a bedroll
against the far wall. She could see nothing that would endanger Robo, nor were there any suspicious-looking nooks and
crannies that might be hiding a stash.

She leaned down to pat him on the side. "Do you want to
go to work?"

He came to his feet, tail waving.

"Okay," she told him. "Find some dope."

Robo turned into a slinking, sniffing machine. With his
ears pinned back, he shifted his nose first to the floor and then
to the air as Mattie directed him around the edge of the room
in a clockwise sweep. She made him take his time, holding his
leash with her left hand while she directed the search area with
her right, first asking him to sniff low and then high. Without
any alerts, they made it back to their anchor point.

Then she directed him in a sweep of the center of the
room. Robo's ears shot forward as he approached the table.
Without warning, he leaped on top. To her relief, the table
wobbled but bore up under his weight. He sat down on top of
it, his indication that he'd found something. He looked at her
expectantly and opened his mouth in a pant, his pink tongue
drooping.

"Good boy," Mattie praised him, thumping his sides in a firm pat. She could see nothing but had no doubt that trace scent from the cocaine that had been bagged and forced down Belle's throat the day before lingered on the table. Had the rest of Mike's dogs gotten the same treatment? Was he using all the dogs as mules?

Had he killed Grace?

They finished up the room with no further alerts from Robo and then moved outside. She mentally marked out a grid on the ground in front of the cabin and asked Robo to search as she slowly led him back and forth. He quartered the area, sniffing from side to side. About halfway through, he stopped and nudged some dirt aside with his nose. He touched something with his mouth, sat, and looked at Mattie.

Her adrenalin surged. Robo had been taught to touch with his mouth—but not disturb—anything outside of the environmental norm when searching for evidence.

"Did you find something?"

There, in the dirt, lay a spent brass casing, its golden glint evident in the sunlight, upturned from the dusting of earth that had concealed it from human eyes.

Detective LoSasso came from around the cabin's corner just as Mattie was raising her eyes from the casing in disbelief.

"What?" Stella asked.

"Robo found a brass cartridge case."

A look of intensity filled Stella's face. "That's one hell of a dog you've got there, Deputy."

Chapter 10

Cole hit the speed dial on his cell phone for his home number, and Jessie answered. "How's Angela doing now?" he asked.

"She's a little better. Pretty washed out, but she's starting to keep liquids down, I think."

"I've called Tess to come in and help me with surgery on this dog. Its leg is swollen and cold this morning, and the bullet needs to come out. Can you hold down the fort a little longer?"

There was a silence that stretched out for several seconds before Jessie answered. "I suppose so. I have no choice. But when are you going to tell Angela about her friend? You can't keep it from her forever."

Cole groaned. "Come on, Jess, don't bust my chops. I'm doing the best I can here."

"I'm just calling it the way I see it, and I'm seeing things more clearly now. I'm thinking your lack of involvement with your kids has something to do with your wife leaving."

Cole rubbed his forehead, trying to unwind the painful knot that was forming there. He heard Tess coming in the back door of the clinic. "I can't talk right now. Tess just came in and we need to get this dog into surgery. I'll come down to the house right after, okay?"

"Where have I heard that before?"

Cole gritted his teeth. *Damn, this woman is impossible.* "Good-bye, Jess."

"You need to be prepared to talk with Angela by the time you get home."

"Good-bye," he said firmly, a grim feeling taking hold of him. He disconnected the call.

For the love of Pete, Jessie was more tenacious than a pit bull.

From the other room, Tess called out in a singsong, "Hi, hi!"

Pulling himself back to the task at hand, Cole left the office and went into the surgery room where Tess was already getting out supplies and setting up the stainless steel surgical tray.

"The sheriff is sending over a deputy to be here when we take out this bullet." Cole had tried to reach Deputy Cobb, but she'd evidently left the office and couldn't be reached. "He should be here any minute."

"Okay."

Cole went into the kennel room to get Belle. She lifted her head and regarded him with a stoic expression. He'd bathed her and run lab tests earlier this morning, and he thought she would tolerate the surgery. Her wound had been seeping during the night, so her blood volume was slightly low and she was still dehydrated. But he couldn't wait any longer to remove the bullet; he didn't want her to lose that leg if he could help it.

When he led Belle into the surgery room, he saw that the deputy had arrived and he was standing back in the corner. He was a tall, lean kid who introduced himself as Deputy Johnson.

"I asked him to stand back out of the way," Tess said.

"Do you want to stand by the table to watch?" Cole asked.

"No, sir. This is okay over here. I just need to be present when you remove the evidence."

"All right. We'll get started."

Cole pulled preanesthesia medicine into a syringe, and Tess held Belle still while he found a vein and injected her. After she slumped to the floor, they lifted her to the stainless steel surgery table. Out of the corner of his eye, Cole saw Johnson sway. The kid's face was pale, his freckles standing out like tiny copper pennies.

Good Lord, we've barely gotten started.

"Sit down on the floor, Deputy. Bend over and lower your head between your knees," Cole told him.

Tess glanced at Johnson while he did as he was told but continued to help Cole position Belle on the table.

"Tell you what. Don't watch us at all. When I'm about to take out the bullet, I'll tell you and you can look up," Cole said.

"Okay," Johnson said, head lowered and voice muffled.

Even though Tess had put on a surgical mask, Cole could read her smile in her eyes. He injected a small amount of barbiturate in Belle's vein, placed a tube in her throat, and hooked her up to the anesthesia machine. He picked up the electric clipper and shaved the inside of her thigh over the area where he knew the bullet had lodged.

Tess cleaned the surgical site while he moved to the sink to scrub. He took off his wedding ring to put in his pocket, pausing for a moment to examine it and wonder why he still bothered to wear it. After washing, he put on surgical gloves, the latex cuffs snapping into place. From the open surgical pack, he removed green draping to place over Belle's leg. "I need you to stay on top of her pulse and oxygenation. She's dehydrated, and I don't want the anesthesia to put her too deep."

"You got it," Tess said.

"You okay, Deputy Johnson?" The kid remained sitting on the floor with his back to the wall, knees bent and head between his knees.

"Doing great, Doc." Head still down, voice still muffled.

Cole shook his head slightly at Tess and then focused on his work. Planning his first incision, he glanced at the radiograph hanging in the light box. While his eyes found the bullet on the x-ray, his fingertips gently palpated the dog's inner thigh, searching for the leaden lump.

He made an incision through the skin and then dissected the glossy, opaque layer of fascia immediately below. He inspected the opening, looking for the thin white nerves and the dark red arteries and veins. He avoided slicing into the large thigh muscle as he dissected around it, going toward the bone.

Once he'd cleared an opening, he probed the surgical wound with his finger and felt the hard lead bullet at the bottom.

"Okay, Deputy, look here for a moment," Cole said. Taking up a forceps, he used it to grasp the slug and pull it out.

That's when things headed south.

The incision filled with blood and overflowed onto the surgical drape. Dropping the bullet and forceps into the pan that Tess held ready, Cole put his finger down into the hole, trying to staunch the flow that he realized now had been plugged somewhat by the leaden slug.

"Sponges and a clamp. Now."

Tess was already moving. She peeled open a sterile packet of cotton gauze, holding it close for him to reach. Cole grabbed the cotton and started cleaning out the wound, but the blood was flowing faster than he could blot it. Tess kept opening packages while he tried to spot the bleeder at the bottom of the incision. It was like trying to see down into the bottom of a murky well.

Using the index fingers of both hands, Cole spread the tissue enough to give him some space to work. Alternately blotting out blood and peering into the hole, he spied the end of the bleeding vessel. Grabbing up the clamp, he clipped it on and was relieved to see that it made a huge difference in the amount of blood flow.

Tess had turned to monitoring Belle's pulse. "Her heart stopped!"

Cole could hear the panic in her voice. With the sudden drop in Belle's blood volume, he knew the anesthesia had become too concentrated. "Stop the gas, leave the oxygen on, and start bagging her. I think it'll start again once the gas dissipates." Cole worked to tie off the bleeding vessel. "Do you have a pulse yet?"

Using the stethoscope directly over Belle's heart, Tess concentrated on listening. "Yes! Yes, her heart's beating again."

"Keep bagging and increase the fluid drip. I've gotta get this incision closed ASAP so we don't have to put her under again. Are you still with us, Deputy?"

"Yeah, still here." Johnson's head was down again, and he appeared to have no intention of looking back up.

"Good man."

It took a few minutes for Cole to tie off some minor vessels that were bleeding. Then he worked to repair the internal damage left by the bullet and his surgical incision. Finally, he was able to suture the skin, setting a line of neat stitches across Belle's thigh.

During the process, Belle started breathing on her own. Tess was able stop monitoring her long enough to put the lead bullet into a baggie and send Deputy Johnson proudly on his way.

By the time they could move Belle back to a cage to recover, her heart rate and breathing were stable. Now all they needed was a little time to see if they would be able to save the leg.

As Tess gathered her things to leave, Cole decided to broach the subject of having the girls at the clinic while they worked. "I need a place for the kids this next week. Would it bother you if they stayed here?"

"Not at all. They're old enough to put to work. Angie could learn to run the computer, and Sophie will love to clean things."

Cole kind of liked the idea of his daughters having jobs. It would be good for them. "Thanks, Tess. I appreciate it."

Tess left, and Cole decided it was time to go tell the kids about Grace. He might as well get it over with.

At the house, he found Sophie and Jessie in the kitchen cooking something on the stove.

"Daddy!" Sophie ran across the room and thudded into his legs.

"Hey, squirt," he said. "What ya doin'?"

"We're making soup for lunch." She skipped across the room to rejoin her aunt. "I'm stirring it."

"Sounds good," he said.

Jessie turned and gave him a tired—or was it sad?—smile. "I thought I'd make something that Angie might be able to eat. It's just a light broth with a few vegetables. Thought I'd stay away from chicken."

"That's a good idea," he said. "Where is Angie?"

Sophie piped up. "She's in the living room watching a movie."

"Oh, maybe I'd better leave her be then."

"No," Jessie said, "I think you'd better have that talk while you can."

"What talk?" Sophie said, ever alert to any disciplinary action her sister might need.

Cole looked at her. "You might as well come in and join us. I only want to have to do this once."

Jessie adjusted the flame under the soup. "Come on, Sophie, we'll all go."

He led the way, Sophie hurrying to keep up. Angela, pale and drawn, looking even thinner than usual, reclined on the couch, a chocolate-colored fleece throw pulled up to her chin.

"Hi, Angel, how are you feeling?"

"Not too bad."

"Can we stop the movie for a minute?"

Angela hit the pause button on the remote.

Cole noticed a glass of bubbly liquid on the end table beside her. "Is that ginger ale?"

"Yeah, I can drink it now."

"That's good," he said. "Here, can you scooch up your legs so I can sit beside you?"

"I wanna sit beside you, too, Daddy," Sophie said in a plaintive tone.

"You can sit right here, on my other side," he said.

Cole found himself wedged between his two daughters, while Jessie sat in the chair on the other side of the coffee table. He reached out a hand, and Angela slipped her cold fingers into it. He felt a slight tremor in them before she clasped his hand. He rubbed her fingers, trying to warm them.

"What is it, Dad? What's wrong?" Angela asked.

"How do you know something's wrong?"

"You look sadder than usual. Have you heard from Mom?"

He shook his head. He felt adrift in unfamiliar waters. At the clinic, he was used to being in charge, and he could handle emergencies, sickness, or even death. But this, this was something for which he felt ill-prepared. There was only one way he knew how to do things, and that was to tackle them head on.

"Angela." He paused and looked at his youngest, too. "Angela and Sophie . . . I hate so much to have to tell you this, but I have some very bad news."

Tears sprang to Sophie's eyes. He could feel her become tense as a taut wire fence beside him. "Is it Mom?"

"No, honey, this isn't about your mom. It's about Grace. Grace Hartman. I don't know any way to cushion this, so I just have to say it. I found out last night."

"What, Dad?" Angela's voice sounded thin and pinched.

"Grace is dead."

For a moment, everything in the room went still. He met Jessie's eyes, and she gave him a slight nod of encouragement.

Sophie began to sob. Cole put his arm around her and hugged her close.

Angela sat immobile; a shattered expression gradually took over her face. Her voice quivered. "Did she wreck her car?"

There was nothing else to do but just get through it. "No, honey. Someone killed her."

Angie gasped and put her free hand up to her throat, fingers fluttering. Cole had to stop himself from squeezing the one hand he held even harder. It felt fragile and cold inside his, and he didn't want to crush it.

"Someone killed her?" Sophie said between sobs. "A bad person?"

"Yeah, sweetheart, I think it's safe to say a bad person did it."

Cole had been watching Angela, and he saw her slowly start to crumble. Her lips trembled, and her eyes filled, spilling over. He felt himself melt at that moment, too, and the sorrow he'd kept in check for so many hours finally took over. Gathering his daughters into his arms, he allowed his own tears to flow.

Soon Jessie joined them on the sofa, spreading her arms wide, trying to hold and comfort them while all four of them wept.

Chapter 11

After spending the morning at the cabin and gravesite, Mattie and Stella finished up and started the drive back down the mountain. The Crime Scene Unit had arrived from Byers County and had gathered information, some of which answered a few immediate questions.

"So now we know the blood on the cabin deck is human," Mattie said.

"Yeah. CSU can have that blood type for us before the autopsy. DNA will take longer. At least we'll be able to match type by this afternoon at the latest."

"Could they tell anything else by the stain?"

"It's fresh, although they couldn't say exactly how old. It's feasible it got spilled there in the last twenty-four hours. Looks like the victim got shot, dropped right there, and bled out. She was shot in the chest; probably hit the heart, so that fits. Someone took a swipe at cleaning it up but didn't work at it too hard. They might have thought no one would pay attention to blood at a hunting cabin."

Stella settled into the passenger seat, hanging onto the safety strap above the window, while Mattie steered the cruiser back down the steep mountain road. "Your dog made a valuable find back there, Mattie."

Mattie tried to tamp down the pride she was feeling. She could hear Robo panting in his compartment behind her. She turned the air conditioning on and directed the flow back to him. "I know it."

"We'll be retrieving the slug from the girl at the autopsy this afternoon. If the calibers match, it's safe to say this casing came from the bullet that killed her."

"And we'll know the shot came from a handgun, not a rifle," Mattie said. "That pretty much eliminates accidental death from a hunter's stray bullet."

"Since the casing can be matched to the weapon that fired it, we'll be able to identify the gun that killed her if we find it," Stella said. "In the meantime, CSU will try to get a fingerprint or a print fragment off of it this afternoon. Maybe that will lead us to our killer."

They'd reached a spot lower in the foothills, and Mattie's cell phone beeped, letting her know simultaneously that they'd driven back into cell phone range and that she'd missed a call.

"Let me pick up this message," she said.

It was from the vet. She summarized for Stella. "That was from Dr. Walker. He said he needs to remove the bullet from the dog's leg this morning, and since he can't reach me on my cell phone, he'll try to reach me at the station. Last night, I told him one of us needed to be there when he took the bullet out to protect the chain of custody on the evidence. I hope someone was available."

"His daughter's the one we have to interview, right?"

"Yes. She was also the one who was sick all night."

"Call him and tell him we'll swing by now to talk to the girl."

Mattie knew it might not be that easy. The vet seemed pretty protective of his daughter. "I'll see what I can do."

"I want to talk to her before I get tied up in that autopsy this afternoon, so don't take no for an answer."

Walker answered on the first ring.

"This is Deputy Cobb. I'm just coming down from the mountain. I see that you called."

"Yes. I ended up reaching Sheriff McCoy. He sent Deputy Johnson over to attend Belle's surgery, and he took the slug with him when he left."

"That's good. Thanks for taking care of that."

"I'll do whatever I can to help you catch this guy."

"Did you tell your daughter about Grace?"

"Yeah." He sounded grim. "She finally fell asleep. She had a tough night and now a bad morning."

Mattie cringed inside, but she had to push. "We need to talk with her as soon as possible. We're moving forward with the investigation and time is of the essence. The detective is with me now. Could we talk to your daughter in about twenty minutes?"

He paused long enough that Mattie was beginning to construct an argument in her mind.

"Yes, we can work that out," he said at last. "Just come to the house. Angie will be awake when you get here."

Whew. "That would be great."

"I already talked to Angela about speaking with you. She wants to do whatever she can to help. I think it gives her something to do so she doesn't feel so helpless."

Mattie felt grateful for the vet's proactive attitude, and it sounded like he was trying to impart that to his daughters as well. Nothing at all like her own father, but it reminded her a little of Mama T.

"We'll see you soon," she said, and she disconnected the call.

"Good work," Stella said. "And Mattie, one more thing."

"What's that?"

"Would you take the lead on establishing rapport with this girl?"

It was an unexpected request, and Mattie gave the detective a searching look. "Why's that?"

Stella shrugged and made a squeamish face. "I don't do kids."

★

If there were two species on the face of the planet that Mattie could relate to, they were dogs and kids. She'd spent years in foster care surrounded by all kinds of kids, and she understood them. Sure, she understood their dreams, their goals, their puppy-love interests. But more important, she understood their fears: the fear of not fitting in, the fear of not having enough food to eat, and the big one—the fear of getting hurt.

Mattie found an old cottonwood tree in front of the vet's house that she could park under. Pulling up so that the cab of her car was in the shade, she rolled down the front windows.

"Let me pour some water for Robo and put it in the back for him before we go inside," she said.

She kept his supply of water in a gallon jug in the trunk of the car, and she made sure it was full and fresh daily before leaving her house. By the time she finished, the vet had opened his front door and was standing out on the wide covered deck, waiting for them. He opened the door as she and Stella approached.

"Come in," he said.

Mattie recognized his grief in his red-rimmed and swollen eyes. As she entered the room and encountered the rest of his family, she saw that they all suffered the same.

"This is my sister, Jessica Walker," the vet said, introducing a tall, slim woman. A small girl with brown curls came forward to hang on Walker's left forearm. He indicated her by flexing his bicep and lifting her up. "This is my youngest, Sophie. And my oldest, Angela."

The girls were as Mattie remembered them, and they couldn't have been more different. The youngest looked adorable with her freckles and short, solid build, while the older one stood tall, willowy, with pale skin and white-blond hair. She could tell they'd both been crying, and her heart went out to them.

"Okay, Sophie, time for you to go upstairs with Aunt Jessie," Walker said.

"Dad-dy," Sophie said in a quiet but decidedly whiny voice, looking up at her father with wide, beseeching eyes. "Can I stay here with you?"

"Nuh-uh," Walker said. "Nope. We talked about this, half-pint. Now upstairs you go."

"Come on, Sophie," the aunt said, holding a hand out toward her. "Let's go read some stories."

Although she made a show of not wanting to, the young girl did as she was told.

Just like Robo.

Walker gestured toward the living room while Angela led the way. It had a huge vaulted ceiling and was dominated by a fireplace made of rock. Leather furniture, oak end and coffee tables, Navaho rugs, and pillows and throws made the room homey and inviting. Walker waved Mattie and Stella over toward some chairs while he and Angela seated themselves side by side on the couch.

"Thank you for talking with us, Angela," Mattie said, starting out by giving the teen lots of eye contact, making sure she knew that Mattie was talking directly to her and not to her father. "I'm sorry for your loss."

Angela's eyes filled, and she looked down at her hands for a moment.

"And I want you to know," Mattie continued, "that we'll do everything in our power to find out who did this to your friend. Your talking with us is very important, and I believe you might be able to help us understand some things about Grace that could give us leads. We plan to search for her killer until we find who did this."

Angela had regained control and was now looking directly into Mattie's eyes. She liked the teen's serious demeanor and guessed there wouldn't be much drama from this one.

Mattie glanced at Stella, and the detective gave her a nod.

"Do you know of anyone who might want to hurt Grace, Angela?"

The girl shook her head. "No one. There's no one who would want to hurt Grace. She's one of the most popular girls in school."

Angela seemed to be having trouble speaking of her friend in the past tense. "Is there anyone who might have been jealous of her? Anyone at all?"

Angela seemed to be looking inward, thinking. "Well, maybe. I mean, some of the girls might be jealous, but . . . well, no one ever acted mean to her out in the open. I don't even know of anyone acting mean behind her back."

"Did Grace have a boyfriend?"

"No, not a boyfriend really."

"Someone she likes, someone that likes her but she doesn't like him back?"

"Well, she's liked someone for a while now, but I don't think he likes her back."

"And who would that be?"

"Mike Chadron."

This answer took Mattie by surprise. Chadron had to be at least seven years older than Grace. She glanced at Walker, who looked shocked.

"Do they spend time together?" Mattie asked.

Angela looked at her dad, and he encouraged her with a nod. "Well, at first he was helping her train Belle. And then he told her he was too busy to help anymore and that she'd better stop coming over. I thought maybe he wanted some space, like maybe he thought she was being too intense or something. Grace can be that way sometimes when she decides she wants something."

"So did Grace quit going over to his place?"

"Yeah, but once she got her driver's license, she'd spy on him sometimes, follow him places. I told her she was, like, stalking him, and it was ridiculous. But she just laughed."

Stella leaned toward Angela, tense and direct. In a brassy voice, she asked, "Are you sure they weren't involved with each other and Grace just didn't tell you about it? Maybe she kept secrets."

A look of confusion crossed Angela's face. She hesitated, appeared unsure of herself. "I, uh, I don't know."

The doctor placed a protective arm along the back of the couch behind his daughter's shoulders. One look at his face told Mattie he wasn't pleased with Stella's confrontational approach. She scooted to the edge of her chair, hoping Stella would get the signal that Mattie was supposed to be taking the lead.

"That's all right, Angela," she said. "It's okay for you to stick to telling us the things you know." Then giving Stella a pointed look, she added, "You can leave the speculation for us to do later."

Stella raised her hands slightly, as if in surrender, and settled back in her chair.

Mattie tried to get back on track with the teen. "So as far as you know, Grace had a little crush on Mike, followed him sometimes. Did she ever say where she followed him?"

Again, Angela appeared to search her memory. "Not really. Grace thought it was fun, you know, trying to follow him in the car without him seeing her."

"Did she ever mention following him up into the mountains or anything like that?"

Angela shook her head. "No. Not that I can remember."

"Did Grace like to drive up to the mountains?"

"I've been away most of the summer, and she got her license while I was away. I mean, we talked on the phone all the time, but we never talked about where she was driving her car."

Stella spoke up again, this time in a more modulated tone. Maybe she'd been listening more carefully to Mattie's approach. "Angela, do you know if Grace was involved with drugs of any kind?"

Angela looked at the detective, her face remaining certain, sure of her answer. "No, Grace didn't want to have anything to do with drugs. Her parents would've killed her—" Her wan face blanched even more. "I mean, she knows how her parents feel about drugs."

"And how did Grace get along with her parents?"

Angela's eyes welled with unshed tears. "Are they doing okay? Have you seen them yet?"

Stella's voice actually sounded kind when she answered. "No, I'll be visiting with them this afternoon. I just wondered if Grace got along with them."

Suddenly, Angela folded forward, put her hands to her face, and sobbed. The vet leaned over his daughter, trying to provide what comfort he could. Mattie could tell how much the thought of the Hartmans' pain affected them both. She met Stella's eyes and settled back in her chair, sending her a silent message to wait a few moments.

Soon father and daughter regained control, and he reached for a box of tissues beside him on an end table. "Here, Angel," he said, before looking at Mattie. "Are we about done?"

"No, Dad. I'm okay," Angela said, wiping tears and blowing her nose in a dainty way. "It's just that, well, if you'd met them, you'd know they're older than most of our parents." Her lip trembled, and she bit it for a second, struggling to maintain her composure. When she continued, her voice was high pitched and quivery. "She's their only kid, you know, and they love her so much. They give her everything she ever wants, but she doesn't act spoiled about it. They just . . . love each other. That's all."

Through her tears, the girl glanced at her dad. He hugged her tightly against him with one arm.

Mattie cleared the tightness from her throat. "So from your perspective, they had a good relationship, right?"

Angela nodded.

"And as far as you knew, Grace didn't use drugs," Stella added.

"She would've told me. She didn't." Angela's eyes moved from the detective back to Mattie. "Wait . . . do you guys think this has something to do with drugs?"

"We don't know yet, Angela. But what if it did? Do you think there's anyone, oh say, someone at school or maybe someone out in the community, who might have approached Grace to buy drugs?" Mattie asked.

Angela's face took on a guarded look. "There's always kids at school with something."

"Don't worry. You probably won't be telling me anything I don't already know, Angela. And anything you tell us is strictly confidential, our secret. Are there any kids you know of that are selling drugs?"

Again that guarded look. Mattie could tell the girl didn't want to be seen by her peers as a narc. "Well, there's rumors about Tommy O'Malley."

"Yeah, he's been on my radar for a while now. I can tell you the kids in his posse, too." Mattie rattled off a half-dozen names while Angela's eyes widened almost imperceptibly, looking impressed. "So see, I know some things already, but if there's a chance you could give us a lead we don't know about and it ultimately reveals who killed Grace, that would be sweet. Can you think of anyone else?"

It appeared that the girl was right with her. "I'll think about it. If I come up with someone, can I call you?"

"Of course, call me anytime about anything, even if you just want to talk about something that you're not sure about. We never know in an investigation when something small turns into exactly the bit of information we need." Mattie dug a business card out of her pocket, pulled out a pen to write a number on the back, and handed it to the girl. "That's my cell phone number on the back. Don't hesitate to use it. Talk things over with your dad, see what memories come up. Let us know about anything that concerns you, okay?"

"Okay," Angela said, looking down at the card.

"Anything else, Detective?" Mattie asked, turning to Stella.

"Not for now. We'll be in touch."

"I may want to see you again tomorrow, Angela. By then we could have more questions." Mattie looked at the doctor. "Can I call in the morning to set something up if we need to?"

He nodded.

"How's Belle?" Mattie asked.

Angela looked surprised. "Belle? That's Belle you have up at the clinic?"

"Yeah, Angel. I guess with you being so sick and everything, I forgot to mention it. Deputy Cobb brought Belle in because she'd been shot."

"Like Grace?"

The doctor looked at Mattie, as if tossing the question to her.

"Yes," Mattie said. "It looks like she was with Grace, and they were both shot."

"Grace always had Belle with her."

"That's what I've heard."

"Poor Belle!" The girl looked at her dad. "Dad, you can't leave Belle at the clinic all by herself. You've got to bring her here to stay at the house."

Looking a bit besieged, the vet said, "She's just coming out of the anesthesia, Angie. She needs to stay there for a while."

"Well, she's not sleeping there by herself tonight. I'll go and stay with her if I have to."

Relieved that the heroic dog had a champion, Mattie had to suppress a smile as she watched the father cave.

"Oh, all right," he said. "She has to stay there for a few more hours, but if she's awake enough, I'll bring her here for the night. I bet the Hartmans will want to pick her up tomorrow. I'll call Garrett and see." The grim expression had returned to his face, and Mattie knew that he was dreading the task.

Mattie and Stella said good-bye and went back out to the cruiser. Robo stood up, yawning, obviously having napped while they were gone. The temperature in the car was cool enough, and after Robo took a few slurps of his water, Mattie emptied the rest, put the bowl away, and settled into the driver's seat.

"Now that is one good-looking hunk of male, Mattie. Makes me want to forget I've sworn off men lately," Stella said, with a grin.

Mattie shrugged. "I hadn't noticed."

"What are you, blind, girl? Or just not interested?"

Mattie had had her share of boyfriends in high school—that is, until Mama T put a kibosh on it. Once she got into junior college and police academy, she'd had a few longer-lasting relationships, but nothing permanent. Yeah, she found the vet extremely attractive, but that's not what their relationship was about. "He's married."

"He doesn't wear a wedding ring."

Mattie could have sworn she'd seen one last night. "Well, I'm just not interested, I guess."

"Ha! You crack me up. You're as easy to read as an Amber Alert. Of course you're interested in the man."

Having had enough of the detective's teasing, Mattie changed the subject. "Let's get back to the office and check in. We need to tell the others about Mike Chadron's relationship with our victim. Maybe Brody has a warrant by now and we can search his property."

Chapter 12

When Mattie and Stella arrived at the station, they found Sheriff McCoy and Chief Deputy Brody in the report room together, and both were pretty well steamed. Evidently, Judge Taylor had denied their department a search warrant.

"The judge is an old hunting buddy of Chadron's dad," Brody explained, his voice gruff. "Says we don't have enough evidence to treat Mike like a common criminal."

"That's one judge that needs to be voted out of office during the next election." Stella paused, pursing her lips. "Well, the evidence against Mike Chadron is growing. We just learned that our victim followed him around in her car. Chances are good that she followed him up to that cabin."

"That's significant," McCoy said.

"No word yet on the BOLO we put out on Grace's car or Chadron's truck?" Mattie asked.

"None," McCoy said. "I still believe her car got ditched near the crime scene. I heard from Ranger Benson. She hand-picked some volunteers who know the area and won't get lost to help them look for it, but they have a lot of country to cover. I don't know why we can't turn up Chadron's truck, unless he switched license plates on it or something."

"You'd think the description of a truck and dog trailer would be enough. Not very common," Stella said.

McCoy nodded. "I think I'll give Mike Chadron's father a call and see if he knows where Mike is. I'll avoid mentioning we suspect his son of illegal activity."

"Sounds like a good idea," Stella said.

McCoy looked at Mattie. "This afternoon, you and I are going to meet with John Brennaman at the school. He heard about Grace's death and called me."

Mattie's gut tightened.

"Mr. Brennaman is pretty shaken up over the death of a student and wants to see if he can help. I figure there's no time like the present to get him involved in our school drug intervention program. And we'll see what he knows about Grace and her friends."

"When is our appointment?"

"We have a little over an hour. Get some lunch and meet me at the school by two o'clock."

"I'll be at the autopsy this afternoon," said Stella. "Afterward I'll interview our victim's family. Unless I turn up something else to do today, I'll go home for the night and be back tomorrow morning by seven."

"Okay, we have a plan," McCoy said. "Let's get to it."

On the way home, Mattie tried to ignore her dread. The run-ins with Brennaman happened a long time ago.

You'd think I'd be over it by now.

After pulling up in her front yard, she let Robo out the back of the cruiser. He bounded off toward the side gate.

"You want that bone I gave you yesterday, don't you? Come on through the house, and I'll get you some fresh water first."

Inside, Robo rushed to the kitchen door and stood by it.

Mattie picked up his water bowl and carried it over to the sink. "Just cool your jets—have some water. It's starting to heat up outside."

Robo lapped a few times and then went back to the door.

"One-track mind. Do you want to go outside?"

He danced on his front paws.

"Here you go."

Mattie stepped outside and stood on the porch to watch him.

He darted toward the bone but, at the last second, crouched and slunk up to it, sniffing furiously. The shift in his demeanor made Mattie follow him out into the yard.

He scooted around the bone, nose to the ground, and went out to the spruce tree as if on the trail of something. At the fence, he turned and gave Mattie a quizzical look, then trotted back toward her. He gave the bone a soft touch with his mouth, sat, and stared at her.

Mattie approached him and knelt to examine the bone. The bottom of it was plastered with hamburger meat, brown and dried at the edges. She knew it hadn't been there last evening.

Thoughts spun through Mattie's mind. She'd heard that drug runners sometimes paid to have narcotics dogs killed. Had someone poisoned the hamburger meat to get rid of Robo?

"Come with me."

Planning to have the meat tested, she carried the bone into the house and put it into a plastic bag. Sealing it, she leaned on the kitchen counter, her hands shaking. What might have happened if Robo didn't have such a well-trained and sensitive nose?

She took a moment to wash off any poison that might have lingered on her hands and then sank down on the kitchen floor, patting her leg. "Come here."

Robo leaned into Mattie as she hugged him, burying her nose in his silky fur.

There's nothing like the comfort of a good dog.

"I'll buy you another one." After a few minutes of cuddling, she knew what she needed to do next. "You wait here."

Mattie went out to her car to get Robo's work collar and leash. There would be no better way to assure his living quarters were poison free than to have him do a sweep of the area.

Robo got excited when he saw his equipment. After putting it on him, Mattie picked up the bag holding the bone, opening it carefully. She held it so he could get a whiff without touching it.

"Let's go find the poison," she told him.

Going out into the yard, Mattie led Robo on a sweep of the area. He alerted once more by his water dish. Made sense.

"Christ," Mattie muttered as she led Robo back to the house so she could get a container for the water. She planned to put in a request for razor wire for the top of the fence first thing tomorrow. But now, she needed to call Sheriff McCoy to report this crime and file a report. An attempt on the life of a K-9 was serious criminal activity and needed to be handled as such.

By this time, Mattie was no longer shaken; she was just plain mad. She vowed she'd find whoever had messed with her dog. She'd track him down and nail his hide.

★

After talking to the sheriff, Mattie felt too worked up to eat anything. She decided to give Robo a quick brushing so he wouldn't shed while inside the school building. Then she changed into the newest everyday uniform she had in her closet, since her dress uniform had been trashed the day before. She had no time to style her hair, so she ran a comb through her short bob and tucked the sides behind her ears.

As she drove, Mattie analyzed her nervousness. She knew it had everything to do with the past and nothing to do with the present. She was more confident in Robo's performance now than she had been yesterday when she'd last faced this meeting. She knew he was capable of finding even invisible amounts of the drugs he'd been trained to detect, and his obedience training was spot on.

But she couldn't shake the memory of how Brennaman belittled her. Yes, she'd been a wild student, but an educator shouldn't try to browbeat a kid into submission. Well, she'd have to show him that she'd changed. She'd hold her head up and show him she knew her business.

Mattie pulled up to the school, a building made from brown native stone and cream-colored aluminum siding nestled against the hillside. The sheriff's Jeep was already parked, and he was sitting inside it, talking on his cell phone. She parked beside him, got out of her cruiser, and released Robo from the back.

Robo was beginning to prance in place to show how excited he was. Mattie snapped a leash onto his collar and ran through a few quick obedience drills to get him into the right mood.

When Sheriff McCoy ended his call, he exited his vehicle, speaking to Mattie as they walked up to the building. "Mr. Chadron says that Mike is at a dog show and should be back late tonight."

"Why would he have been up in the mountains yesterday if he was headed for a dog show?"

"Good question. I wish he was here so we could ask him."

They entered the building together, and Mattie saw that things hadn't changed much in the past decade. The glass case filled with old trophies and framed photographs of past championship teams still sat against the wall, and the oak counter still separated the lobby from the administrative offices.

The receptionist was new, a plump thirtysomething bottle blonde, with teased hair and a frazzled attitude. "You must be Sheriff McCoy," she said. "I'm Betty Potts."

The two shook hands while McCoy introduced Mattie.

"I feel just awful about not noticing that Grace was absent yesterday." Betty shook her head, looking teary.

"Were you expecting her?" McCoy asked.

"Yes, she's our student volunteer. At first I thought she was late, but I've been so swamped, and I got busy with things. And then I guess I forgot she was coming."

"Did you know Grace well?"

"She started working for me just this week, so no, I didn't know her well. But she seemed like such a good kid. Very respectful, responsible."

"Do you have any idea who might have hurt her?"

Tears welled, and she brushed at them. "No, I'm sorry, but I don't even know who her friends are or anything like that. School hasn't started yet, and she wasn't here in the office last year."

"Perhaps Mr. Brennaman can help us."

"Oh. Oh, yes. I'll tell him you're here." She turned and hurried down a hallway leading toward the back of the office.

Feeling a tug on the leash, Mattie glanced down at Robo. As typical, he'd picked up on her nerves and was trying to see around the end of the counter to keep an eye on Betty. She corrected him and told him to sit. By the time the receptionist returned, Robo was sitting at heel, panting.

"Come with me back to the conference room. Mr. Brennaman will join you there."

Just shoot me.

Keeping Robo in heel position, Mattie followed Sheriff McCoy down a long hallway and into a room that was carpeted in cheap-looking but serviceable brown Berber and dominated by a large, walnut-grain Formica-topped table.

"Can I get you something to drink?" Betty asked, looking as if serving them was the last thing she wanted to do.

"No, thank you," McCoy said. "Deputy?"

Mattie felt like she couldn't swallow anything around the nervous lump in her throat. "No, I'm good. Thanks."

They sat in silence for a few minutes. Apparently growing antsy, McCoy pushed back his chair and got up to circle the room. Robo raised his head to watch, prompting Mattie to tell him, "Stay."

"This place hasn't changed much," McCoy said. "I've been here a few times since I graduated, but when I was a student here, I never knew this room existed."

Mattie was familiar with the room; the table was the same. "Mr. Brennaman put me in here for detention before I got on the track team and cleaned up my act."

The sheriff's eyes narrowed as he came back around the table and took his seat. Mattie felt her cheeks flame with heat.

"I thought you might need to know," she said. She reached down and stroked Robo's head.

The door opened, and Brennaman bustled in. McCoy stood, so Mattie did, too. Robo stood when she did, and his hackles raised on his shoulders. She could see him assuming a "guard" position, so she quickly intervened and told him to sit. He obeyed, but his eyes remained pinned on the principal. She didn't know why he was acting so protective, but it was probably her fault. Emotions from a handler ran right down the leash, and she assumed Robo could sense her nerves. She hoped no one else in the room could.

Brennaman was dressed casually in denims and a light-blue shirt, probably since school wasn't in session. Mattie would guess he was in his early sixties, and he was of average build though fit and muscular for his age. His gray hair was short, military style. "Sheriff," he said, offering a handshake. Then he turned and offered her one. "And is it Mattie Lu Cobb?"

His grip felt solid and firm. Robo's training held, and he remained seated at Mattie's heel, hackles still raised. "Yes, Mr. Brennaman. Good to see you again."

"And you." He turned his attention back to the sheriff and took a seat at the table, gesturing for them to be seated as well. "We're terribly disturbed by this tragedy."

"It's a blow to the whole community," McCoy said.

"I heard from Mr. Hartman that Grace was shot, buried in the mountains."

"That's right."

"Terrible, just terrible," Brennaman said, shaking his head. "I hope you find her killer and bring him to justice."

"We plan to." The sheriff paused, spreading his hands out on the table in front of him. "What can you tell me about Grace Hartman?"

"Well, let's see. Grace would be a junior this year. She was bright, popular with both teachers and students, did well in her studies, and participated in sports." He looked at Mattie. "Not as fast as you were, Mattie, but she did go out for track. This was her first year volunteering in the office, so I didn't know her as well as I would have by the end of the year. Betty feels responsible for losing track of her yesterday morning, but things were hectic. I got called to an unplanned meeting, had to cancel the one I had with you." He nodded at McCoy. "Well, these things happen. I'm glad you could come by today."

"Do you know of anyone who might have been mad at Grace? Anyone who might want to hurt her?"

"No, no." Brennaman was shaking his head. "We all loved Grace around here. I can't even imagine anyone wanting to hurt that girl in any way."

McCoy nodded. "That's what we've heard. Mr. Brennaman, I can tell you that our investigation has turned up the probability that Grace's death is drug related."

Brennaman's gray brows shot up. "Drugs? Grace?"

"That surprises you."

"Of course it does! I can't imagine Grace having anything to do with drugs."

"We don't necessarily believe she was involved with drugs herself. But we believe her killer may be involved with drugs in some way. In light of that possibility, can you think of anything that might help us with our investigation?"

Mattie watched Brennaman pause to digest the information. "Not anything that comes to mind immediately, but I may need to ponder that for a while."

"Fair enough," McCoy said. "That brings me to what Deputy Cobb and I would like to talk to you about. We'd like to develop a presence here at the school with our new narcotics detection dog. Did you get a chance to look at the letter I sent about this dog being added to our department?"

"A few weeks ago, I believe. Perhaps you should brief me."

"We've already started combating drug traffic on our highways with road blocks and vehicle sweeps, and we'd like to do something similar here at school. We'd like to provide an antinarcotics education program and combine that with occasional unanticipated locker checks. We're here to offer these services and gain permission to start."

Frowning, Brennaman tapped a finger on the table, setting up a muted drum. "Grace Hartman's death was a tragedy, but this isn't a police state. The drug education program's one thing, but I don't like the idea of a police dog roaming our halls."

McCoy sat back in his chair, relaxed and casual. He steepled his fingers against his chin. "A narcotics dog wouldn't be roaming. He's on leash and under the control of his handler. Other communities have found the use of a dog very effective, and the animal becomes a mascot for the program. A dog can make inroads with some kids that teachers and law enforcement officers have found difficult to reach."

"And this dog's handler is Deputy Cobb, here?" He looked at Mattie.

"Yes, sir," she said.

Brennaman smiled at her and then shifted his attention to Robo. Mattie quickly checked him, too, and saw that his fur was smooth again, hackles dropped, but he was still staring at the principal.

It felt like Brennaman was legitimately concerned about having a police dog at school. Or maybe he was afraid of dogs.

"Robo was raised with kids," Mattie said. "He acts like a family pet. And he's completed more obedience training than most other dogs."

"I still don't like the message we'd be sending by having a police dog and an officer here at school, but I'll consider it. I'm just not convinced drugs are a big problem here at Timber Creek High."

"We believe one child lost is one too many," McCoy said. "We'd like to do what we can to prevent further harm to our community's children."

Brennaman nodded. "We're in agreement there. The drug education program sounds worth taking a look at, depending on who's teaching it. We would need to review that individual's credentials to ensure an appropriate match. We have our standards here for teachers and recognize the kind of influence a good teacher can have on students of this age."

Mattie felt anxiety wash through her. Was Brennaman trying to find a way to block the program because she would be involved? Or was she being too sensitive?

Sheriff McCoy leaned forward in his chair. "Deputy Cobb completed twelve weeks of K-9 Academy training, and she and this dog were at the top of their class. Part of her training included using him in schools and public relations. Her qualifications are impeccable."

Brennaman looked at Mattie, giving her another brief smile. "I'm sure they are. It's good to hear what training you've had, Mattie. You'd make a great role model for the students."

She lowered her head in a slight nod to acknowledge the compliment. "Thank you. I'm excited about the program. I received a training curriculum and materials at the academy that I'm happy to share with you."

He nodded. "That would be good. I'll have to look them over, talk to the superintendent about this, and then get back to you in a few weeks."

"Perhaps Deputy Cobb can drop off the materials on Monday." McCoy stood and Mattie rose to stand beside him. "It sounds like a good idea to involve the superintendent, but we'd like to move forward with this as quickly as possible. I'll check with your secretary on my way out to get started on setting up a meeting with the two of you as soon as possible."

McCoy extended his hand, and Mattie followed suit, realizing that McCoy had taken hold of the meeting and didn't plan to let Brennaman delay implementation of the program. She followed the sheriff to the front desk but passed by to go outside when he and Brennaman stopped to talk to the receptionist.

The air felt clean and fresh, and Mattie drew in a deep breath, feeling a huge sense of relief that the meeting was over. Brennaman appeared to accept her; it was Robo he seemed to have problems with.

While she was putting Robo back into the cruiser, McCoy exited the building and walked down the sidewalk to join her. "Be sure and get those materials you mentioned over to Mr. Brennaman on Monday."

"Yes, sir."

"Spend some time this afternoon writing up a proposal that I can use with the superintendent. Have it on my desk by the end of the day. I'll set up that meeting with the superintendent and Brennaman next week." McCoy looked off to the distance, thinking. "We didn't learn anything useful about Grace here. Right now, Mike Chadron is the best lead we've got. If he doesn't come back to town tonight, I'll resubmit an affidavit for search in the morning. I'll take it over to Judge Taylor personally, and we'll have a little talk. He won't deny us again."

McCoy went to his Jeep and got inside, leaving Mattie to get into her own vehicle. She couldn't help feeling drained from the stress she'd put on herself prior to the meeting. She'd always known that she would stand a better chance of leaving her past behind if she moved away from Timber Creek, but this was the only place she'd ever called home.

Besides, she couldn't help but believe that one day her mother would come back to look for her here. And more than anything, Mattie wanted to be found.

Before starting up the cruiser's engine, she turned to Robo, putting her hand into the steel cage to pet him. "Hey, buddy. I know I got a little hyped up in there, and you did, too. But remember I'm in charge, okay? You don't have to protect me just because I'm a basket case."

Chapter 13

Since writing wasn't her strong suit, Mattie wrestled with the proposal until her shift ended. After finishing up, she drove over to Crane's Market to get Robo another bone. Starving after going all day without lunch, she went home to make herself a ham and cheese sandwich for dinner.

When her cell phone rang, she noticed it was the vet calling. "Mattie Cobb."

"This is Cole Walker."

"Hello. How is Angie feeling tonight?"

"She's better, almost recovered from the food poisoning."

"And how's Belle?"

"She's not bearing weight on her leg yet, but it's still early for that. I guess I'll have to figure out a way to get her down to the house for the night. Neither of the girls will have it any other way."

"I'm glad to hear she'll get some special attention. All three of them have had a tough day. They'll be good for each other." Mattie paused, unsure if she should go this next direction. "I hope it'll be okay with your wife."

"What's that?"

Her curiosity embarrassed her. "Oh, you mentioned to me yesterday that your wife didn't allow dogs in the house."

"Oh. Oh, yeah. Well, it won't be a problem."

Maybe the rumors around town are true.

"Thanks for handling the questions with Angie so well today," Walker said.

"Sure. Just doing my job."

"Well, you seem to do it better than the detective."

"Not necessarily. I think I've just had more experience talking to kids. I think she's really quite good at what she does."

"I hope so. But the reason I called is I got some lab results back from Belle that you'll be interested in."

"Oh?"

"It wasn't just the foreign bodies that caused the diarrhea. She had salmonella."

Mattie's mind made the connection immediately. "Clucken House."

"Yeah." He paused for a moment. "It got Belle and Angie, both."

She also remembered that Mike Chadron cooked at Clucken House. This was more proof that Chadron had been the one to feed Belle the meat after forcing the balloons filled with cocaine down her throat.

But Walker was the one to say it. "You know that Mike Chadron works as a cook at Clucken House, right?"

"Yes, I do."

"Have you questioned him yet?"

"He's out of town. Supposed to be at a dog show and back home tonight. We'll visit with him first thing in the morning."

"Is he a suspect?"

"I'd say more a person of interest."

"Can you let me know how it turns out?"

"I'll keep you informed about what I can." Mattie paused. "Thanks for calling to let me know about the lab results. It's important information."

She ended the call feeling like they'd both left several things unsaid. Since he seemed to want to be involved, she wished she could bring him more fully into the investigation. She also knew how badly he must want justice for the death of this child. But there was only so much she could say under the circumstances.

Thinking it over, she grew impatient. She hated to sit around waiting for Mike to turn up, and she began to wonder if there might not be a justifiable reason to do a welfare check on the guy. After all, it was well known that there'd been a salmonella outbreak at his place of employment. Maybe he'd been sick in bed and unable to answer the door when Brody checked earlier in the day. Just maybe she'd better run over there and check on him herself. And she'd keep her eyes wide open for probable cause to get a warrant while she was at it.

If Mike Chadron killed Grace, he should be considered dangerous, but she rejected the idea of calling in backup. And since she'd be acting unofficially and on her own time, she wouldn't subject Robo to the risks either. Besides, she'd already set him up in the kitchen on its old linoleum floor with his new bone. She wouldn't ask him to leave it again. So after tucking her second handgun, a Smith & Wesson .38, into her waistband at the small of her back and pulling on a jacket to cover it, she headed out to her patrol car alone.

Chadron lived on the west edge of town in a run-down log house with dried adobe in the chinks. Shaped like a cracker box, it might have been built a century ago. There were chain-link dog runs out back attached to an old shed that served as indoor dog shelters and a kennel office. The back of the property sat next to a hay field adjacent to the city boundary, and the lots to each side were empty of houses but filled with junk. Bare dirt beneath towering ponderosas made up the front yard. A path made of flat shale stepping stones that must have been put into place decades ago led to the front door. Most of the stones were all but obscured with dirt. Chadron's vehicle was still not visible, but that didn't mean it wasn't parked in one of the old sheds out back.

As Mattie approached the house, she went into that hyperalert state associated with going into a risky situation. She could hear a truck gear down out on the highway, a woman call her children down the street, a breeze sigh through the ponderosa. She continuously scanned the house, checking windows, the edge of the building, and the door. As she drew near, she saw it had been left open a few inches.

Someone must be here. Brody didn't mention a door being open when he checked the place this morning.

She knocked on the door jam. After a short wait and no answer, she called inside. "Mike? You home?"

Mattie listened intently but could hear nothing. She knew she was taking a risk if she entered Mike's home, and not just a physical risk—she could also threaten the investigation. Any evidence found by entering a suspect's home illegally couldn't be used in court, even if she left the premises and tried to get a warrant. But if she could see something to give her probable cause, she could enter.

She went to the window off to her right and peered in: a messy living room with a big-screen TV. A recliner sat in front of it, the back of the chair toward her. She thought she could see the back of a person's head at the top of the chair. No movement. Who was it? Sleeping or sick?

Mattie pushed the door open enough to step inside. "Mike? You in here?"

She stood in a boxy entryway with log walls and a filthy wood floor. The place smelled musty and unclean. And there was another odor she couldn't place. She walked farther into the living room, scanning as she went: sparse, worn furniture and glass and wrought iron end tables. Close enough now to tell it was definitely a person's head she'd seen.

"Mike?"

She knew he was dead before she reached him. A bullet hole in his right temple, blood saturating the chair's back. A handgun in his lap, near his bandaged right hand. No decomposition noticeable. She thought of a hunter's phrase . . . fresh kill.

Mattie drew her weapon. Holding it ready, she strained to listen, wanting to hear any movement, any rustle of sound that could tell her if she was alone or not.

The place sounded dead. Cautiously scanning the room, she checked for a pulse at Mike's neck. Nothing. She'd known he was dead, but she had to check. Using standard operating procedure, she raised her weapon in both hands and slipped quickly toward an open doorway that led to the next room.

The kitchen was awful: food-encrusted dishes were piled on counters and the floor and appliances were covered with years of grime. From there, she cleared two bedrooms and a bath, finding no one.

Once again in the kitchen, her eyes swept the countertop but were riveted by what she spotted toward the back, halfway behind a stack of dirty dishes.

A box of rodent poison.

Moving into the living room, Mattie stared at the dead man and felt a moment of regret. Son of a bitch. Her gut told her this was the man who tried to poison her dog . . . and she'd never have the pleasure of kicking his ass.

Chapter 14

In the dim evening light, red-and-blue strobes circled from atop three Timber Creek County Sheriff cruisers, throwing a cyclical colored wash on the log walls of the Chadron house. Yellow tape enclosed the crime scene. Despite seven years of police service, the effect still gave Mattie an eerie feeling. She approached from down the street where she'd been knocking on doors, asking neighbors if they'd heard or seen anything unusual that day. Everyone she'd turned up had denied it. Homes were thinly scattered on this edge of town, so it could be possible.

Detective LoSasso arrived in her silver Honda. After parking her car, LoSasso strode up to Mattie, face rigid with anger, an icy glint in her blue eyes. "What made you decide to come over here tonight?"

"I learned that our dog victim had salmonella, and I knew Chadron cooked at the restaurant that was shut down yesterday because of the same illness. I thought he might be incapacitated or sick. I did a welfare check."

"And you didn't think of calling me first?"

The question surprised her. "I knew you'd gone home for the night. There'd be no reason to call you before doing a welfare check."

Sheriff McCoy came up to join them. LoSasso narrowed her eyes and stared at Mattie. "We'll talk later."

"Thanks for coming back, Detective," said McCoy. "From the looks of things, we've got a suicide on our hands. I'm eager to see what you think."

Still giving Mattie a hard stare, LoSasso paused. She turned away without speaking and walked toward the house with McCoy. Mattie followed behind, keeping her distance. She'd let the detective have a few minutes in the house before requesting what she'd been wanting to do ever since she found the body: sweep the area with Robo.

Inside, LoSasso appeared to take in the scene. Doctor McGinnis, who also acted as Timber Creek's coroner, stood near the body.

"Good," the doctor said in lieu of greeting. "You're finally here. I'd like to get this body transported as soon as possible, but Sheriff McCoy wouldn't let me move it until you'd seen it."

Mattie noticed that LoSasso stiffened. The detective had driven more than one hundred miles this evening just to go home and then turned around and drove back to Timber Creek. The delay was not her fault.

"Simply following protocol," McCoy said. He introduced the doctor to the detective.

Silent, LoSasso squatted down next to the corpse and studied it. The odor assailed Mattie, and now she recognized it for what it was: a cross between raw meat and the ironlike taint of blood.

"Cause of death is a gunshot wound to the head. Time of death, according to degree of rigor mortis, I'd guess two to six hours ago," McGinnis said.

LoSasso glanced at him. "Can you tell me something I don't know, Doc?"

McGinnis looked offended. "I'll leave that up to the medical examiner, Detective. That's why I want to transport the body as soon as possible."

"Is the CSU done with taking pictures?" LoSasso stood to take latex gloves from her pants pocket.

"Yes," McCoy said. "They got here about a half hour ago."

"Then let's start bagging this evidence." She picked up the handgun with gloved fingers, handling it delicately. "We've got a neat little Walther P22 here, semiautomatic, uses the same caliber ammo as the casing Robo found."

She bagged the handgun and then lightly touched a bandage on the dead man's hand. "Would you help me take a look at this, Doc?"

Dr. McGinnis moved forward, gloving up once again. "If you'll just step aside a moment, Detective," he said, and he began unwrapping the bandage.

The wound that he uncovered looked nasty, the fleshy part of the hand torn and bruised and bearing two obvious puncture marks that even Mattie could see.

"Looks like a dog bite," McGinnis murmured.

"Um-hmm," Stella said, meeting Mattie's gaze.

Mattie wondered if this was how Belle had gotten away after being force-fed balloons filled with cocaine. "I'd like to go get Robo now if it's all right with you, Sheriff."

Attention fixed on the dead man, McCoy agreed, allowing Mattie to leave the house and return to her cruiser. On the way out, she met Brody.

"What were you doing here, Cobb?"

"Welfare check."

"What made you think a welfare check was needed?"

Although he used a combative tone, she reined in her temper and told him about the salmonella concern. "And by the way, Chadron's door was open. Was it that way when you checked this morning?"

He frowned. "No, it was not. He must've come home tonight."

"Must have. Now, the sheriff wants me to go get Robo to do a drug sweep here, so I'd better go do it."

"Did any of the neighbors see anything?"

"I couldn't find anyone who'd seen or heard anything, but not everyone was home. We might have to check that again tomorrow."

"I'd think it would have been called in if someone heard a gunshot," Brody said.

"People still take potshots at coyotes and skunks over here on the edge of town."

"Okay," he said, waving her off. "Go on, now."

As she drove down the street to get Robo, Mattie thought about Chadron trying to poison him. She assumed he'd been planning it for a while, possibly even before Grace's death. She realized how easy it must've been for him to scope it all out, since he lived so close to her.

Robo met her at the door with his usual exuberance, loading up quickly when she told him he was going to work. Back at the crime scene, she left him in the car until the detective told her to bring him in. Using the same approach she'd used to sweep the cabin, it took Mattie the better part of an hour to sweep the house. Robo alerted twice, once at the kitchen cabinet under the sink and once at the living room sofa. In both instances, they found what appeared to be a packet of cocaine.

By the time Mattie finished, things were wrapping up. Brody had searched the outside premises and found Mike's truck parked inside an old shed, but the dog trailer and dogs were still missing. The CSU had gleaned all they could from the scene and had left. After putting Robo in the car, she went to make sure it was all right with the sheriff if she clocked out.

McCoy was talking to the detective. "It's late. Let me offer you a place to stay tonight in our guest room. My wife would be glad to have you."

LoSasso turned her frosty-blue stare on Mattie. "Thanks, but I'm staying at Deputy Cobb's house. We need to work through some things."

Taken aback, Mattie swallowed. She'd never had a house-guest before, and the last thing she wanted was a hostile one. But she didn't feel she could protest, so she nodded agreement despite the pit in her stomach.

Mattie watched the detective's headlights in her rearview mirror as LoSasso followed her home. Once parked, LoSasso stepped out of her car and then turned to retrieve a small over-night case and a hanging bag from the back seat. Clearly, she'd come prepared to stay the night somewhere.

Robo dashed over to welcome her, apparently delighted. *Traitor!* LoSasso set her bag on the car trunk, clicked the door lock on the remote, and patted Robo's side while he leaned on her legs.

"At least someone's happy to have me stay. Let's go inside."

Robo led the way, tail waving, while Mattie stepped up on the porch to unlock the door. She entered the house, switching on lights as she passed through the front room. "I'll get you sheets and a blanket. You can have the couch."

"First, let's get this other thing out of the way," LoSasso called to her.

LoSasso was standing by the sofa when Mattie reentered the room. She'd hung her bag of clothing on the door jam and placed her overnight bag on a chair. She was removing her jewelry, her hands at her ears. She took off one turquoise, bear-claw earring and put the small piece back on the post. She raised her hands to take off the other.

Mattie placed the bedding on the sofa and then stood with her arms at her sides, waiting for LoSasso to speak. Robo lay down near her, ears pricked, looking back and forth between them. Mattie could tell he sensed the tension.

LoSasso pinned the small piece to the post of the second earring, examining it as if she'd never seen it before. "I'll tell you what pisses me off the most. The fact that you went ahead on your own and left me out of this investigation."

Mattie lifted her chin. "When I went to Chadron's house this evening, there was nothing to investigate. I was simply doing a welfare check."

"Just don't forget that this is my case."

"It's *our* case, Detective. I know you're the lead, but this is our jurisdiction. I have as much ownership in solving this case as you do, possibly more." Mattie drew a breath to steady her temper. "Have you ever lived in a town as small as Timber Creek? We check on each other. It's the way we do things."

LoSasso pursed her lips. "If you were a man, I'd have your ass in a sling. But since it's hard to find a good cop, much less a good female cop, I'm going to let this one go. Just don't ever cross me again."

Mattie was in no mood to accept the left-handed compliment. "I'm not quite sure what your problem is, Detective, but I've worked with a lot of decent cops before. And if I see a situation where I need to act, I can't promise that I'll take the time to decide if I'm crossing you or not."

They stared hard at each other for several seconds. Robo barked once, followed by a deep rumble in his chest causing them both to look at him. He was staring at the detective.

LoSasso's lips started to twitch at the corners, ending in a slight smile. She said, "Well, I can see that I can't bully you into submission, especially with your bodyguard ready to pounce."

Mattie raised a brow. "Why would you want to?"

LoSasso shrugged, slipping a silver bracelet off her wrist. "It's what I do."

"Okay . . ." Mattie raised the tone of her voice to indicate she believed there must be more.

"Suffice it to say, I've had some bad experiences in the past. Used to be married to a cop who was a real asshole. It . . . colors my perspective." LoSasso sat down on the sofa, her voice taking on a sweet tone while she patted her thigh. "That's okay, Robo. I'm done being a bitch. Come here and see me."

His tail thumped once, but he didn't budge.

LoSasso gave an exaggerated sigh. "Maybe later. Would you have a beer for me, Mattie?"

Amazed at the swing in the woman's mood, Mattie responded, "Sure, I'll get you one. But if we're done with this, I think I'll go to bed now. I get up early in the morning to take Robo on his run."

LoSasso kicked off her shoes and put her feet up on the coffee table, stretching her legs out in front of her. "Don't get unfriendly on my account. Have a beer with me."

Mattie went to the kitchen, popped the tops on a couple beers, and returned to hand one to Stella. Even though it wasn't very comfortable, she settled in the only chair in the room so she wouldn't have to sit next to the detective on the sofa. Not sure how to start a conversation, she focused on sipping her beer, hoping it would relax her.

Stella didn't seem to have a problem with starting conversations. "Brody was sure mad at your ass."

"Oh, yeah?"

"Came in all ruffled up and complained to the sheriff about you not following protocol. McCoy seems to have your back. Told Brody, 'Since when have we changed the protocol to do welfare checks on citizens of Timber Creek?' Brody grumbled about you going off half-cocked and acting on your own."

"I guess you and Brody have something to agree on."

Stella made a dismissive sound. "Then I seriously doubt that we could find two things to agree on. Just thought I'd let you know that he seems to have it in for you. What did you ever do to him?"

Mattie shrugged. "He's been mad ever since I got back from the academy. We had a cross-country competition to see who would be Robo's handler. He seems to resent that I beat him."

Stella made a low whistle. "Wish I'd been here to see that. Well, as far as I'm concerned, the best man won. He'd have made a lousy K-9 handler."

Mattie peeled part of the label on her beer, which was now near empty. It had calmed her somewhat, and it felt good to be able to talk to someone about Brody's attitude, especially someone who agreed with her about Brody's disposition to be a handler. The thought of him being in charge of Robo soured her stomach.

Stella changed the subject. "Our crime scene tonight may have looked like a suicide, but I'm not convinced."

Mattie had begun to wonder about that herself.

"I think it was staged." Stella continued. "The way the gun lay in his lap looked like someone placed it there. No gunpowder at the entry wound and no suicide note. But now we probably have the weapon that killed Grace Hartman. Ballistics may let me know as early as tomorrow if that gun matches the casing Robo found and the slug taken from her body. After Chadron's autopsy, they can tell us if it's the same weapon that killed him, too. But I'm not buying that he used it on himself."

"I agree. I thought the scene looked staged, too." Mattie wanted Stella's opinion on something dear to her heart. "What do you think about that box of rat poison in the kitchen?"

"The rat poison? I don't know. Maybe Chadron came back to town earlier in the day and tried to kill Robo, but it seems like a long shot. We're checking the box for fingerprints. If he did it, his prints should be on it. I'll know more about that tomorrow."

"I think he would have had easy access to my yard. You see how close our houses are."

"Yes, but has he been back in town that long?"

Mattie shrugged.

"And then we have the cocaine packets," Stella said. "I have to wonder if they were planted. At this point, I'm pretty sure Mike Chadron is guilty of drug traffic, and he may even be the guy who killed Grace. But I don't think he committed suicide. I think someone killed him."

"And if so, his killer might be the one who killed Grace."

"Right." Stella drained her beer and raised the bottle toward Mattie. "You got another one of these for me?"

"Sure."

Mattie took their empties to the kitchen and reached into the refrigerator to take out two more bottles. She hesitated and replaced one, deciding she'd had all she should allow herself. She popped the top on the other and carried it back into the living room. She sank down onto the far end of the sofa as she handed Stella her beer and began to unlace her boots. After slipping them off, she put her socked feet up on the table and slumped down into the sofa's cushions. Robo lay with his head on his paws, eyebrows twitching, looking torn between keeping an eye on the detective and falling asleep.

"What makes you tick, Mattie Cobb? You seem like a smart officer, independent. You seem capable of standing up to my shit."

"I've had a lot of practice," Mattie said.

"With Mom or Pop?"

"My dad. He beat all of us, but mostly my mom." Mattie slumped down even further into the cushions. "He was killed while serving time in prison for trying to kill her."

Stella remained silent and took a sip.

"I'm the one who called the cops and got him arrested."

"Sounds like he deserved it."

Mattie told the story. The drinking, the yelling. Punches so hard, she could still hear the smack against her mother's body. The knife in her father's hand. How she'd sneaked into her parents' bedroom and dialed 9-1-1.

"You know, you probably saved your mother's life that night," Stella said.

Mattie shrugged. "Maybe. Mom was in the hospital for a while. Dad went to jail, then prison. My brother and I went into foster care. When Mom recovered enough to come home, she didn't want to. She said she couldn't take care of us anymore and gave us over to the county. Then she disappeared. Haven't heard from her since."

Stella sipped her beer, pursed her lips, and thought. Robo had let his guard down and seemed to be sound asleep.

Eventually, Stella said, "Sounds like tough times. You still did the right thing."

On an adult level, Mattie knew that. But she also suspected her brother blamed her for splitting up the family, and she wondered if her mother blamed her as well.

"It's getting late." Feeling older than her years, Mattie pushed herself up out of her chair. Robo's eyes popped open and he stood, too. "Let me help you make your bed."

"No, I'll do it."

Already, Mattie regretted sharing her story. She didn't know what had gotten into her. "I shouldn't have spilled my guts like that."

Stella shrugged, giving Mattie one of her searching gazes. "You needed it. Don't worry, it doesn't change anything between us."

Mattie gave her an abashed smile and then looked away, avoiding eye contact. "I'll say good-night then."

As Mattie turned to leave, Robo dogging her tracks, Stella called her back. "And Mattie . . . don't worry about me talking about it. I carry things to the grave."

This time Mattie looked Stella in the eye, liking the warmth she saw there. At least with the detective, a girl knew exactly where she stood. "I think I must have known that."

Chapter 15

Sunday

When Mattie got back from her run with Robo, she discovered that Stella had already left. She hurried to shower so she wouldn't get to the office too far behind.

At the station, she spotted Stella's Honda parked with Brody's and Sheriff McCoy's county vehicles. Since the department was small and anyone could be called to cover an emergency, staff used their assigned vehicles to go to and from work. It also made law enforcement more visible throughout town during the night, when only a skeleton crew was on duty.

Mattie entered the building with Robo walking obediently at her side. His early morning run ensured his best behavior at work.

Rainbow, dressed in an expensive-looking silk blouse and tailored slacks, an unusual outfit for the department flower child, greeted Mattie with her usual friendly smile. "Good morning! I'm sorry you couldn't come to my house for dinner last night. I mean, I know you said you probably wouldn't, but I was hoping you'd change your mind at the last minute, and I've got so much leftovers, well, you know how it is." She finally paused for a breath.

Mattie had forgotten all about it. "Did you hear what we were doing last night?"

Rainbow sobered. "About Mike Chadron?"

"Yeah."

"I did when I got in this morning. That must've been a shock, huh?"

Brody came out of the sheriff's office, and his gaze went straight to Mattie. "You're on patrol today, Cobb."

"I'm on it. Do we have report first?"

"Nah, we'll skip it since most of us were at the scene last night."

"Do you have someone to canvass that neighborhood today?"

"What? You think you need to tell me how to do my job now?"

Geez, sensitive.

Mattie shook her head, holding out her hands in a submissive gesture. "No, Brody, just trying to help out if you need me over there."

"Johnson and I can take care of it."

She didn't like the idea of having to take patrol while the rookie got to investigate. It didn't make sense. But Brody was her superior in the department's loosely linked chain of command, so she'd have to deal with it.

"Well, I'll grab a cup of coffee and get started early." She wanted Brody to realize it was still a half hour before the start of her shift.

He glanced at the clock, and as if somewhat mollified, he said, "Okay, then."

Brody left, went into his own office, and closed the door.

"Okay, then," Rainbow said, making a stern face and imitating Brody's tough guy voice. Then back to normal: "There's fresh coffee and some doughnuts in the break room. The sheriff brought in some fruit, too."

Mattie had never really joked around much in the office, even with Rainbow. Not knowing quite how to respond, she tried to keep it light. "Thanks, I'll grab something, and Robo and I will go out there and try to track down some speeders."

After selecting an apple and pouring herself some coffee, Mattie left the break room and encountered Stella and the sheriff leaving his office.

Mattie raised her cup. "Coffee?" she said to either or both of them.

"Had some," Stella said. "Thanks for the sofa last night. Do you have a minute?"

Mattie glanced at the clock. "Sure, I have a few minutes before I need to get out on the streets."

She led Stella back to the staff office, where the two of them had the room to themselves.

Mattie said, "What's up?"

"I just finished telling the sheriff that I doubt Mike Chadron died by suicide. He says he agrees."

Mattie took a sip of her coffee. "What's the plan?"

"This morning I'm talking with Chadron's family and whatever friends they can give me, give forensics time to do their thing. By noon, we'll have more information. I've set up a meeting then to go over the case. I want you here for it."

"Thanks for keeping me in the loop."

"Of course." Stella paused. "There's one thing you could think about this morning. The money. We need to follow the cash on this drug deal. Is there anyone who seems to have hit the jackpot lately? Anyone who seems to have more money than usual?"

Instantly, Mattie thought of the hot springs crowd. Setting up a resort would take lots of money, but she knew nothing that tied them to the drug trade. "I'll keep that in mind and get back to you later."

Rainbow appeared at the staff office doorway. "Mattie, there's a call from Crane's Market about a shoplifter. Mr. Crane is holding the suspect in custody."

Mattie looked at Stella. "Duty calls. I'll see you back here around noon."

"Sounds good."

Robo was lying on his dog bed watching them.

"Robo? You ready to roll?" Mattie said.

He jumped up and trotted toward the door.

Stella returned Mattie's grin. "Looks like he is."

Outside, the morning air still felt crisp, but the sun's rays promised a hot day. She drove the few blocks between the department and Crane's Market. Mr. Crane, an older man with a stained apron covering his potbelly and a white butcher's cap on his gray head, stood out front. He had a small boy in tow who looked to be around five or six years old.

Oh, man . . . looks like the perp is just a little kid.

Quickly, Mattie hit the lights and whooped the siren once as she pulled to a stop, hoping to make a stronger impression on the young thief. Maybe she could add to his discomfort and stop him from continuing his wayward ways.

The boy wore a ragged denim jacket over his T-shirt and shorts. His blond hair was a mess, and his knees looked like grimy knobs.

Mattie left the cruiser running, air conditioning vented toward Robo, windows halfway down in the back. As she approached, Crane handed her a brown paper bag.

"This is what I found in his jacket pockets," Crane said.

Mattie peered inside the bag. Two jars of baby food, two cans of formula, four sticks of beef jerky. Strange items for a child to steal. She'd expected candy.

"Do you know his name?" she asked Crane.

"Sean O'Malley. His mom's a regular customer. Down and out. Lives over in that trailer house beside the Catholic church."

O'Malley, like Tommy O'Malley, the troublemaker at the high school. Was this his little brother?

She looked at the boy. He stood with eyes downcast, hands thrust in pockets, and chin set in a belligerent attitude. She remembered using that posture herself as a young girl.

"Do you know that stealing is wrong, Sean?" she asked him.

His eyes flickered up to touch on hers for a brief moment and then went back to studying the ground. But in that brief moment, Mattie connected with her own childhood, and she knew she'd have to side with the boy on this one.

She turned back to Crane. "I'll take him home and speak with his mother, investigate the home situation. You noticed the items he took were probably not for himself, right?"

"Yes. I won't press charges this time, but I don't want him coming back in my store without his parents again."

"Did you hear that, Sean?" Mattie asked.

Silence.

"You'd better answer. Mr. Crane is letting you go without sending you to jail. You should never do this again, because you might not be so lucky next time." Mattie paused to let that sink in. "Now, did you hear him say he doesn't want you coming back into his store without your parents?"

Sean shifted his weight. "Yes."

Mattie had an inkling that the parents were part of the problem. Why else would a child come into a grocery store to steal baby food?

"Do you understand that stealing is wrong?"

"Yeah," he said, begrudgingly.

"Is there a baby at your house that needs this food?"

Head down, he nodded.

"Just so you know, there are other ways to get food when you need it besides stealing. I'm going to pay Mr. Crane for the baby food this time, and we'll take it home to your mom. Then we'll look into getting some help for her to get more food."

Silence.

Crane screwed up his face in distaste. "Aw, hell, take the damn baby food. Take the jerky, too."

"What do you tell Mr. Crane for giving you the food?"

Sean looked at her as if he were clueless.

"You need to tell him thank you."

The kid squinted as if in pain, but he lifted his chin. "Thanks."

"Now get out of here," Crane said to him, turning away to go back inside, disgust evident.

"Come on," Mattie said, leading the way to the passenger side of the cruiser.

Robo barked a greeting and leaned out the open window, panting and showing his teeth. Sean stopped in his tracks, eyes wide.

"Go ahead and get in the car," Mattie said, opening the door. "There's a wire screen between you and him inside. He wouldn't hurt you, anyway."

Sean climbed in but perched on the front of the seat, twisting toward the back so he could keep his eye on the dog. Robo moved up to the front of the cage, eager to make friends.

"He's friendly, but don't reach your hand through the wire to pet him. It's never a good idea to do that with a strange dog." Mattie walked around the cruiser and sat in her own seat.

It would only take a few minutes to get to the boy's house, but Mattie hoped to get some information out of him before they got there. "How old are you?"

"Six."

"Do you have a dad at home?"

Perched on the front of his seat, grubby hands clutching the dashboard, Sean looked out the windshield. "Yes."

Mattie thought of her own father. "Did he tell you to steal the food?"

"No."

"Did your mom?"

"No."

Mattie thought he must be lying one way or the other. "Put on your seat belt so we can go."

Gingerly, Sean inched back in the seat, reaching for the belt while still keeping an eye on Robo.

Mattie put the car in gear. "Are you afraid of dogs?"

"No."

"He's a big one, I know." Not to mention he could be ferocious when necessary. She paused while she drove out into the street. "Who all lives at your house, Sean?"

He gave her a sideways glance and a shrug. "My mom and dad and baby sister."

"Is that all?"

"My big brother and sister." Sean pointed at the trailer house just past the church. "That's where I live."

"Any other grown-ups live with you, Sean?"

"No."

Mattie parked the car on the street in front of a ramshackle mobile home. The yard surrounding it had long ago gone to weeds. "Let's go talk to your parents."

"My dad's at work."

"Your mom then."

Leaving Robo in the car, she followed Sean through the clutter of junk left out in the yard: a rusted-out washing machine, numerous toys, the shell of an old Chevy auto body up on wooden blocks. They stepped up onto the splintered wooden deck.

Before Mattie could knock, a tired looking woman opened the door. She was holding an infant who had a runny nose. Her eyes shifted between Mattie and Sean, and Mattie could see her putting two and two together. She'd bet that the mother was the one who sent the boy out to shoplift.

"Mrs. O'Malley?" Mattie said.

"Yes."

"Mr. Crane caught Sean stealing food over at the market."

The woman's eyes misted, and her shoulders slumped as she turned her head aside, trying to hide her emotion from Mattie.

"Come inside, Sean," she said, her voice barely audible. She stepped out onto the deck and closed the door behind her, shutting Sean inside. "I'm sorry, Officer. I'll see that he's punished."

Mattie observed the woman's whipped demeanor, her old-fashioned and threadbare house dress, her rail-thin body that looked like it hadn't been fed a good meal in quite some time. "I'm not sure punishment is in order, Mrs. O'Malley. Did you tell Sean to get the food?"

A spark of anger flickered in the woman's eyes, long enough for Mattie to know it was there before the woman extinguished it. "Why would I do that?"

"Money's short, your children are hungry. It's understandable."

As if to reinforce Mattie's words, the baby whimpered half-heartedly. Mrs. O'Malley shushed her and patted her gently on the back.

Behind her, Mattie heard gears grind and gravel crunch. She turned to see an old beater pickup truck, blue paint showing between rusty dents, pull up and park behind her patrol car.

A man with a thundercloud on his face got out of the vehicle. Tall and lean with brown hair grown halfway down his neck, he crossed the yard in a few quick, angry strides.

"What's the police doing here?" he asked the woman.

Mattie assumed the man was Mr. O'Malley. Two teenagers, a boy whom she recognized as Tommy and a girl, got out of the truck on the passenger side and came around where Mattie could see them. The girl's short hair was dyed bright red and Tommy's was bleached blond. Mattie guessed they were close to the same age, although Tommy appeared to be older. They stayed by the truck.

Mrs. O'Malley shrank away from the angry man. "The . . . this officer brought Sean home."

He looked at Mattie, his dark eyes demanding an explanation.

Mattie instantly disliked him. "Your name, sir?"

"Patrick O'Malley. Who wants to know?"

"I'm Deputy Cobb from the sheriff's office." She held out the paper bag in a slight gesture. "Sean was caught taking food from Crane's Market."

Patrick snatched the bag and looked inside. He glared at his wife, who was trying, in vain, to comfort the baby. "I'll take care of this," he said to Mattie.

She wasn't sure what he meant, but she didn't like it. "Mr. Crane gave the food to your family with a warning that he doesn't want Sean coming back into the store without his parents. He isn't going to press charges. I've warned Sean that he won't get off so lightly if it happens again."

"It won't happen again," Patrick said. He thrust the bag toward his wife, forcing her to juggle the infant into one arm so she could take it. "Take her inside and see if you can shut her up."

Mrs. O'Malley went inside the trailer.

"I'm going to ask social services to make a visit today so we can get you the resources you need." She knew they wouldn't visit on a Sunday, but she thought an eminent home visit might protect his family.

Anger darkened his face.

Tommy left the truck and sauntered up. "Dad's been out of work, but he has a job now, and I have a job."

Mattie read the kid as wanting to help diffuse the situation. "Hi, Tommy."

The girl had come up behind him. "Hi," Mattie said to her. "And your name is?"

"Molly," Tommy said before the girl could speak.

"Why do you know my son?" Patrick said, clearly unhappy about it.

Mattie decided not to mention that she'd first met Tommy months ago when she confronted him and his friends for littering in the park. "I met Tommy in the park a while back, sir. Him and some of his friends." She addressed all of them. "I know times have been rough, but it sounds like you'll have more income soon."

She withdrew several business cards from her shirt pocket and gave one to Patrick and each of the kids. "You can reach me at this number if I can do anything to help. Tommy, could I have a word with you out by the car?"

Patrick opened the trailer door. "Come inside, Molly." Giving Mattie a mean look, he disappeared into the trailer with Molly following.

After moving toward the car, Mattie faced Tommy. "Has your father even been violent with anyone in your family?"

He smirked. "Nah, he's a pussycat."

"Don't hesitate to dial nine-one-one if you fear for your safety. Or the safety of anyone else."

"Sure thing," he said with a smart-alecky tone.

She decided to move on. "Did you hear about Grace Hartman?"

The smirk left his face. "Yeah, I heard. Everybody's talking about it."

"Were you friends with her?"

"Are you shittin' me? Grace ran in a different crowd."

"Did you want to be friends with her?"

"Nah, I have friends of my own. She was too stuck up for us."

"Sounds like you didn't like her."

Tommy shrugged and put his hands back in his pockets. He seemed to take the question seriously. "Nah . . . it was more like we just didn't have any use for each other."

Mattie hadn't been out of high school so long that she couldn't remember how cliques could coexist peacefully in a small town. She believed he was telling the truth.

"Do you know Mike Chadron?"

"Knew who he *was*."

"So you know he's dead, too."

"Yep."

"How'd you know that?" she asked.

"One of my friends told me."

His eyes slid away when he said it, and she suspected he was lying. But she didn't know why. "What did you hear about it?"

"Just that he killed himself last night."

"Anything else you know about Mike?"

"Why would I know anything else about him?"

"Just tell me what you know."

"I know he has a bunch of dogs he brings to the park. That's about it."

She figured he was back to at least partial truth. Tommy spent a lot of time hanging out at the park; he'd probably seen Mike there. She wondered if he knew anything about Mike and their suspicion of him transporting cocaine, but she couldn't ask him about it directly.

"I'm on a mission to clear drugs out of Timber Creek, Tommy."

He looked back toward his house. "What does that have to do with me?"

"I believe you may know something about drugs around here."

"Well, I don't."

"I'm not trying to bust you. I just want to know who's selling."

He shifted away from her, and she could tell she was losing him. "I don't know anything about that, I'm telling you."

"Is there anyone you've noticed who has more money than usual? Someone with cash?"

"That guy out at the hot springs. The owner. I hear he's rich."

She'd expected him to mention Mike or one of his peers. She was surprised he'd bring up the owner of the hot springs. She doubted they ran in the same circles.

"Anyone else?" she asked.

"No." He looked sullen. "I don't even know anything about him."

"That's okay. You think about this conversation and let me know if you can come up with anyone else. I'll check back in with you later."

Avoiding her gaze, he turned away and headed for the trailer. As he entered, he looked back to see her watching him. Giving her a little finger wave, he closed the door.

Feeling unsettled, Mattie climbed into her cruiser and drove away, wondering why a teenager would notice that the hot springs owner had a lot of cash.

Chapter 16

During the next hour, Mattie patrolled the streets of Timber Creek thinking about her conversation with Tommy O'Malley. She'd expected him to deny any knowledge of drug use or Grace's killing, but she'd been surprised when he mentioned the hot springs owner. Had he blurted out the name of his supplier when he'd felt pressured?

The killing of Grace Hartman and Mike Chadron had to be related to the drug trade. Yesterday, when Angela Walker said there'd been rumors that Tommy O'Malley might be selling, she'd backed off from pressing her, both for the sake of establishing rapport and because she felt sympathy for the girl's grief. Now she needed to know if Tommy had a reputation as a dealer at school or not. She needed something more solid the next time she questioned him.

Perhaps Angela's grief wouldn't be as new and raw as it had been yesterday. She reached for her cell phone, swiped to Cole Walker's business number, and dialed.

"Hello, Deputy Cobb," he said.

"Good morning. How are the salmonella patients doing today?"

"They're better, thanks, at least from a physical standpoint. From the looks of things, I'd guess that they're both a little depressed though."

"Yeah." Mattie's mind conjured pictures of both dog and teen from the day before. She sighed and said in a tone meant to show her sympathy. "Why wouldn't they be, right? You, too, I imagine."

He cleared his throat. "I'll be all right."

She adopted a more businesslike tone. "Have you heard about Mike Chadron yet?"

"No, what's up?"

"We found him last night at his home. Deceased. Apparent suicide."

"Good grief! That's not like the Mike I know. In all the times he brought his dogs in, he never once seemed despondent or depressed."

His comment backed up their theory. "Really?" she said, inviting more.

"Well, maybe he hid it, like some people do." He paused. Mattie waited to see if he'd continue. "My wife has been dealing with depression all summer, earlier than that, really, unbeknownst to me. So who am I to be able to recognize it?"

"I'm sorry about your wife's troubles," Mattie said, surprised that he would share something so personal.

"Ex-wife, I should say. I'm not used to that yet."

So the rumors were true. "I'm sure it's been hard on you. The kids, too."

"Yeah." He paused again.

Mattie switched the topic back to business. "I wondered if I could talk to Angela again this morning."

"Yes, but later. My sister will be leaving, and we need to spend some time with her first. Maybe you could come by around eleven thirty?"

"House or office?"

"House."

"I'll be there."

After disconnecting the call, Mattie realized she felt flushed. She'd never been comfortable discussing people's personal lives unless the discussion had something to do with the job. Surely that was the only reason.

She decided to call Stella to tell her about the hot springs lead, and the detective answered immediately.

"LoSasso."

Mattie told her about her conversation with Tommy and how he pointed to the owner of the hot springs as someone who had a lot of money. She shared her suspicion that the group could be involved with drug running. "One of us should go out there and meet him. See if he could also be a suspect for our killings."

"I'm on my way to meet Chadron's parents now. You go ahead and see what you think. When we meet at noon, we'll share info and set up a plan for next steps."

"All right."

Mattie checked in with dispatch, telling Rainbow that she was headed out to patrol the highway. She didn't want Rainbow to call ahead and inadvertently alert her new friends about the visit, so she didn't mention her destination. Taking Highway 12 out of town, she passed the turnoff to the vet clinic and realized she'd be back just about the right time to stop in for her appointment.

Their route also led to Ute Canyon, and Robo stood behind her, watching intensely out the windshield. She realized he remembered the drive from both days before and thought he was going back up to work.

"We're not heading up there today. Not that I know of anyway. We're going to Valley Vista hot springs. You'll see."

During the ten-minute drive through dry grassland on the valley floor, the elevation rose slightly so that she could see Timber Creek, like an oasis surrounded by trees, behind her.

She turned east onto a county road that stretched in a gray line running upslope and ended in a pocket of aspen growing in a canyon at the base of the mountains. Although Valley Vista was located only halfway up the road, Mattie had been to the end many times, hiking the trails that led to crystal-clear lakes nestled between the peaks above timberline.

Valley Vista itself couldn't boast the jewel-like appearance of the lakes in the high country. Instead, it was more like a concrete-lined mud hole in the middle of nowhere, surrounded by buffalo grass and rabbit bush. Abandoned for years, the only structure at the place was a tumbledown bathhouse that had been built decades earlier. There were no trees to block the high-altitude sunlight that beat down on the valley, creating solar waves that bent the atmosphere.

As Mattie approached, she could see the cluster of large, white tents that had been pitched around the premises. The old bathhouse had been taken down and a new one had been partially framed to take its place. Three workmen paused to observe her as she parked her patrol car on the far side of the pool and turned off the engine. Since there was no shade to park under, she decided to take Robo with her. Besides, an alert from a narcotics detection dog provided probable cause to search, something she would just love to do.

She remembered the name of Rainbow's new friend. "I'm looking for Anya Yamamoto," she called to the workers.

A well-muscled, young Hispanic male, shirtless and with sweat glistening on his brown skin, pointed his hammer toward the nearest tent. Now that she was closer, she could see that it was actually a yurt. "Should be over there. If she's not, someone should be there to help you."

"Thanks."

The rotten egg smell from the sulfur springs was decidedly unpleasant. She opened her mouth slightly so she wouldn't have to breathe through her nostrils and made her way toward the yurt, a white nylon structure supported with a wooden frame. Its flaps were pinned back, and as Mattie approached, she could see that it contained a floor made from a wooden platform, two desks with computers on top, printers, telephones, and other equipment that made up an office. Mattie figured the entire setup, including several other yurts and electrical installation, must have cost a bundle.

She wondered where the money to front this enterprise was coming from.

An Asian woman was seated at one desk, a man at the other. The woman rose to greet her while the man's attention remained fixed on his computer screen. He was tapping away at the keyboard.

The woman said, "Mattie Cobb . . . welcome."

Surprised, Mattie said, "You know me?"

The woman smiled. "From Rainbow's description. None other could be dressed in officer's uniform, leading a large, black dog."

The man glanced her way and then moved his computer mouse in a furtive way, closing down his screen.

"I'm Anya Yamamoto and this is Valley Vista's owner, Dean Hornsby. We're delighted you came to pay us a visit."

Mattie shook hands with the woman. She looked to be thirtysomething and a little more than five feet tall. She had black hair in a straight bob, almond-shaped eyes, and flat cheekbones. She held her small mouth slightly pursed.

"I'm pleased to meet you," Mattie said. "Rainbow mentioned you to me, too."

"I'm sorry we missed meeting you last night."

Mattie dipped her chin in acknowledgement and turned to Dean Hornsby, offering a handshake. "Mr. Hornsby," she said.

He arose to shake her hand. He stood slouched with rounded shoulders and a protruding belly, his body looking as soft as his handshake. He wore his brown hair in a bad comb-over, and he peered at her through Coke-bottle lenses. "Welcome, Ms. Cobb."

"That's Deputy Cobb, sir." She wanted him to know this was more than a social call. "Rainbow told me about your spa, and I was hoping to take a look."

Anya wore a white flowing garment that gave the appearance of being gauzy and cool. She reminded Mattie of a Bedouin, which suited the surrounding encampment. Hornsby had on khaki shorts and a tan shirt with a button-down collar, making him look like he was just about ready to go on safari. All he lacked was the hat.

Anya stepped toward her with a slight smile. "I'll be glad to show you around. It will give us a chance to get to know one another better."

Motioning toward his computer, Hornsby said, "I have some work to do, so I'll leave you girls to it."

"Mr. Hornsby, I want to speak with you, too," Mattie said.

"Certainly."

"Rainbow says you have big plans for out here."

"Yes, we do. I'm sure Anya can explain everything to you while she gives you the tour."

Mattie waved a hand toward the tent opening. "Place like this must cost a lot of money to set up."

"I have the capital for it, but I'm not sure I understand why it's any of your concern."

"What brought you here to set up a business in such an isolated place?"

Hornsby looked impatient, making Mattie wonder why he felt so pressed to get back to his computer. "The hot springs. I wanted to set up a resort that was far from the crush of the city. So here we are."

"Where are you from, Mr. Hornsby?"

"Phoenix."

Mattie knew little about Phoenix except that Brody liked to go play golf there almost every time he took vacation. "What did you do there?"

Hornsby began to bluster, growing red in the face. "I need to get back to work. For some reason, I'm beginning to feel like this is an interrogation. What's your concern?"

"My concern is stopping drug traffic in Timber Creek." Mattie observed him to see his reaction.

Hornsby sputtered. "You can't possibly think that we have anything to do with that."

"Do you?"

"Of course not."

"Then you won't mind telling me how you got the capital to front this operation."

Hornsby glared at her. "I'm a legitimate businessman. And I raise capital like any businessman does, through past earnings and investments."

"From what source?"

"Technology and soft goods! Now, I must excuse myself and get back to work."

"Just a few more questions, Mr. Hornsby. Do either of you know Grace Hartman?"

"She is the young girl who was killed," Anya said. "No, I did not know her."

"Mr. Hornsby?"

"No."

"Do you know her parents?"

Both indicated they did not.

"How about Mike Chadron?" Mattie asked. "Do you know him?"

Anya shook her head. "I do not know this person either."

"What is this all about?" Hornsby asked. "Why all these questions? Who is this Mike person?"

"Mike's a local resident who was found dead last night."

Anya frowned. "Also killed?"

"His death is under investigation."

"It's ridiculous for you to imply we might have something to do with these deaths," Hornsby said.

"I implied nothing. I'm simply asking you if you knew these people."

"No, I didn't." Hornsby gestured toward the door. "Now, I insist that you leave. I must get back to work, and I think you've wasted enough of my time."

He sat down at his computer and put his hand on the mouse, making Mattie's fingers itch to get at it herself.

Anya stepped forward. "You're welcome to stay, and I'll show you around. We have nothing to hide here."

Hornsby's reaction to her presence had been strange from the beginning, and she wondered why. She decided to see what she could discover through Anya. "Thanks, I'm still interested in a tour."

Anya smiled. "Let's go outside."

Mattie turned to Hornsby. "Thank you for your time, Mr. Hornsby. If your business is legitimate, of course you're welcome here." *If not, we'll find out about it and shut you down.* "I'm sorry if my questions disturbed you. I'm just doing my job."

He gave her a brusque nod of dismissal.

She followed Anya out into the hot sunshine, Robo close at her side.

As they walked, Anya said, "Your suspicions are misdirected, Mattie. May I call you Mattie?"

"You may."

"I expect that you are suspicious of almost everyone, and we are no exception. Is that true?"

"Part of being a law officer."

Anya gave her an appraising look that made Mattie wonder if the woman could read her mind. Just before she got really uncomfortable, they reached the next yurt. Pulling aside the flap, Anya gestured with a delicate hand for her to step inside.

"This is where I work."

The yurt was as large as the other. It was filled with the clean aroma of sage, and a padded massage table covered with lavender-colored sheets stood in the center. One of the walls was lined with floor cupboards containing Lord knows what.

Two end tables, one holding a large bowl filled with black stones and the other a small CD player, sat against the opposite wall.

Anya flipped a thumb switch on a cord leading to the bowl filled with stones, turning it into a circling fountain accompanied by the soothing sound of bubbling water. "Has Rainbow told you about our health spa?"

"Not in detail."

"We'll be providing a variety of health services in conjunction with the healing qualities of the mineral hot springs. Several of our yurts are set up for guests. Though our bathhouse isn't yet completed, we have already hosted a few guests."

Drawn by the bubbling fountain, Mattie touched one of the black rocks; its surface felt smooth as glass. Robo raised his nose up to the table to take a drink. Mattie quickly stopped him. "No, Robo. I have water for you out in the car."

Anya's laughter sounded like a tinkling bell. "Let me get him some when we go outside."

Remembering the tainted water in Robo's water bowl in her backyard, Mattie said, "No, he's fine, really. We won't stay long, and I can take care of him."

"He's a beautiful dog. May I pet him?"

"Sure, just hold out your hand for him to sniff first." As Anya complied, Mattie said, "Robo, meet Anya."

He waved his tail while he was being petted, and Mattie noticed he seemed to have no concerns about the woman. She'd also noticed him sniffing around at the unusual scents the room contained, but so far, no alert.

Anya finished petting Robo and straightened. She went to one of the cupboards and opened it. "You might be curious about some of our equipment."

Mattie did want to know more, and she moved forward to peer inside. This cupboard contained a soft felt strip of fabric with pockets holding tuning forks and several small bells. She saw numerous small bottles and read the labels on some: sage, lavender, peppermint, frankincense.

What the hell is all this used for?

Though the scents made Robo sniff toward the closet, he still showed no sign of alert for narcotics.

"Let me show you the rest of our resort. It's rustic now, but we have great plans."

Anya showed Mattie one of the guest yurts, set up with two twin-size beds and a small dresser, a lounge chair, and an ottoman. Nice little home away from home. When they stepped outside, an attractive blonde wearing white shorts and a pink tank top was passing by on the gravel path.

"This is Adrienne Howard, one of our massage therapists," Anya said, introducing Mattie.

The woman's handshake was firm and the gaze from her gray eyes direct. "It's nice to meet you," she said. "I've heard about you and your dog."

"Wow," Mattie replied. "And who's been talking about us?"

Adrienne smiled. "Various people, Rainbow among them."

"Oh, yes. Rainbow is excited about your work out here."

"She's a sweetheart."

Not knowing exactly how to answer that, Mattie glanced at her watch and realized her appointment with the Walkers was approaching. She'd seen enough to know that everything else she'd be shown today would look like a legitimate health spa, whether it was or not. "I have to go now. It's been nice to meet you both."

After returning a polite response, Adrienne said good-bye and left.

"I appreciate you showing me around," Mattie told Anya.

"I hope you'll come back for a treatment."

"I'm not sure I'll be able to take the time."

"I could give you Reiki. We could start with only a half hour if you are short on time."

"And that is?"

"A type of treatment, very relaxing. Then we could start revitalizing your heart chakra."

Mattie had no possible way she could respond to that.

Anya smiled slightly, as if understanding Mattie's discomfort. "I'll teach you what I'm talking about. I hope we can put your mind to rest about our business. We have nothing to do with the criminal element you have to deal with here in Timber Creek, and I wish you the best in eliminating it. Even though Dean is uncomfortable talking about his income, I can assure you he comes by his money honestly."

Mattie said good-bye and headed back to Timber Creek. Though Anya Yamamoto spoke a language that Mattie was unfamiliar with, she seemed sincere and truthful about her profession.

Dean Hornsby, on the other hand, lit up Mattie's radar. Though he didn't seem like the sinister type, she suspected he was hiding something. There was something about him that she found hard to put a finger on. She decided to run her interview past Stella and recommend that the detective also pay him a visit.

Chapter 17

When Mattie rolled into her now familiar parking spot in front of the Walker house, she saw Cole Walker and his daughters out in the front yard with Belle on a leash. The large dog was walking gingerly on three legs, barely touching the ground with the fourth. Mattie paused for a moment, enjoying the sight of little Sophie carefully guiding Belle from flower bed to rose bush, offering her each tantalizing blossom to sniff. Smiling, she rolled down the windows for Robo and got out.

"Hey, Sophie," she said as the girl slowly led Belle over to greet her.

"Hi!" Sophie called. "See Belle walk."

Robo barked from his cage in the back of the cruiser.

Mattie turned to give him the look, but this time it didn't work, and he barked again. "Robo, quiet."

He settled down with a whimper.

Walker and Angela joined them.

"I see her," Mattie said to Sophie. "It looks like she's doing real well for the day after surgery." She glanced at Walker for confirmation.

"She is," he said. "We just said good-bye to my sister and decided to give Belle a little exercise. She's had about enough now, Sophie. Let's go up on the porch."

"Okay." Sophie said to Mattie, "She can do stairs, too, even on three legs."

"Oh, wow," Mattie replied and then turned her attention to Angela. The girl's face had better color than it did yesterday morning. "How are you feeling today? Did you get over the food poisoning?"

"Yes, that stuff was nasty."

"I'll bet. Clucken House is still shut down today."

"It doesn't matter to us, we won't be going back there for a while," Walker said. "Do you want to get Robo out of the car? The girls would like to meet him, and it looks like he'd like to meet them, too."

Mattie turned back to the cruiser to see Robo grinning and waving his tail. When he saw her turn, he started doing his happy dance.

Mattie remembered the face-off over Grace Hartman's grave between Robo and Belle a couple days ago. "I don't know. He's friendly with kids and well socialized with dogs, but he and Belle squared off the last time they were together. I wouldn't want them to mix it up and hurt Belle." She observed the two dogs—Belle seemed to be ignoring Robo for the most part, and Robo just wanted to play.

"Sophie, I think it's time for Belle to go inside and lie down on her bed for a while anyway. Why don't you and Angie go put her there and then come out and meet Robo?"

It looked like Belle was happy to follow the two girls as she limped after them. Mattie waited with the doctor and watched the dog take the three steps up onto the deck and hobble inside.

She turned away to get Robo out of the car, and Walker followed her.

"I told the kids that Robo found Grace. He's something of a hero in their eyes." He wore a somber expression. "I didn't tell them that Belle dug up her body."

The memory of finding Belle trying to protect the teen's body would stick with Mattie for a long time, and she shared in the vet's sadness. "Robo was in a down-stay, showing me what he'd found. He didn't want to fight with Belle, but she was protecting the girl's body from him."

"That must have been hard on you, too." He searched her face as if trying to read her feelings, looking away when his daughters came out of the house. "Well, let's let him get out now so he can play. He can distract Sophie while you talk to Angela."

"I'll put him on a leash."

Robo worked his magic on the girls, and Mattie could tell they were just as taken with him as they seemed to be with Belle.

As Sophie led Robo around the yard, the other two Walkers and Mattie settled into wrought iron patio chairs that were circled around a matching table. Angela sat on her hands and leaned forward in her chair. Mattie noticed she had a pink flush on her pale neck.

Trying to put her more at ease, Mattie relaxed back into her own chair. "Angela, thanks for talking with me again. You don't have to answer any question you don't want to. I think you're brave, and I admire you for being so willing to help."

Angela nodded, her eyes lowered.

"We're pretty sure that Grace's death had something to do with drugs." Angela looked up sharply, frowning, but Mattie continued. "Now, you said yesterday that to your knowledge Grace never had anything to do with drugs, and I believe you. But I want you to keep an open mind and think. Is there a chance that she got involved with the drug scene this summer while you've been away?"

Angela started shaking her head even before Mattie had finished her sentence. "No, Grace wasn't like that. She wouldn't even smoke a joint."

"I hear ya. So what I'm searching for is someone else then. Someone who might have been involved with drugs that she hung out with." She was thinking of Mike Chadron but needed Angela to be the one to say it.

Angela expelled a breath of air and swiped at a lock of hair that had fallen toward her face. "Okay, some of our friends smoke weed. Once in a while. But I'm not going to tell you who they are." She met Mattie's gaze with all the teen defiance she could muster under the circumstances.

The vet fidgeted in his chair, and Mattie could guess how hard he was working to keep silent.

"You don't have to tell me, Angie," she said in a soft voice. "I'm not interested in those kids right now. But I do need to know of anyone involved in cocaine. Not just students, anyone around town."

"None of the kids I know use cocaine. I mean, like I told you before, maybe Tommy O'Malley and his crowd, but I'm not even sure about them. That's just something I heard from someone who heard, you know? Rumor." Angela moved around in her chair as if trapped. "I don't know for a fact about anyone using or selling hard drugs at school or around town. I don't hang with kids that do hard drugs. And Grace didn't either. I do know that."

Walker leaned forward. "She's telling you the truth, Deputy. We've talked. I believe she can't give you any more information to help you with that line of your investigation."

Mattie was quick to agree. "Oh, I believe she's telling the truth, too. I'm grateful for that, Angela. And don't think you're not helping. Anything you tell us about Grace and what she might have been doing this summer could help us find her killer, even though you might not be able to point a finger at anyone. Let's shift gears for a minute and talk about Tommy O'Malley."

Angela's eyes opened wide and then narrowed as her brow knit. "Is Tommy a suspect?"

"Not necessarily."

Sophie skipped up with Robo gamboling at her side. "Tommy O'Malley smokes weed," she piped up.

"Good Lord," Walker muttered.

Frowning, Angela asked, "How do you know that?"

"His little brother was my kindergarten partner last year."

"Kindergarten partner?"

"The teachers gave each of us second graders a kindergarten kid to read to. I got Sean."

Mattie checked in with Walker by giving him a direct look. It was one thing to interview a teenager with her parent's permission but quite another to question a child Sophie's age.

Walker took over. "Did Sean ever say anything about his brother using cocaine? I'm assuming you know all about cocaine, too, you being such an expert."

Sophie smiled at him, looking wise beyond her years. "Sure I do. Nope, he only talked about Tommy smoking weed. He says he does it at the park with his friends."

"And you know that's against the law, and if you ever do something like that you'll not only be in trouble with me but with the police, too?"

"Drugs are bad, Dad," Sophie said. "I know that. Mom told me."

"I'm just saying, Sophie. So you know what I think, too."

Mattie decided to switch topics, trying to see if Angela knew anything about Chadron's involvement with drugs. "Just one more thing, Angela. Did you happen to remember anything else Grace said about Mike Chadron that could help us?"

"Dad said he heard Mike killed himself last night," Angela said.

"That's what it looks like."

"Grace talked about him a lot, but it was just silly stuff. Nothing about drugs."

"Did she happen to mention any of his friends?"

Angela was shaking her head when a blue Ford pickup truck turned into the lane. Mattie paused her questioning to see who had arrived. The truck parked beside her cruiser, and she recognized the man exiting the vehicle as Garrett Hartman.

"Oh, no . . ." Sophie moaned. "Here, Angie, take Robo." The child stuffed Robo's leash into her sister's hand and darted into the house, firmly closing the door behind her.

Mattie wondered what was wrong with her.

"Uh-oh," Angela said, tears welling in her eyes. She turned to Mattie. "Mr. Hartman's going to take Belle home."

"Excuse me," Walker said, pushing up from his chair and going out to greet the man.

Garrett Hartman stood well over six feet with a rangy build, his craggy face sheltered by a worn felt Stetson. A Viking of a man, he was a familiar figure in town, one of the community's leaders. His startling blue eyes found Mattie up on the porch, and he seemed to watch her even as he greeted Walker.

"Here, I'll take Robo," Mattie said, reaching for the leash. She moved off the porch, Angela and Robo following.

"I'm Deputy Cobb, Mr. Hartman," she said as she approached the two men. "I'm sorry for your loss."

"I know who you are," he said, clasping Mattie's extended hand in both of his. "You and your dog found my Grace."

Apparently that was all Angela could take, because she burst into sobs.

"Angie, come here, honey." Hartman stretched out a long left arm and tucked Angela against his side while still holding Mattie's hand in his right.

He continued to speak to Mattie as he gave Angie a comforting squeeze. "My wife and I are eternally grateful. Without you, we might never have known."

"I'm glad we were in the right place at the right time. Without the ranger's call, we wouldn't have been up there at all."

Hartman nodded, his eyes reddened and sad. He gave Mattie's hand another squeeze and released it. Then he enfolded Angela in both arms and bowed his head over hers, dwarfing the slim girl. "Ah, Angie," he said quietly. "We're going to miss her."

Feeling awkward and out of place, Mattie wanted to leave, but interrupting their grief seemed inappropriate, so she took a step backward to allow them privacy. Walker placed a comforting hand on Hartman's shoulder, and his dark eyes searched out hers, including her in the circle. She wished she knew what to say but didn't, so she waited in silence.

After gathering himself back into a semblance of control, Hartman squeezed Angie and then set her back away from him, putting an arm over her shoulders. The girl had also quieted her sobs. "There'll be a funeral for Grace this Wednesday at eleven. You're welcome to come," he said to Walker and Mattie.

"The girls and I will be there," Walker said while Mattie merely nodded.

"I can take Belle off your hands now."

"She's inside the house. I'll go get her," Walker said.

"I'll settle up my bill, too."

"No, you won't. There's no charge."

"I can still pay my way."

"Of course you can, but it's the least I can do to help you and Leslie. If there's anything else you need, please let me know." Walker turned and headed toward the porch but hesitated when a charcoal Toyota 4Runner turned up the driveway.

He changed directions and walked toward the Toyota. Mattie recognized Principal John Brennaman as the newcomer. He exited his car and, holding a covered dish in his left hand, shook hands with Walker. He glanced her way, appearing as surprised to see her as she was to see him.

"Mattie," he said to her by way of greeting.

"Hello, Mr. Brennaman."

Robo took a step toward the principal and bristled. "Heel," Mattie told him, using the leash to give a correction and put him back at her side.

"Garrett, I see you're here, too," Brennaman said in a voice filled with sympathy. "I am so, so sorry. Words cannot express . . ."

The two clasped hands.

"Thank you, John. It's been a horrible shock to Leslie and me."

"Of course it has. If there's anything I can do, anything at all. Well, you know how to reach me." Brennaman turned his attention to Angela. "Angela, I'm sorry for you, too. I know you'll miss your friend."

Angela remained by Garrett Hartman's side, droopy and all cried out. She nodded at him, keeping her face slightly downcast. "Thanks."

"Cole," Brennaman said, handing the dish over. "Rosellen baked casseroles today. I've been sent to deliver one to you, and then I was planning to take one out to you and Leslie, Garrett. You've saved me a trip by both being here in the same place."

Walker's brows shot up as he took the casserole dish. "That's really nice of her, John, but why is she sending one to us?"

"Just being neighborly. We hear you've been batching it this summer."

Walker's face took on a trace of disgust. "Word does spread around town."

Brennaman had the decency to look embarrassed. "I'm sorry, Cole, we're not a couple of old gossips. Yes, stories spread through this town like wildfire. Besides, I wanted to speak with Angela for a moment if I might."

He moved a hand in his daughter's direction. "She's here."

"I just wanted to let you know, Angela, that we need a student volunteer for the office this year." He threw an apologetic look at Hartman who bowed his head, allowing the broad brim of his Stetson to shield his eyes. "I'm not sure this is the time to talk about it, so I'll just mention it and let you talk it over with your dad. It would look good on your high school transcript. I know you're only a sophomore this year, too young to be thinking of applying for college, but it never hurts to start early."

Mattie couldn't help but compare the principal's demeanor toward Angela to the way he used to treat her when she was that age. His manner wasn't quite ingratiating, but it was a long way from the derision he'd once passed her way. Well, she'd be the first to admit she'd been a difficult teenager to like in those days.

Brennaman made a gesture toward his car. "I should go. Like I said, this isn't the time for us to talk about it, but maybe you could call me tomorrow to let me know if you're interested or not. I need to fill that position before school starts if I can." He paused. "I hope you had lots of time to spend with Grace this summer, Angela."

Angela's face crumpled, and Mattie knew she regretted being away most of the summer. The girl nodded, looking as if she didn't trust herself to speak.

"Well, those memories should lessen your pain in time." He moved to get the second casserole dish to hand to Garrett Hartman.

The sound of Belle barking furiously came from inside the house. Mattie turned and saw the big dog standing at an open window on the main level, pressing her nose against the screen. She hoped she wouldn't try to break through it and hurt herself. Walker must have had the same concern, because he quickly shook Brennaman's hand. "I need to go get Belle. Sounds like she might have heard Garrett and is eager to see him. Please thank your wife for the casserole." He took the dish with him as he left.

"Oh, Grace's dog?" Brennaman said.

"Yes," Hartman said. "She got shot, too, but survived."

"Oh my . . . what a tragedy. I must go, Garrett, but I hope to see you soon." As he shook hands with the man, he glanced at Mattie. "I'll see you tomorrow, Mattie?"

"Yes, sir."

"I'll be at the school. Just come anytime. Seems like I live there." He said good-bye, got into his car, and drove away.

Mattie noticed that Robo seemed happy to see him go. He looked up at her and waved his tail gently. She smoothed the hair on his back, thinking it was way past time for her to leave. But then, Walker came out of the house, leading Belle with Sophie trailing behind. The young girl carried a large stuffed rabbit that looked like it had seen better years. Even as Mattie watched, she stuck one of the rabbit's ears into her mouth and clamped her jaw down on it. She appeared even more upset than she'd been yesterday.

Belle sniffed the yard where the group had been standing as she approached Hartman. He bent to pat on her side, and she leaned against him. When he straightened, he gave both of Walker's daughters a searching look, and Mattie felt certain that he didn't miss the girls' distress over Belle's departure.

Sophie continued to suck on the rabbit's ear as the men loaded Belle into the passenger seat of the pickup. Angela drifted over to her sister, put an arm around her, and stood looking stricken. Mattie could hardly stand it. She led Robo over to touch Angela's shoulder while Sophie put a hand on Robo's head.

"She's better off going home," Angela said in a quiet voice.

Mattie wasn't quite sure if she spoke to her or to her sister, but she replied, "She'll be fine." Belle stared out the windshield at the two girls, though, and Mattie had to wonder.

Hartman rounded the truck to go to the driver's side but paused and turned back as if he'd remembered something. "Angie," he said, "I need to ask you something. Leslie and I noticed that one of Grace's rings was missing."

"Which one is it?"

"The one we gave her for her sixteenth birthday this summer. Do you know what it looks like?"

"The gold band with the ruby?"

"Yes, that's the one. It's the only ring she has of any value. Do you think she'd give it to someone?"

"No way."

Hartman looked at Mattie. "It's missing then. It could've been stolen. By . . . by the person who . . ."

Mattie felt a little surge of adrenalin. This could mean something. "Have you told Detective LoSasso yet?"

"No, I wanted to check with Angie first."

"I'm on my way to meet with her, so I'll tell her about it. She'll call you if she needs more information."

Hartman drove away, and when Walker joined them, she could see that he wasn't immune to his daughters' feelings.

Static erupted from the radio inside Mattie's cruiser followed by Rainbow's voice. "K-9 One. Copy."

"Excuse me," Mattie said. She hurried to the car, Robo trotting beside her. Pressing on the transmitter, she responded with her location, "Timber Creek Veterinary Clinic. Go ahead."

"Code ten-nineteen to the station at your earliest convenience. Over."

"Ten-four. I'm on my way."

Mattie keyed off the transmitter and hung it in its cradle. "I need to get back to the office now," she said. "But I'll be in touch."

After letting the girls say good-bye to Robo, she loaded him up and got into the cruiser. When they reached the porch, the girls turned to wave. Mattie waved back, thinking they looked awfully lonely, but there was nothing she could do about that. She fired up the engine, eager to get back to the station to see what Stella thought about the missing ring.

Chapter 18

Back at the station, Mattie found Sheriff McCoy, Stella, and Brody in the report room gathered around a dry-erase board that had been wheeled from its usual place beside the wall and positioned up front and center. McCoy was seated at a table taking notes in a small spiral booklet while Stella was writing on the board, adding final touches to an information grid she'd made that appeared to outline the current information, evidence, and clues she'd compiled regarding the two Timber Creek deaths. Brody sat at McCoy's table, arms crossed on his chest.

Mattie took a seat at the table behind them and told Robo to lie down beside her. He did so immediately but remained crouched, ears pricked and alert.

"I'm glad you're here, Mattie," Stella said. "We've had a great deal of information come in from forensics this morning. I'm getting ready to start going through it."

Brody cleared his throat and twitched his shoulders, rolling his head from side to side as if to release tightness. Stella pointed to the upper middle of her grid where she'd written "Victim 2: Mike Chadron." Her finger moved down the grid as she described each point.

"The ME has agreed with me that Mike Chadron doesn't look like a suicide. He doesn't have gunshot residue on his hands, and there was no gunpowder stippling at his temple. Most importantly, though, there were no prints on the gun. It appears to have been wiped clean, and suicide victims don't wipe their weapons after shooting themselves." Stella gave them a grim smile. "So we're ruling it death by gunshot wound to the head, manner undetermined. I'm assuming this is another homicide, and we're going to work it that way."

"The crime scene was unorganized," McCoy said.

"Yes. In fact, we can say that about both our crime scenes."

"Not done by a pro," Brody said.

Stella moved her hand to the upper left side of her grid where she'd written "Victim 1: Grace Hartman." "We've uncovered quite a bit of information about our first victim, and I've narrowed down a few key points here. First, I got word that the blood type at the cabin matches Grace's. Let's assume she was killed at the cabin, moved a mile away, and buried."

Mattie raised a hand to interrupt. "I just talked with her father. There's a ring from one of her fingers missing, a plain gold band with a ruby. He said it's the only ring of value that she wore."

Stella's brow raised as she turned to write the information on the grid. "What can we make of that?"

"Theft?" Brody asked.

"Could be. Or maybe a trophy? Whatever the reason, it could become valuable evidence if it turns up." Stella pointed to the next items on the grid as she read them aloud. "Her car is missing. There's no identifiable history of drug involvement. And last, she stalked our second victim."

Stella faced her audience. "Let's talk about that."

"The Hartman ranch is adjacent to the national forest and farther north from Ute Canyon Road," McCoy said, "past the road where you turn off to go to the cabin."

Mattie leaned forward. "She would have driven right past the turnoff on her way to school that morning. What if she saw Mike Chadron's car and decided to follow him?"

"I think it's likely," Stella replied. She turned back to her grid and pointed to the upper right, where she'd written "Injured Dog." "What is our dog's name, Mattie?"

"Belle."

"Yes, Miss Belle," Stella said as she wrote in "Belle" at the top of the grid. "Here's what we know about Belle. First, she was used as a mule. Second, she was shot with the same gun that shot Grace and Mike Chadron. Which now leads me to jump over to our final spot on the grid . . . the weapon."

Stella indicated the far right of the grid where she'd written "Walther P22" at the top. "Ballistics has tied this handgun to all the bullets retrieved from our victims. This information would be invaluable if we knew who fired this weapon, but unfortunately we don't. Yet."

She paused to give them a pointed look and then continued. "This .22-caliber handgun is an interesting little semi-automatic weapon. It's small and light and so might be carried for self-defense, which, thanks to its serial number, I happen to know is exactly why it was originally purchased."

This new information caused a spike in Mattie's interest.

"Dr. Dennis Brinkman, a dentist living in Phoenix, purchased the gun and kept it in the glove compartment of his car. In March of this year, he reported it stolen, which a Phoenix detective that I spoke to this morning verified. There's a report filed, all tidy and legal. His car was broken into while he was playing at a golf tournament there, and the gun was the only thing taken at the time."

McCoy turned to Brody. "I wonder if that's one of the tournaments you went to, Chief Deputy."

Mattie saw the back of Brody's neck flush deep red.

"They have all kinds of tournaments in Phoenix," he said. "I'd have to check the dates."

"Follow it up," McCoy said. "I'd like to make sure that gun was truly stolen and out of Brinkman's hands. See if you played golf with someone who knows him. Let's verify if his word is reliable."

Brody shrugged. "All right."

Stella pointed to another spot on the grid. "The most promising evidence we have at the moment is the brass casing that Robo found."

Though Robo had relaxed down and laid his head on his front paws, he now lifted his head, pricked his ears, and stared at Stella.

"Yes, I'm talking about you," she said, giving Robo a half smile. "Firing pin and ejector marks on the casing show it was fired by this handgun. They've taken a fragment of a print off the casing and are running it through AFIS. We can hope for a match."

"Wow! Good work, Robo. You, too, Deputy." McCoy turned to acknowledge Mattie.

Mattie shrugged slightly and looked down at Robo, who'd broken into a light pant. She hated group recognition, and it appeared to make Robo nervous, too. But she knew that the Automated Fingerprint Identification System might need something larger than a fragment to successfully pull up a match. The system also needed to contain the shooter's fingerprints, and since the database contained primarily known criminals, a first-time offender might not be in it.

"Let's go back to Mike Chadron now and finish him out." Stella pointed back to the grid under Victim 2. "He and his dogs were seen at the cabin prior to, and the morning of, the Grace Hartman shooting. Trace cocaine was found on the table inside the cabin. Belle was carrying balloons filled with cocaine, and we might infer that those balloons were filled in the cabin. By Chadron? By Grace Hartman? By Chadron's killer? Anyone else care to take a guess?"

"From what we've learned about Grace Hartman, I believe we can eliminate her," Mattie said. "I'm convinced she wasn't the type of person who would abuse her dog, or any dog, for that matter."

"How about Mike Chadron?" Stella asked.

"Your guess is as good as mine," Mattie replied. "The vet thinks he took good care of his dogs, but he's also showed up with more cash than usual lately."

"He could do it, all right," Brody said.

"And you know that because . . ." Stella said.

"Came from poor white trash, lived on the west side. He worked as a cook at the local greasy spoon. Had ambition to get ahead, make a living off his dogs. Had the motive and the opportunity. Yeah, he could do it."

Brody's reference to poor white trash made Mattie uncomfortable. A lot of good people lived on the west side. But she held her tongue; now wasn't the time for a debate.

"Okay," Stella said. "Let's say that Chadron participated in drug running. Let's say that he was using his own dogs as mules. How did Grace Hartman's dog end up with cocaine in her belly?"

"What if Mike did it after Grace was killed?" Mattie asked. "He had a dog bite on his hand. Maybe it didn't come from one of his dogs. Maybe it came from Belle, and that's how she got away."

McCoy nodded. "What if Grace was driving to school, spotted Mike Chadron, followed him up to the cabin, and ran into someone involved in bagging the cocaine? That someone might've killed her and then killed Mike, the only witness, a day later."

"That's what I've been thinking," Stella said, giving them her too-sweet smile. "Now, just a couple more points here. One, Chadron's truck was parked in a shed on his property, but his trailer and dogs are still missing. God knows what happened to those poor creatures. And two, both the box of rat poison and the packets of cocaine that we found at his house were wiped clean. No fingerprints at all. Why would a person wipe these items clean and then leave them in spots where we'd be most likely to find them? They were planted."

Mattie agreed with Stella's reasoning, and she decided she might have jumped at too quick a conclusion that Mike Chadron tried to poison Robo. She felt some guilt for wanting to kick a dead man's ass, but only a small amount, because it still looked like the guy had abused his own dogs and possibly Belle, too.

"So," Sheriff McCoy said. "What's our focus?"

Looking reflective, Stella said, "We've got to stay on this drug trafficking lead. That means we've got to follow the money. Identify anyone who seems to have come into a windfall lately. Talk with people who might be users or dealers.

Mattie, you went out to the hot springs. What did you find out?"

"The new owner at Valley Vista hot springs seems worth checking out. His name is Dean Hornsby." Stella wrote that down on her board while McCoy appeared to record it in his notebook. "He seemed to overreact when I asked him about his business. Seemed too sensitive. Acted like a man with something to hide."

"Nah," Brody said. "I stopped in there and met him a while back. The guy's an idiot, but he's not the drug-boss type."

"Okay . . ." Stella raised her eyebrows at Mattie, inviting a response.

"He says he's from Phoenix, as is our murder weapon," Mattie said. "And drug traffic through here started after he moved to town."

"I'll check him out," Stella said. "Anyone else?"

Mattie noticed a muscle bulge at Brody's jaw as he clenched it. "Local lawyer," he said. "Justin McClelland. Drives around in a brand-new Caddie with plates that say, 'Hot Shot.' Moved to town a year ago, set up a law office. Not much business here, but looks like he can afford an expensive new car."

"Okay," Stella said, writing down the name. "I'll check him out, too."

Mattie added to the list. "There's Tommy O'Malley, a local teen. I talked to him yesterday. Denies any knowledge, but rumor has it that he might sell drugs, smokes pot, but no known report of cocaine use."

"Got a juvie record?" Stella said.

"No, just littering and loitering, small-town trouble-making. No arrests yet."

Brody muttered, "Soft."

Mattie ignored him and went on. "Money's tight with the family, and he says he and his dad just found work. I'll follow up on that and find out if it's legitimate work or not."

"Let's poke around some before we jump on him. It's unlikely he's a drug boss, but he may be on the verge of getting involved on some level. Mattie, can you take the lead on him?"

"Sure. We've already mixed it up a time or two. I can take him."

"See what you can find out about his new place of employment, and see if you can uncover a cocaine connection. Since he's a minor, let's keep him off the board but still keep him in our sights," Stella said. "Anyone else?"

Stella waited and then continued when there was no response. "We've still got a BOLO out on the dog trailer and our first victim's car. If we find the dog trailer, maybe we'll find the dogs, but it's probably too late to determine whether or not they've been used as mules. What's your take on that, Mattie?"

"Twenty-four to forty-eight hours. If they ate meat tainted with salmonella, sooner."

"So we're at forty-eight hours this morning." Stella screwed up her face in a grimace. "They've pooped out the cocaine by now."

Mattie agreed. "Most likely."

"We've still got Belle."

Again, Robo raised his head to look at Stella.

"What, now you know your girlfriend's name, too?" she asked him, and then went back to business. "I agree with Sheriff McCoy that we need to look for any connections between Dr. Dennis Brinkman, that Phoenix golf tournament, and

Timber Creek. I'll work that angle, ask this Mr. Hornsby if he plays golf, and Brody, you see if you can come up with something, too."

As Mattie noticed Brody's neck flush red again, she realized with a start that if this were a poker game, she'd been observing a series of "tells" in the man throughout the meeting.

Interesting.

"I still need Cobb on patrol this afternoon," Brody said.

"I've got it," Mattie said. "That'll work out fine. I need one more contact with the O'Malley family today anyway."

Brody turned to stare at her in his "big boss" sort of way, but Mattie responded with a little shrug to indicate she couldn't care less, and he turned back to Stella.

"Is that all?" he asked.

"For now," she said. "We've got a good case building here, troops, even if we don't have someone to arrest yet. We're making some good progress."

On their way out of the report room, Rainbow stopped them by holding up one finger. Taking her phone from her ear and pressing the hold button, she said, "Sheriff, I've got that ranger you've been talking to, Sandy Benson, on line one. She says she needs to speak with you ASAP. She's got urgent news. I don't know what about, she didn't want to tell me."

"Wait here," McCoy told the group, hurrying to his office. "I'll take it in here, Rainbow."

Mattie felt like she'd been left hanging. She glanced at Brody, curious if she could observe another strange reaction, but he had gone to his in basket and was shuffling through his mail. Stella opened a notebook she carried and started making notes, presumably from the meeting.

When her gaze traveled to Rainbow, the dispatcher smiled and asked, "Do you have time for lunch, Mattie?"

Stella glanced her way and raised one brow.

"No, I'll have to grab something on the run."

"I wondered if you wanted to sit here, you know, if you brought your lunch with you today and didn't want to eat in the car or back in your office or something. I thought we could just sit here and talk, you know, pass the time."

Mattie liked to eat lunch alone, but Rainbow looked so hopeful that she hated to disappoint her. "Maybe another time."

Stella pursed her lips with distaste and went back to her notebook. Thankfully, the sheriff came out of his office to break the tension.

"Good news," he said, his face set with purpose. "A ranger found Grace Hartman's car. I've got a location. Deputy Cobb, I want you and Robo to come with us. Detective, you ride with me."

Brody glared at Mattie.

"I'll get back on patrol as soon as I return to town," she said. "I'll report back in."

McCoy looked at Brody and spoke in a voice that discouraged argument. "We need the dog's nose to check out this car for even the slightest amount of drugs. This is priority for the K-9 unit. I think we can be a car short on patrol for a few hours."

"You're the boss," Brody muttered as he headed toward his office, and this time Mattie could see that the red flush on his neck suffused his face. The man was as mad as a hornet.

Chapter 19

As she drove toward the mountains to get to the car's location, Mattie searched her memory, trying to connect her observations of Brody's stress indicators with specific points in the discussion. Although she couldn't vouch for exact detail, she remembered that the chief deputy's mannerisms had demonstrated tension from the very beginning of the meeting. That in itself didn't seem too unusual, since Brody had always been wound pretty tight. The man could crack walnuts with those jaws of his.

But the telling signs began when Sheriff McCoy pointed out that Brody had played golf in Phoenix during the same month the dentist's gun had gone missing.

So what about Brody being in Phoenix? Her own shoulders tightened as she continued to think along that line. If Brody had stolen that gun, then he might have used it to kill Grace Hartman and Mike Chadron. It was unthinkable, but she couldn't keep it out of her head.

Where had Brody been on Friday morning between eight and ten o'clock, the time period when Grace was killed? She went over the morning to recall where she'd been herself. Seven o'clock—report. She'd been there, but Sheriff McCoy had led report that day. As far as she could remember, Brody hadn't been at the station at all. She felt a moment of vague light-headedness as the blood drained from her face. Surely not. Surely Brody couldn't be involved with these crimes.

What would be his motive? Was he involved with drug running? No one could get rich on a deputy's salary, but you could still earn a good living. A dirty cop wasn't unheard of, but Brody?

It would be easy enough to look at the duty roster from the week to check Brody's schedule, and she planned to do it as soon as she returned to the station. Realizing that a slight thrum, like the vibration of a guitar string, had begun to quiver inside her, she took a deep breath to calm down. Thankfully, they'd reached the turnoff to Ute Canyon, and the sheriff was booking it in his Jeep, staying well ahead of her. She'd have to pay attention to her driving if she was going to keep up.

Twenty minutes of climbing and hairpin turns later, they drove past the cabin and up the road another mile. The sheriff stopped behind a light-green SUV with a US Forest Service logo on the door, which was parked at the entry into a rugged logging trail that looked like it was no longer in use. Sandy Benson stood by her vehicle.

"You'd better climb into the back, Deputy," McCoy said, getting out of his vehicle and opening the back door. "I don't think your patrol car can make it in there."

"Let me get my equipment," Mattie said.

Making sure to remember all her supplies, she gathered them up and loaded them into the back compartment of the Jeep. Then, after snapping a leash on Robo, she led him to the back seat, where he jumped in easily, getting more excited by the minute and panting like crazy. Stella stayed in the front passenger seat.

Typically, police vehicles were designed with washable seats in back and a steel mesh grill to separate the driver from the bad guys, but the sheriff's Jeep lacked these modifications. It was decked out like any standard Jeep Grand Cherokee except for the law enforcement technology in front. Although her surroundings promoted comfort, Mattie sat on the edge of her seat.

"How much farther?" she asked.

"About a half mile in."

They followed the ranger's SUV along a narrow two-track filled with potholes; sharp stones; and half-buried, small boulders. Branches screeched against the side of the vehicle, sounding much like fingernails on a chalkboard. Mattie put an arm around Robo to brace him as the Jeep bumped along, tipping side to side.

As they approached a steep, rocky grade, Stella glanced back over her shoulder. "Hold on, Robo."

Mattie gave her a quick smile, acknowledging the detective's concern for her dog. "He is," she said, gripping him as the front end rose at a steep angle and then jolted into a small chasm. The engine growled and the four-wheel drive gripped as the Jeep maneuvered the deep erosion in the track.

After a grueling ride that made Mattie's teeth rattle, the sheriff pulled to a stop behind Sandy Benson. She'd reached a point where they could glimpse the sheen of a red vehicle partially hidden behind pine trees.

"Great work, Sandy," McCoy said as they all unloaded from the vehicles. "It took a lot of effort to locate this one. It's well hidden."

Benson approached their vehicle. "It was a team effort, and we were determined to find this car. But it also took some luck, since we came down this trail once before but stopped back there where the road's washed out. We didn't think someone could navigate this little SUV over something that deep. Must have been really motivated."

"I expect so," McCoy said. "Let's get your equipment, Deputy, and go on over there."

Mattie strapped on her utility belt, gave Robo some water, and then put on his working collar. Robo settled in immediately and followed her at heel. McCoy carried Stella's kit, a hard-sided container that looked like the kind of tool case you'd buy at a hardware store. Behind the trees, they found Grace Hartman's brand-new, dark red Honda CR-V looking none the worse for wear.

"The CSU vehicle will never be able to get back here," McCoy said to Stella.

"They're on their way, too. Sandy, would you go back and meet them? Have them transfer their equipment into your vehicle and drive them back up here."

"Sure. How far are they behind you?"

"Hard to say, maybe a half hour, maybe less."

"I'll go wait now, then." And she left.

Stella began handing out latex gloves. "This is sort of like, what came first, the chicken or the egg? Who searches first, the CSIs or the K-9? This one is up to me, so I choose Robo. But let's preserve this scene for the CSI unit as much as we can." She looked at Mattie. "Do an exterior sweep first and then we'll see if we can open it up."

Mattie led Robo to the car and said, "Search," directing with her right hand. Robo pinned his ears and started sniffing, paying extra attention to wheel wells and door panels. Mattie even had him sniff what undercarriage they could reach, spending more time at the rear. Not once did Robo indicate a find.

"Nothing," Mattie said.

Stella approached the car and peered into the front window on the driver's side. "That's handy," she said. "Our perp left the keys."

She reached for the handle, and the door opened with a soft, new-car click. Mattie and the sheriff peered through windows, watching Stella as she leaned into the driver's side and sorted through items carefully, using only her gloved fingertips.

"Tell us what you find, please," McCoy said.

"She must have been a tidy girl," Stella said. "No trash. But there is a lot of black dog hair here in the passenger seat. Looks like lip gloss here, an iPod plugged into the stereo. I'll just open up this middle compartment so Robo can sniff inside it in a minute. Here are some CDs and, get this, a pair of binoculars." She looked at Mattie with one eyebrow raised. "Good little detective. How long has she had this vehicle?"

"A little over a month."

"I'll open the glove box, too. Not much in here. A flashlight, car manuals, tire air gauge. Not very interesting."

Stella got out, peered under the driver's seat, and then went around the car, opening all the doors. "Let me do a quick check under the seats, and then we'll let you and Robo have it."

She peered under the front passenger seat. "What's this hidden down here? Something tells me I need to take its picture before I move it."

With not just a small amount of excitement building, Mattie watched Stella use her cell phone to snap a photo.

Then Stella extracted a slim volume with a flowery cover. "Oh my god!"

"What?" McCoy asked, his tone imperative.

Stella looked at both of them with an astonished expression. "It's a diary."

This time, that burst of adrenalin hit Mattie square in the chest.

"We've hit the jackpot," McCoy said.

"Let's bag it," Stella said. "We're taking this back with us."

McCoy reached into the kit for an evidence bag, and Stella placed the diary inside, giving it back to McCoy to keep. Stella searched the side pockets, the back seat pockets, and under the back seats but found nothing more than an ice scraper and a can of windshield deicer. The back compartment of the vehicle held a few emergency flares. Mattie's heart ached at the thought of Garrett Hartman equipping his daughter's first vehicle with so many safety supplies, an obvious labor of love.

"There's blood here on the carpet in back," Stella said. "The perp must've used her own vehicle to move her body."

"Christ," Mattie muttered.

"Scum," Stella said, backing off from the Honda. "Okay, Mattie, your turn."

Mattie directed Robo into the SUV and together they completed a thorough sweep. Like during the exterior sweep, Robo didn't hesitate, nor did he indicate the presence of narcotics.

"This vehicle is clean," Mattie announced, confident in Robo's skill. "Grace never transported any drugs in it."

"Don't quibble, Mattie, tell us what you really think," Stella teased.

Mattie gave her a half smile. "Robo's nose knows." She tried not to sound too smug, but she felt terribly proud of her partner.

Sandy Benson's engine growled as her SUV made its way up the steep track to the trees and then ground to a stop. "Well, I'd better go break the news that we've already been into their crime scene," Stella said, as she watched the same techs who'd worked the other two scenes exit the ranger's vehicle.

Her brassy voice carried as she walked away toward the others. "I had the K-9 sweep the car first so we wouldn't confuse the scent trails inside. You'll just have to deal with it."

Mattie cringed at Stella's choice of words, thinking the detective must have missed the memo on interdepartmental relationships. She followed a few paces behind McCoy as they headed back toward his Jeep.

But the lead tech, possibly used to working with Stella, peeled away from the rest of the group and approached Mattie with a gloved hand, a baggie, and a smile. "Let me get a sample of your K-9's hair, officer," she said. "Can you keep him from biting my hand off?"

★

After returning to the station, Mattie checked in and told Rainbow she would head out next for patrol duty. Before leaving, though, she took a quick look at the duty roster, which told her that Brody had been scheduled a day off last Friday. Yet he'd already been at the crime scene when she arrived. She wondered when he'd been called and where he'd been at the time.

Feeling unsettled, Mattie headed back outside to her patrol car, Robo at her side. Compared to the mountains, the day had turned hot down in the valley, not a cloud in the sky, a dog day of late summer. After loading Robo in the back, Mattie decided not to think about what she was going to do about her suspicion and drove toward the O'Malley trailer house. She would focus on Brody later.

Pulling up in front, Mattie saw Sean sitting out on the front step, listlessly tossing pebbles into an upturned hubcap. His face had been washed and his sandy hair combed, though he still wore the same dirt-smudged T-shirt and shorts he'd had on the day before.

Deciding to use Robo to try to make some inroads into a relationship with the kid, Mattie invited him out of the car and snapped on his leash. His tail waved and he looked toward Sean in a friendly way. At the academy, Robo's trainer had explained how Robo had been socialized with children as a young dog, and he'd taken to it like a duck to water. Mattie realized how valuable that experience had been to round out Robo's usefulness in a community setting such as Timber Creek.

Still, Sean left his play and stepped backward, his face taking on a look of caution.

With Robo at heel, Mattie approached him. "How are you, Sean?"

Sparing Mattie one brief glance, Sean continued to eye Robo. "Okay."

"Robo, sit." Seeing that Robo sat at heel as directed, Mattie looked back at Sean. "Robo likes kids. Would you like to pet him?"

"I guess so."

Mattie stroked the top of Robo's head gently. "First put your hand out low so he can sniff it, and then pet him on his head like this."

It only took about a minute for Robo to make friends. Sean took a step to move closer, smoothing the fur on Robo's shoulders.

"See, he likes you."

Sean glanced at Mattie with a half smile. "Does he like to play?"

"Yeah, he does. He loves to play ball. You wanna come with me to the park someday to do that, if it's okay with your mom?"

"Sure."

"Let's ask her."

Sean hurried into the trailer house. Within seconds, Fran stepped out on the porch carrying the baby. Mattie noticed a fresh purple bruise that hadn't been apparent the day before over Fran's left cheekbone. Sean came out behind her and then moved down the stairs to pet Robo again.

Fran stood with her face turned partly away, fiddling with the baby's clothing, not meeting Mattie's gaze. "Sean says you want to talk to me."

"He wants to go to the park with me someday to play ball with Robo. We wondered if you would allow it."

Fran's eyes darted out to take in the boy and the dog. "We'll see. I'll have to talk with my husband."

A quick glance told Mattie that Sean's attention seemed centered on Robo. She stepped close to Fran and said in a low voice, "You have a bruise on your face. Did your husband hit you?"

Fran shook her head no. "I ran into a doorway last night when I got up to take care of the baby in the dark."

The door opened slightly, causing both Mattie and Fran to step away. Tommy O'Malley came out of the house.

He gave Mattie a smile that seemed contrived. "I see you've come back to see us."

"I see you haven't gone to work yet today."

"Oh, we'll be going later, me and my dad."

"I'm glad you've been able to find a job. Where are you employed?"

Tommy's smile dimmed somewhat, though he tried to fix it in place. His eyes darted off quickly to the side before coming back to focus on Mattie's. "We're going to go work at the mine in Rigby. It's a drive, but I can work weekends when school starts."

Mattie knew she'd have no trouble checking that detail. She decided there was no reason to mince words. "I'm concerned about the bruise on your mother's face."

Tommy narrowed his eyes and studied his mother, as if seeing the bruise for the first time.

Eyes downcast, Fran shifted the baby in her arms as if uncomfortable with her son's attention. "I told her I ran into a door frame last night." Finally, she lifted her eyes to meet Mattie's, but the animosity contained within them was a surprise. "I told you I don't need your help."

"Someone from Child and Family Services will be stopping by today. You can at least get some help with groceries until your paychecks start rolling in." Mattie tried to maintain eye contact with Fran, but the woman avoided her gaze. "If you need help with domestic violence, your caseworker can arrange that for you as well."

Neither of the two O'Malleys responded. Tommy stared at Mattie, but his face was expressionless, and she couldn't get a read on him. Fran avoided her gaze, turning away as if she couldn't wait to go back inside the trailer.

Mattie asked, "Where's Mr. O'Malley, Fran?"

She stopped and looked back at Mattie. "He's at the school, taking down an old shed for the principal."

"I have some questions for Tommy. We can do this now, or I can take him into the station and call his father to join us." She hoped Fran would choose the first option.

Tommy shoved his hands in his pockets and adopted a smirk. "What do you want to know?"

Fran made no verbal protest, so Mattie decided to go for it. "How old are you, Tommy?"

"Seventeen."

"Do you have your driver's license?" She already knew he did but wanted to give him some questions that were easy for him to answer to get started.

"Yeah."

"I imagine you've had a way to earn your spending money this summer—you know, money for going to the movies, going out to eat with your friends."

Tommy removed his hands from his pockets and crossed his arms over his chest. "Yep."

"Hey, Tommy, help me out here . . . don't make me ask how, just tell me."

He shrugged. "I pick up odd jobs here and there. Me and my dad do handyman work around town."

"Now that wasn't so hard, was it?" She paused, knowing that getting an answer to her next question might be harder. "I hear you smoke weed out at the park now and then, Tommy. Any truth to the rumor?"

She observed both Tommy and Fran closely. Fran kept her eyes on the ground, but Tommy didn't glance at his mother. He stared at Mattie and the smirk returned to his face.

"Who told you that?"

"I don't reveal my sources."

Tommy sent a look toward Sean, but the child didn't notice. He was focused on Robo, who was up on all fours, using his nose to nudge Sean's hands while his tail wagged his whole body. They both wore big grins.

"No, Tommy, it wasn't your little brother. I don't use little kids to gain information about their older siblings. I'm just trying to help out you and your family here. I tell you what, let's not worry about whether that's true or not. I withdraw the question. And you know what? I'll give you a pass on any weed that you might've smoked before. I can't make promises if I catch you with it in the future, though, because I'm sure you know that it's still illegal in this state for someone your age to smoke it or have it in your possession. But I'm not interested in that right now."

She'd regained Tommy's attention, and he stared at her, hands in pockets, apparently waiting to see what else she had for him.

"I'm interested in knowing where kids get the stuff."

Tommy snorted. "From their parents, big brothers and sisters, grandparents, aunts and uncles, you name it."

"Do you get it from your parents?" She looked at Fran.

"We don't have money for such things," she said.

Mattie nodded at her, acknowledging her reply and not doubting its truth.

The smirk was back. "I don't get it from anyone. I don't smoke it, remember?"

Lucky for her that this kid was so easy to read. "How about the hard stuff . . . meth, cocaine. What do you know about that?"

He shut down. "I don't know anything."

"Who deals it?"

"Don't know."

"Who uses it?"

"Not my crowd."

"Do you know who transports it through town?"

"You're shittin' me again. How would I know that?"

Mattie let the silence stretch out between them. Tommy bobbed back and forth on his feet a couple times and then broke it. "You ought to ask that big cop what he knows."

A tingle flitted along her neck. "What big cop?"

"That guy that's all pumped up, looks like he uses roids, huge shoulders."

"Deputy Brody?"

"Yeah, he's the one."

"Why him?"

"Saw him hanging out with Chadron and his dogs at the park this summer."

They hadn't released any information to the public about Mike using the dogs as mules. "Why would that make you say he might know something about who transports drugs through town?"

Tommy went very still, looking as if he realized he'd said too much.

Mattie waited, but this time he didn't break. "Tell me why I should talk to Deputy Brody."

"Well, he knew Mike, and Mike's dead. That's all."

"But what does that have to do with transporting drugs?"

"I don't know. You're getting this all twisted up. I'm just saying." Tommy paused while his eyes jumped around the yard, looking at anything but Mattie. "He's always at the school, hanging out with kids."

"Did you ever see him with Grace?"

"Yeah—probably. I've seen him there a lot."

"Patrol is his job. Why would you think he's there for something different?"

"Don't believe me. I don't care. You cops always cover for each other."

Mattie could see him shutting down. "Not true. If there's something specific you know about Deputy Brody, you need to tell me."

"Shit." Tommy toed the ground. "I got nothin' more to say."

"Are you sure?"

"Don't tell him I said anything."

"Like I said before, I don't reveal my sources." Mattie searched him for signs of fear, but what she saw was mostly belligerence. "Are you afraid for your safety?"

Tommy laughed. "Of course not. That's all I got to say."

Mattie studied him for a few seconds. He folded his arms across his chest again and stared back. She could tell he was withholding something, but whatever it was, she wouldn't be able to drag it out of him right now.

"Well, Tommy, if you remember anything else, you have my card. Give me a call if you think of something or if you need my help. You too, Fran. Is there anything you need me to know before I leave? Anything I can help with?"

"No," Fran said. She still refused to meet Mattie's gaze.

"Call me if you change your mind. Thank you both for your time."

Mattie headed toward the cruiser, purposefully luring Sean along with her, using Robo as bait. Fran went inside the trailer, but Tommy stayed on the porch, watching.

"You can help me load Robo in the car," Mattie told Sean. Once they had Robo secured in his area, she wrote her cell phone number on the back of one of her cards and slipped it into Sean's grubby hand. "You call me if you're afraid or if you need any help. Okay?"

Looking up at her with a face that seemed more open and trusting than when she'd first arrived, Sean nodded. He tucked the card into his shorts pocket.

In her rearview mirror, Mattie saw Sean standing at the edge of the street watching her drive away. He looked like a thin little waif, lonely and vulnerable. Suddenly, his head turned toward the house as if something drew his attention. Then, head downcast and shoulders rounded, he slowly walked back toward the trailer.

Mattie wished she had reason to take him away from the home and keep him safe with her. And what was she going to do about Brody?

Chapter 20

Mattie drove to the school. A quick check at the back proved that Fran had indeed told the truth: O'Malley appeared hard at work, loading debris from an old shed into his battered truck. She spent the last hours of her shift driving around town, checking the local hot spots, and pondering what she was going to do with her suspicions about Brody. Checking local hot spots turned out to be easy since the streets and hangouts looked pretty much dead. No one was at the park today, all was peaceful on Main and at the Pizza Palace, and Clucken House was still closed.

But deciding what she was going to do about Brody proved to be much more difficult. She thought about her conversation with Tommy. When he first mentioned Brody, it was in conjunction with Mike Chadron and the dogs. She suspected Tommy knew more about the cocaine traffic through town than he was saying, but why would he implicate Brody? Unless Brody really did have something to do with drug traffic. But Tommy might have also been trying to draw her attention away from himself to mislead her. She shouldn't rush to conclusions too quickly.

But then there was also this golf tournament thing, possibly putting Brody in Phoenix when the murder weapon was stolen.

Shit! There was nothing worse than a dirty cop. She'd known Brody for seven years, and it was hard to believe he might have turned. But the evidence was mounting against him.

On her way back to the station, she drove past the O'Malley place one last time, but there was nothing to be seen. She made a mental note to call the mine in Rigby in the morning to determine if the O'Malleys were on the payroll there.

When she checked in at the station, she learned that Brody had left for the day. The duty roster told her that he'd signed out right at the end of shift, which was unusual for him. He usually hung around for a bit, making sure no one signed out early or put in any unauthorized overtime.

Stella had left for home, taking the diary with her. She would probably be able to brief them on information it might contain about the case by morning. Mattie finished up her paperwork, said good-night to Rainbow, and then she and Robo left for the day.

★

Cole moved about the kitchen, heating the casserole from the Brennamans and guiding Sophie in her salad-making adventure. Angela had taken her cell phone up to her room, presumably to talk to a friend. He hoped the conversation with another girl from their friendship circle would do them both some good. Sophie stood on a step stool while he supervised her using a paring knife to cut celery. She had a pretty good technique going, using the knife exactly how he demonstrated, so he let his mind wander.

After Belle left, both kids had barely picked at their lunch. It had been a hard afternoon primarily filled with movies and television and occasional sniffles as one or the other of them teared up. He was going to have to come up with something to distract everyone, himself included, for the evening.

"These carrots are tough," Sophie said, forcing his attention back to her as she sawed on a baby carrot.

"Let me help you," he said, placing a hand over hers on the knife handle. Together they finished up. "You put the salads on the table, and I'll get out the casserole."

It smelled delicious as he placed the dish on the table and took off the hot lid. It looked like a tuna concoction with soup and broccoli mixed in and crushed potato chips on top. The scent wafted up and made his stomach growl. He realized with a feeling of guilt that his appetite had kicked back in tonight, the first time since learning of Grace's death. "Sophie-bug, go get Angie," he said.

When she returned, she said, "She's not hungry," and took a place at the table, dragging her old stuffed rabbit with her. Until today, Cole hadn't seen that thing in years.

"She's got to eat." Cole went to the bottom of the stairway and called up. "Angie?"

Angie yelled from inside her room. "What, Dad?"

"You've got to eat something. Come join us."

"I'm not hungry."

"Come anyway."

"Dad!"

"Come on, now. Sophie made a salad and everything. You've got to come down and try to eat at least a little bit."

"Oh, all right." There was a long pause while Cole assumed she was saying good-bye to her friend. Then her bedroom door opened, and she started down the stairs looking ashen and weary. Concern made him decide on an early bedtime for everyone.

Once seated, Cole dished out a heaping portion of the tuna casserole for each of them while Angela gave him a stare that would have wilted a lesser man. "What kind of salad dressing do you want, Sophie?"

She removed the rabbit's ear from her mouth to respond. "Ranch."

"Here, let me have that rabbit and put him on the chair over here by me so you can eat."

He tried not to flinch when his fingers learned that the rabbit was wet clear down to its shoulders. He was going to have to lose this thing before bedtime.

They ate in silence, Angela picking at her meal while he and Sophie dug in to theirs. Cole noticed, however, that Sophie picked out the broccoli to leave on her plate while Angela sifted through the casserole, eating bites of broccoli and leaving the chips. "At least take one bite of broccoli, squirt," he said, using Liv's one-bite-required rule. Without thinking, he added, "That's what your mother would want."

Fork poised in midbite, Angela glared at him. "Mom's not here, Dad."

"I guess not, but it's a good rule."

"Then tell her *you* want her to eat it. Don't bring up Mom. She wants nothing to do with us."

Stricken, Sophie rose from her chair and started around the table toward the rabbit. Cole caught her with one arm and lifted her up to his lap. "Sit here for a minute, Sophie. Let's talk."

He wrapped his arms around the child and focused his gaze on his oldest. "Angel, we can't say your mom wants nothing to do with you."

"Well, she won't let us visit her. Even though we've been in Denver most of the summer, she wouldn't let us come over."

"I know, I know. Your mom's having a tough time right now. You know the doctor has put her on some medicine, and she's getting some counseling. She just needs a little time. She'll get better."

"Before she left, I heard Mom tell Marci on the phone that you're never around," Angela said. "You never help her with us kids, and you never listen to her."

A pain flared up in Cole's midsection, and the tuna casserole he'd consumed became a lump in his stomach. Marci, Liv's old college roommate, had welcomed her into her home and made it easy for Olivia to leave her family and never look back. But Olivia's words were what truly hurt. Because even though he wanted to deny it, he recognized them as partially true.

"I know I've been too busy at work, but it's how we make a living. It's how I pay for our house and put food on our table. And what went on between your mom and me is our business alone," he said, giving his eldest a pointed look.

Sophie put her thumb in her mouth, another habit long past, and Cole could feel the tension in her small, sturdy body. He gave her a little squeeze.

"One of the things I've learned lately is that communication goes two ways, you guys," he said. "I hope that's something we can remember as we go on from here."

In a voice that quivered and caught, Sophie said, "Maybe you won't want us either."

"Aww . . . Sophie-bug, it breaks my heart for you to even think that. I want you guys forever and ever. You're the most precious people in my world, and I wish I could make things right for you. It's going to be hard, putting things back together here at home without Mom, but I know we can do it. We need to make a plan."

"Do you plan to keep shipping us off to Denver to stay with Aunt Jessie?" Angela asked.

"Angel, cut me some slack. Maybe that was a mistake, but I didn't know what else to do. I thought you had a lot of things there to entertain you, and it would be a fun summer for you. We just don't have much help here in Timber Creek, and I didn't think it was fair to leave you guys with Grandma or here at home by yourselves all day. How boring would that be? And besides . . ."

Angela gave him a searching look.

"Well, besides, I thought maybe your mom would change her mind and come back by the end of the summer."

Sophie took her thumb out of her mouth long enough to say, "Maybe she will."

Miserable, Cole said, "No, little bit, the divorce is final. None of us should plan on your mom coming home."

Sophie pressed her fingers into her eyes while Angela remained stone faced and silent.

Gently, Cole took Sophie's hands from her face before she could damage herself and held them in his. They felt small and sticky.

"Let's make some plans," he said. "It feels lonely around here tonight without Aunt Jessie and Belle. Maybe we should think about getting a dog."

"You can't just pacify us with a dog, Dad. That won't fix anything," Angela said.

Sophie said, "I just want Belle."

Cole kept himself from sighing. "Okay, let's wait and discuss that again another time. Aunt Jessie plans to put an ad on the Internet and see if she can get us a housekeeper."

Angela nodded, relaxing the stone face somewhat. "She told me that before she left. She said she wants to get someone to cook and clean for us, so I don't have to do that and can still be a kid."

Cole eyed her, thinking she was closer to being a young woman these days than a kid. "Are you on board with that?"

"Yeah. I don't want to be one of those families where the oldest kid does all the work."

"Yeah, I agree, but I'm still going to need you both to help out. Right? You're still going to have to assume responsibilities here around the house. Don't worry, I will, too. And I plan to be around a lot more than you're used to. You might even get sick of me." He tried a slight smile to see if it would bounce off unacknowledged, and he was gratified to see Angela's expression ease and return it in a small way.

"You guys are going with me to the clinic in the morning. Tess is going to show you how to do some of the office work." Cole saw a spark of interest animate Angela's wan face. "But there's always going to be emergencies in the early morning or at night, and we need a plan for that. Especially now, before we get some help. Angela, do you think you could watch your sister if I get called out?"

The two girls eyed one another. "Yeah," Angela said. "Would I get paid?"

"I don't need to be baby-sitted."

"Sophie, you're too young to be left alone for a long time, although I'm sure you'd be fine for a short spell. And yeah, Angie, we could arrange something. As long as you're kind to your sister and you help her if she needs something. You know, do the right thing by her."

Angie made a face at Sophie. "So that means I can't torture her?"

Cole leaned over so he could see Sophie smile back at her sister, and it did his heart good to see that they could still be playful. "Right," he said. "No funny business either. I expect you two to get along."

"Sure, Dad," Angela said and Sophie echoed.

Why did Cole feel like this wasn't going to be that easy? Perhaps because he'd been around the house enough previously to know that things weren't always peace and harmony between the two. At least the truce they'd had in force since returning home from Denver still seemed to be in place.

"Can we watch TV now?" Sophie asked, that whiny tone returning to her voice.

"We've had enough TV for one day. Maybe we should do something else together, like play a game."

"Like what?"

Cole thought for a moment. "I could teach you guys how to play blackjack."

Just then his cell phone jingled in his pocket. *Good Lord, I hope it's not an emergency.* He glanced at the caller ID. "Just a minute, kids. This is Garrett Hartman. Let me see what he needs."

"I hope Belle's okay," Sophie said. Both girls tuned in to his conversation.

He pressed the screen to accept the call. "Hello, Garrett. What can I do for you? Is Belle doing okay?"

"She seems fine, Cole. Physically. But she's gone into Grace's room and won't come out. She won't take anything to eat or drink since she came home. All she does is lie on the floor by Gracie's bed and look at us with the saddest eyes you can imagine. We can't stand it."

"Oh, man . . ."

"Leslie and I've talked it over. She seemed to be doing okay at your house with your kids. We'd like them to have her if it's okay with you. We think it would be best for us all."

The kids couldn't hear Garrett's side of the conversation, and they looked worried as they watched, trying to determine what was being said, perhaps imagining the worst about Belle. Cole couldn't wait to see their faces change when he told them the news.

"That would be great, Garrett," he said. "We'll come right out to get her."

Chapter 21

Almost midnight. Moonlight streamed through the window, striking Mattie's face. But that wasn't the reason she couldn't sleep.

The walls kept closing in on her.

She'd had this problem as long as she could recall, and sleeping with the window open usually helped. Even in winter, she would pile on quilts so that she could leave her window open a crack.

Nothing seemed to help tonight. Thoughts about Brody kept circling through her mind.

With a sigh, she pushed off her covers and sat up on the edge of the bed. From his dog cushion on the floor, Robo raised his head, alert.

"Want to go for a run?"

He was out of bed in a flash, toenails skittering on the wooden floor.

After putting on her running shorts and a white tank, Mattie strapped on a shoulder holster to carry her Smith & Wesson .38 revolver. She wasn't in the habit of taking a weapon with her when she went out to run, but in light of the recent attempt on Robo's life, she felt it necessary. She covered the handgun with a light sweatshirt that zipped up the front.

After pausing to stretch in the shadows on the porch, she opted to head out to the highway to run on its wide shoulder where the moon could light her path. She expected very little traffic this time of night.

Mattie stayed on the left side with Robo trotting beside her. It didn't take long to warm up; despite the daytime heat, the night had turned cool, a sign that autumn was coming. She lengthened her stride, her feet pounding the asphalt in a rhythm she found soothing. She let her mind release and focused on her breath, feeling her muscles loosen and working out the knots that had formed in her shoulders.

While she was out, she might as well take another look at Brody's house. There'd been no one at home when she'd driven by earlier in the evening. He lived in a white clapboard house with blue trim, the paint job looking tired and old, built close to the highway on the way out of town. Not much in the way of a yard: some tall, old spruce trees growing beside the driveway. Nothing fancy, but he kept the place tidy; there was very little clutter. For a single guy, he picked up after himself pretty well.

She slowed as she approached his house, peering toward it through the darkness. He'd turned a light on at the front porch, and she could see his cruiser parked out front. The main level of the house was lit behind the curtains. Seemed rather late for him to be awake, but then, who was she to talk? She couldn't see any activity or tell where Brody was within the house.

After jogging past, Mattie once again picked up her pace. Soon she ran beyond the city limits, where the jagged silhouette of the mountains on her left stood out black against a sky lit by a moon that was almost full. The valley on her right stretched out flat and empty. She'd chosen the highway instead of her usual route up T-hill because tonight she needed a clear path to run. So she continued to go all out on the pavement, making Robo break from his trot into a lope.

Headlights breeched a curve up ahead and tires squealed, bearing down the highway at a speed that had to be exceeding the limit. She wished she was in her cruiser with her radar so she could bust the son of a bitch. She got off the highway and pulled Robo in close, bracing herself to get a make on the vehicle and read the license plate, but the lights blinded her as it raced by, buffeting her with its backlash.

Robo went crazy, barking and trying to chase the vehicle.

"Stop that." Mattie gave him a quick correction with his leash. She tried to read the rear plate, but the plate light was out. She could tell that the vehicle was a dark four-wheel-drive vehicle of some kind, boxy in back, but that's all she could get.

Robo continued to bark, staring at the fading taillights, lifting his front feet up off the ground with each woof.

"No, Robo! Stop your barking," Mattie said, giving him another correction.

Must be the darkness making him so squirrelly.

Knowing she could do nothing about the speeding vehicle right now, Mattie turned to resume her run. She hesitated, though, when she spotted another figure approaching in the night, running along the opposite side of the highway. She unzipped her jacket and touched the handle of her .38, making sure she could get to it.

Charging out to the end of his leash, eyes pinned on the other runner, Robo barked again.

"Is that Robo?" the runner called.

It took only moments for Mattie to place the voice.

"Dr. Walker?"

"Yes, it's me. Cole."

"Stop that, Robo."

Walker slowed his pace, crossing to join Mattie on her side of the highway. "What are you doing out this time of night?"

"I could ask you the same thing."

"Couldn't sleep."

"Ditto."

He was breathing pretty hard. "Did that guy almost run you down?"

"No, we were well off to the side of the road. He was sure hauling."

"He caught some air back there by the curve. Too bad you weren't in your patrol car."

"Maybe the night shift will spot him when he hits town. We can hope."

Walker was patting Robo's side. The dog had greeted him like an old friend, fawning against his legs. She decided to let him, giving him a moment to bond with his new doctor.

"Aren't you concerned about being out here at night by yourself?" Walker asked.

"I have my partner with me."

"True, and he's pretty protective, but still."

"I'm not sure you should be out here alone either, but sometimes we do what we gotta do."

"I know. I didn't think twice until that guy passed me, and then, well, it kind of gave me the creeps for some reason. I think I'll head back home now, so I'll turn around and go your way."

Mattie resumed her jog with Walker falling in beside her. His pace was quite a bit slower than hers, but she felt odd running off and leaving him. Before she could decide what to do, he initiated conversation.

"Do you run at night very often?"

"No, I run in the mornings. How about you?"

"Haven't done this for a long time." He puffed for a few moments. "Should do me some good, if it doesn't kill me."

That decides it, Mattie thought. She had to stick with him until she could escort him safely to the top of his lane.

"Seems impossible," Walker said, his short breath making him speak in bursts. "Danger in Timber Creek."

"Timber Creek has always had its pockets of danger for some." Didn't she know from experience? "These homicides just make it more obvious to the general public."

"I guess . . . you see . . . the bad side."

Mattie slowed even more so the vet could catch his breath. With a grim tone, she said, "I've lived the bad side."

He paused. Then after a few more strides: "I saw you run once . . . at the high school. My last year of vet school, home on break. You were good."

"Running reformed me. I was raised in foster care, had a chip on my shoulder. But that's behind me now."

"Yeah." He paused a few beats. "What's past is past. Or should be."

They continued on, the darkness feeling intimate as they ran side by side, accompanied by the rhythm of their tennis shoes on the pavement, the puffing of Walker's breath, and the jingling of Robo's tags. Every now and then, Robo would sniff the air and make a huffing sound in his chest. He continuously checked behind him, giving Mattie sort of a hinky feeling. She wondered what was out there that caused him to act so worked up.

They stopped at the lane that led to Walker's house. Mattie opened her mouth to say good-bye, but he spoke before she could.

"One minute." He leaned against his mailbox, taking in huge breaths of air, his lungs sounding like a bellows. "I've got a question."

Mattie waited for him to catch his breath.

"It's just the kids and me at home nowadays," he said when he could talk again. "I've told them that if I have to leave the house at night on an emergency, I'll leave them a note. They can call me on my cell if they wake up. The doors are locked, and we have Belle inside. Do you think that plan is safe enough?"

"You have Belle back? Did she take a turn for the worse?"

"No, Garrett and Leslie couldn't stand watching her pine for Grace. They gave her to the kids."

The news filled her with joy. "I'm glad. They seem to love her."

"They do. They're pretty sad themselves now. I hope this will help them feel better. Although I kind of doubt if it will make up for everything."

"It's a hard thing for you all, losing Grace."

"Yeah, it is. So do you think they're safe if I leave them home alone for a few hours when I get called out?"

"Yes, I think citizens are still safe in their homes."

"What you said earlier, about how running reformed you. It looks like you turned your life around and made something good out of a bad situation." He paused, apparently taking time to choose his words. "I hope I can help my kids make the right choices. They're faced with more challenges than I was at their age."

"You have a strong relationship with your kids. That was something I never had with my father."

"Yeah, well, it may look that way. But to tell the truth, I haven't been around much in their lives."

Mattie sensed the vet had more on his mind.

"I got word that my divorce is final last week, and it hit me pretty hard."

Christ! She wished she'd never entered into a personal conversation. "I'm sorry to hear that."

"I'm trying to sort out how much supervision my kids need so I know what kind of help to arrange."

"I wouldn't know how to advise you."

"No, that's not what I'm asking you. I guess I just wanted your opinion on how safe this community is now."

Mattie could handle a cop question. "That's hard to say. Even a year ago, I would've said we didn't have a drug problem in Timber Creek. But as you know, things changed real fast. We believe we can stop the drug traffic through our town, but now here's this thing with Grace. Do I think parents should be concerned? Yes, I do. But do I think Timber Creek is a dangerous place to raise kids? Not any worse than any other place in the state and still a lot safer than most."

Mattie leaned down to brush her fingertips across Robo's head. He'd settled down and sat quietly at her feet, panting lightly.

"Can I drive you back home, Deputy Cobb? I hate for you to be out running alone this time of night."

"Don't worry, I can take care of myself. And call me Mattie. It's simpler."

He extended his hand, and it warmed hers when she took it. "And I'm Cole. Thanks for the advice, and thanks for being there for the kids today when Belle left. Like I said before, I appreciate the way you interact with Angie. I believe she trusts you."

Flustered, Mattie withdrew her hand. She started to leave but then paused to say one last thing. "Don't worry so much about your kids. The fact that you're a part of their lives and you care so much will go a long way. It's a lot more than I ever had."

"Well, sometimes you have to ask yourself, is loving them enough? Sometimes things happen that make you wonder." His voice sounded wistful.

Feeling warmer than her night's exercise warranted, Mattie made a sound of acknowledgement, said good-bye, and headed back home. She felt all mixed up about her feelings toward the vet, so she turned her thoughts to subjects she was more comfortable with: drug traffic and murder. She planned to check on Brody again as she returned home.

After running along the curve that led into town, she approached his house and slowed to a jog. His outside light had been turned off and the main level of the house darkened. The moon provided enough light to see a dark SUV parked now behind his cruiser. Was it the same one that had passed her on the highway earlier? The shape was similar. Without thinking it through, she stopped and led Robo to the spruce trees that towered beside Brody's driveway. Slipping sideways between two of them and getting pricked by the sharp needles, she stilled her breath to listen. All she could hear was Robo panting a few feet away where he'd stopped, being smart enough not to follow her into the prickly spruce.

One dim light lit an upstairs window, covered by a curtain. Even as she glanced upward at it, a shadowy silhouette appeared, its shape nipped in at the waist. Arms came up in the easily recognized movement of a woman taking off a bra. Feeling like a Peeping Tom, she realized that Brody must have a girlfriend up there. Two thoughts occurred almost simultaneously: Could this woman be part of the drug ring? And who the hell would want Brody?

Moonlight illuminated the white letters on the Colorado license plate, and she made a mental note of it. She could tell that the vehicle was a Ford but still couldn't determine the model.

Again without giving it too much thought, because if she got caught it would be disastrous, she decided to ask Robo to do a quick sweep of the vehicle's exterior. His mouth was probably dry after his run, which impaired his scenting ability to some degree, but it couldn't be helped. She needed to move quickly while Brody was still occupied in the bedroom.

Moving out of the trees, she led Robo to the back of the SUV and whispered, "Search."

He looked up at her as if puzzled. She realized she hadn't prepared him by putting on his working collar or jazzing him up about going to work. Thinking that maybe this was a bad idea and not wanting to mess with his training, she decided to give it up. But at that moment, Robo began to sniff. He completed the sweep with his standard mode of operation but didn't indicate any detection of narcotics.

The light in the house went off suddenly, startling Mattie, and she broke away from the vehicle, leading Robo along with her, praising and patting him as she went. Okay, so the vehicle appeared to be clean on the outside, but that really didn't tell her much. And it certainly didn't tell her enough to justify the risk she'd just taken.

It was time to call it a night and get to bed. Doubt nipped at her heels while she ran. Maybe her suspicion of Brody was unwarranted. Maybe her attraction to the vet was silly. Maybe the lack of sleep this weekend was starting to make her go batshit crazy.

Chapter 22

Monday

Somewhere, muffled under the downy veil of sleep, Mattie heard the phone ringing. She cracked open one eye and glanced at the clock. A quarter to six.

Sonofabitch. The answering machine could field this one. She pulled the quilt over her head and nestled under it.

Robo nudged her arm.

Without moving, she muttered, "Go back to bed."

She heard the click of his toenails as he walked back to his cushion. She heard him heave a sigh, signaling he'd finished circling and had lain down. She imagined the stoic expression he'd have on his face. She wondered if he needed to go outside to pee. She peeked out from under the cover.

Robo instantly raised his head, ears pricked, staring at her hard.

"Oh, all right!" Mattie threw back the cover and got out of bed. She made her way through the living room and kitchen to the back door, Robo gamboling alongside. Once out in the yard, he headed for the tree, sniffing the air and the grass. Then he circled the area, apparently checking things out.

She stood on the porch watching him, afraid to leave him alone for fear someone had planted something in the yard again. Wearing only the long T-shirt and boxers she'd slept in, she shivered and wrapped her arms around herself, goose bumps rising on her arms.

Robo huffed several times, sniffing the breeze and standing at the chain link against the north side, his posture that of the alert guard dog. He circled the perimeter again and then finally went back to the tree to relieve himself.

"It's about time. Come back inside now."

She held the door while Robo trotted through. He immediately went to his food bowl, looking up at her, evidently having decided it was time for breakfast. When she'd finally gone to bed last night, Mattie had decided to skip their morning run and sleep in. So much for plans.

After giving Robo his food, she checked caller ID and saw that her early morning wake-up call had come from Mama T. She dialed voice mail and listened to the message: "Mattie? I want you to come to breakfast, *mijita*. I have something to tell you. Call me."

Even as she listened, Mattie could hear the call-waiting beep that signaled another call coming in. Quickly, she pressed the flash button to take the call.

"Mattie? This is your Mama T."

"Good morning. What has you up so early?"

"Ha! The sun can't catch me sleeping."

"No, I guess not. I just got your message."

"Come over."

"I don't have much time, Mama."

"I made your favorite—breakfast burrito."

Mattie could smell it: scrambled eggs with green chili peppers, chorizo, and a homemade tortilla. Instantly, her mouth watered.

"I'll be there in fifteen minutes."

Robo had already scarfed down his breakfast, so he followed Mattie into the bathroom and watched her wash her face and brush her teeth. Then he padded after her to the bedroom to lie down and watch her dress.

"What are you, some kind of a watch dog?"

Robo sighed, putting his head down on his front paws.

"Yeah, it's a tough life, bubba."

Going back to the bathroom, she dampened her hair and slicked back the sides to tuck behind her ears. She grabbed Robo's leash from its hook by the door but let him run free while going out to the vehicle. He loaded into the back compartment, eager to embrace a new day. Lack of sleep didn't seem to be a problem for Robo.

Mattie knew the kids would still be asleep this early in the day, and she would have her foster-mother all to herself. She could smell delicious odors coming from the kitchen as she approached its door. And from the amount of food she saw cooking on the stove after stepping into the room, it appeared as if Mama had been out of bed for quite some time already.

"Will you have coffee?" Mama T gestured toward the white-spotted blue porcelain pot on the stovetop.

"Sure. Can I pour you a cup?"

"*Si, gracias.* I'll fix you a plate."

Mattie poured black coffee into thick, white crockery mugs, appreciating its heady scent.

Mama set a plate holding a monster burrito smothered with shredded pork and green chili in front of Mattie on a wooden table that had seen its share of meals. Mattie scooted up a chair, eager to taste it. "Will you eat with me?"

"Sure."

She waited until Mama had filled her own plate and sat down across from her. Mama bowed her head and murmured a blessing in Spanish. Mattie bowed her head, too, but remained silent.

"Now, dig in," Mama said.

The first bite was heaven. "Mama, you said you had something to tell me."

"Eat first, then talk."

They ate in silence, savoring the spicy food. Mama T rose from her chair at the end of the meal to refill their coffee cups. After settling herself back in her seat, she folded her hands on the table and said, "Now I will tell you."

Sensing the gravity in Mama's manner, Mattie experienced a sinking feeling. "What is it? Is something wrong?"

"No, no. Do not worry, *mijita*. I have news that will surprise you, that's all."

Usually, being called *mijita* warmed Mattie, but this time she was afraid the endearment meant to cushion a blow, and it only served to enhance the sense of dread that was slowly starting to blossom in the pit of her stomach. Mattie waited while Mama seemed to be organizing her words.

"Your brother called."

Or maybe she had just paused for effect. Hard to say, because Mattie suddenly felt herself reeling. She hadn't heard from her brother since grade school. He'd been one of those incorrigible kids the county had found hard to place, and he'd never received the benefit of living with Mama T.

"Why would he call you? He never lived here."

"No." Sadness creased Mama's face. "My home was full when he needed me. He was sent out of town. You know this. I was lucky I had an opening later so I could take you in."

"Why did he call?"

"He wanted me to ask you a question. He knew you lived here once."

"A question?" Why wouldn't her brother just call her directly?

"He said he's kept track of you, but he doesn't know if you want to talk to him. He doesn't want to bother you with a call if you don't want it. He says he would understand if you didn't want to talk to him."

Mattie was speechless. She'd always hoped she would hear from her brother, but she thought that *he* was the one who didn't want to talk to *her.* What would make him call after all these years?

"He said to ask you if you want him to call you."

"Did he leave a number?"

"No, he will call me again later to find out what you say."

Mattie glanced at the old-fashioned, rotary-dial phone hanging on the kitchen wall. No star key, no caller ID. "Did he say where he's living?"

"California. Los An-gel-eees."

"Oh my gosh," Mattie whispered. She looked down at her empty plate, trying to focus her thoughts.

Willie always took the heat; he bore the punches. Mattie was the good girl; she called the police. What would she say after all this time? What would he?

"Let him call you," Mama said, as if she sensed Mattie's trepidation.

Mattie looked at her with watery eyes. "Of course, Mama. Please tell him to call me. Thank you for this."

"My pleasure, *mijita*." She pushed back her chair. "I want a full report after you've talked to him. Now, I got to get back to work. Laundry day."

Mattie hugged Mama T good-bye and then went outside to the car and Robo. He rose from lying on his platform, a sleepy look on his face. He yawned and slowly wagged his tail, his usual exuberance dampened.

"Lazy dog." Mattie ruffled the black fur at his throat. For a few heartbeats, with her arm sticking through the heavy gauge wire mesh, she held onto him, staring at nothing, seeing Willie's childish face in her mind: thin features, their mother's Spanish ancestry showing in his brown hair and dark-tan skin like hers, troubled brown eyes almost black with torment.

The last time she'd seen him, they were on the playground at school; she was eight, and he was ten. Earlier in the school year, he'd been removed from the foster home that they'd been living in together—a home out in the country—after he'd set fire to the haystack. Willie wouldn't tell her why he'd done it; maybe he didn't know himself. After that incident, the only time they got to see each other was at school. He was telling her that their social worker was sending him to another family in Colorado Springs.

"Why, Willie?" she'd asked, her heart beating like a sparrow's wing.

"Because I'm trouble." Willie's face went dark with anger. "And because Dad's in prison, and Mom doesn't want us anymore."

The rest was a blur. She'd been sick to her stomach; she spent the rest of the day in the nurse's office, lying on a cot in a tight little ball, knowing it was all her fault.

As she started the engine, her thoughts in turmoil, Mattie checked the time. She had fifteen minutes to get to work—no time to drive home and digest this new information.

"Damn," she muttered, steering the cruiser out into the street and setting a course for the office.

★

As she pulled into the parking lot, Stella LoSasso was getting out of her Honda. Dressed in a formfitting, gray pantsuit with her honey-highlighted hair pulled up to her crown and anchored by combs, Stella looked the perfect mix of professional and sexy. She stood by her vehicle, waiting for Mattie and Robo to come up to her.

"I checked out Dean Hornsby," Stella said.

"Oh?" Mattie was still thinking about Willie.

"Yeah. He wasn't in our system, no criminal background, so I Googled him. Turns out he's the tampon king of Arizona."

"What?"

"You heard me. Sole heir to the Assurance products fortune. Just sold the company for a couple million."

"You're kidding me."

Stella grinned. "I went out to their new compound to check him out. You're right, he's damn weird. And that Anya, who works for him? She's weird too."

"You can't arrest someone for being weird."

Stella shook her head. "If you could, my ex-in-laws would've been locked up long before I met them."

Mattie smiled.

Stella's demeanor became serious. "I think they're worth pursuing. Hornsby seemed mad as hell to see me, said he was going to sue for harassment. Anya seemed to calm him down, and he made the right choice to stick around for some questions. They say they were both present and accounted for there at the health spa on Friday morning. Of course, they're each other's alibis. Makes it real handy. If we find something else on the guy, we could bring him in and question him here. Or any of the other people out there, for that matter."

Mattie had run the plate on the vehicle parked at Brody's after she returned home last night. It belonged to a dark-gray Ford Escape registered to Adrienne Howard, the massage therapist she'd met at the hot springs yesterday morning. She hesitated to share this with Stella. So far she had nothing solid against either one of them, Brody or Ms. Howard. She decided to sit on it a little longer.

Stella was still talking. "And I made some copies of a couple of pages from the kid's diary last night that I'd like for you to see. It's damn sad reading the thing, and I respect the kid's privacy. Other than these two pages that pertain to the case, I don't plan to share it with others."

"I respect that decision," Mattie replied.

"Can we grab a cup of coffee and meet outside at the picnic table for a minute while I have a cigarette?"

Mattie checked her watch. "I have about ten minutes before briefing."

"Let's postpone the coffee. I'll just go for the cigarette."

Mattie followed the older woman down the sidewalk to the side of the building where there was a covered picnic table meant for employees to have lunch but used mostly as a spot for them to take a cigarette break. This early in the morning, the area was deserted.

While Stella lit up, she said, "You look like someone's holding you hostage this morning? What's up?"

Mattie marveled at the detective's perceptiveness. "My brother called my foster-mom and told her to ask me if I'd want to talk to him."

"This is the brother you haven't heard from since he left town? Years ago, right?"

"Yeah. Since we were kids."

"Hot damn." Stella took another hit on her cigarette. "And you got his phone number, right?"

"He didn't leave it."

"Caller ID?"

"Mama has an old rotary phone."

"We could get her phone records."

Mattie smiled at the lengths Stella seemed willing to go. "That won't be necessary. He'll call her back, and then he'll call me."

"Okay. But what if he doesn't?"

"He will."

"Don't postpone this, Mattie. What are you afraid of? You still functioning under the misconception that what happened to your family is all your fault?"

Mattie paused, no longer sure how she felt but knowing she could never admit it and face Stella's wrath. "No."

Stella gave a skeptical look. "One thing I learned a long time ago, Mattie—and you should remember this—is that it's okay to get out of an abusive situation. You don't have to beat up on yourself just because you refuse to let someone else do it." She sucked another lungful of cigarette smoke while Mattie stared back at her and said nothing.

"Let's move on," Stella said, shifting to a more business-like manner and reaching into her case to retrieve two copied pages covered in plastic sheets. She handed them to Mattie.

Quickly, Mattie scanned the pages for dates. There were only two entries, one made the week before Grace's murder and one made the very day. The first entry read,

Followed M and his dogs to a cabin up Ute Canyon, and I'm parked at a spot just a little ways up where I can watch without him noticing me. He takes a dog inside one at a time and then brings it out to the trailer. WTF is he doing? I wish I could ask, but he'd freak if he knew I've been following him.

Mattie glanced at Stella, who blew a thin stream of smoke out of her pursed lips. She went on to the next one, the one made on the day of the girl's murder.

Followed M back to the same spot. Today there's another car here, a gray SUV kinda like mine. M keeps taking the dogs back and forth. This is so lame sitting here watching him through binoculars. I'm going down there to see what's going on!!!!

With a dull ache in her chest, Mattie looked at the detective.

Mouth downturned, Stella said, "My guess is, they weren't too pleased to see her." She moved her cigarette back up to her lips.

Mattie just shook her head. "I wish she'd written down the plate."

A snort released some smoke from Stella's nostrils. "Tell me about it. We'd be making an arrest about now."

"I'm glad for the parents' sake that there'll be no more speculation about her involvement with the drug ring."

The conversation died while Stella took a last drag on her cigarette, threw it in the grass, and then stubbed it out with the toe of her shoe.

Mattie said, "Guess it's time to go inside."

Brody came strutting around the corner of the building, headed their way. "Cobb! Are you going to work today or just sit around smoking cigarettes with the detective?"

Stella's annoyance was evident.

"I'm on it," Mattie told him, getting up from the bench.

"What?" Brody said to Stella, gesturing with his hands, palms up.

"Just reminded me of an argument that Deputy Cobb and I had about male and female cops," Stella said. "Now, let's go to work and try to do some good."

Chapter 23

"I want braids. Mommy always makes braids for me."

Sophie's whiny voice made Cole wish for a nanny. No wonder Liv was worn down.

"Sophie, I tell you what. If you don't stop that whining, I'm going to send you to your room, breakfast or no breakfast. Do you hear? I can't take it anymore."

Sophie hugged the stuffed rabbit she'd found on the kitchen chair, where, in the excitement of getting Belle last night, he'd forgotten and left it. She stuffed one of its ears into her mouth. Tears streamed down her cheeks as she clamped her teeth. She looked sadder than a wet cat.

Good Lord. The kid was suffering and all he could do was yell at her. He ought to be shot and put out of his own misery. "Come here, little bit."

Cole wrapped his arms around his youngest and rocked her gently until she relaxed into him, sobbing out her lonesomeness.

"I want Mommy," she said between sobs.

"I know, I know." Cole continued to rock her, side to side.

He'd tried to reach Olivia last night by phone, but either she was away from home or she was screening calls and decided not to pick up. He hated to be paranoid, but he thought it was probably the latter. Finally, he'd left the message that he and kids missed her, and he had some important local news he needed to tell her.

He'd hesitated to ask her to call him back; he'd already done that many times to no avail. But it just didn't seem right that she learn about Grace's death on the news or, worse yet, through the grapevine. Olivia had known the girl since the children were first graders, and he knew the news would be a shock to her.

Besides, it would be nice to hear her voice.

Eventually, Sophie settled down, and he set her away from himself at arm's length. "Let's see, now. Did you bring a hairbrush? Yes? Let's see what we can do about those braids."

"Can you braid hair?" Sophie was trying hard not to whine, something Cole appreciated more than he could say.

"How hard can it be? I used to braid reins when I was a kid. I was pretty good at it, too. Can't be much different."

Cole ran the hairbrush through Sophie's brown curls, working with the tangles as gently as possible.

"Did you brush your teeth?"

"Not yet."

"Do that right after breakfast, okay?"

Sophie hugged the rabbit to her chest, head bowed, noncommittal.

Using the brush, Cole made a swipe at parting the hair down the back of Sophie's head. It resulted in a crooked line, off center, so he tried again. The second time was a little better. He parted the hair of one half into four strands and began trying to weave it into a flat braid, like he'd once done with leather. But the curly stuff didn't hold together, and he quickly became all thumbs.

Dropping the hair, he picked up the brush again for another pass. "Where's your sister?"

"She's still in bed."

"Geez," Cole said, irritation starting to give him a knot at the base of his neck. What happened to the excitement about going to work?

"Just a minute, Sophie-bug." Cole went to the base of the staircase and hollered upstairs. "Angela?"

No answer.

"Angela!"

In a grumpy voice, Angela shouted back, "What?"

"Are you up?"

"Yes!"

"Leave the attitude and come down for breakfast."

No response.

"Did you hear me?"

"Yes!"

"Good God," Cole muttered under his breath.

He went back to Sophie, who had settled herself on one of the barstools pulled up to the kitchen island and was pouring milk into a bowl of Cheerios.

"Let's give those braids another go," he said, picking up the brush. This time, it seemed like the extra height lent by the barstool gave him a different angle and a better grip on the silky strands of curly hair. He had one braid done, secured by a rubber band, and was starting on the second one when Angela came into the room wearing denim shorts, a low-cut tank top, and a sour expression.

Angela took one look at the first braid, which was sticking out at a funny angle, shook her head, and snorted.

"Those are sweet braids you've got going on there, Sophie."

Sophie scowled.

"What's wrong with them?" Cole asked.

"You're supposed to divide the hair in three parts, not four."

"So we're doing it a different way."

"Different is not always good."

Cole gave Angela a look.

She shrugged and went to the counter to pour herself some cereal. "Just keeping it real."

"These braids are okay, Sophie. In fact, they look real cute." Cole secured the second braid with another rubber band and stepped back to examine his handiwork. The braids reminded him of Pippi Longstocking's. He moved around the island to get a frontal view. "I like it. It looks great. In fact, you'll probably set a new fashion trend in Timber Creek."

Angela snorted again.

He could tell Sophie was torn between believing him and believing her sister. She started to climb off the barstool, presumably to go take a look at her hair for herself.

"Finish your breakfast, Sophie. We've got to go."

Belle got up from where she'd been lying on the floor and limped over to the door.

"Looks like Belle needs to go outside. We don't have any more time for hair. We've got work to do."

Sophie scooped the last few bites into her mouth and then headed for the door with Belle, letting them both out into the yard.

Cole frowned at Angela. "You need to be nicer to your sister. She's having a hard enough time without you teasing her."

"I wasn't teasing, Dad. You're going to let her go up to the clinic with her hair like that?"

"Good grief, it's only hair. And there's nothing wrong with it." Cole turned to more important matters. "I need your help today, Angel. I thought we had a plan. Let's get it rolling, okay?"

"Whatever." She placed her cereal bowl in the kitchen sink.

"Did you think about Mr. Brennaman's offer to work in the front office this year? You're supposed to let him know today."

She shook her head and frowned. "I think it would be creepy, Dad. You know, to take Grace's job like that."

Cole had wondered how she'd feel about it and had already decided that if she didn't want to do it, he wouldn't push her. She still had two more years after this one to do that sort of thing if she wanted. "It's okay with me if you don't want it. But try to remember to call him sometime this morning. I don't know if I'll be able to remind you once I get started."

"I'll do it. You don't have to nag me about it."

He hoped her mood improved soon. "I wasn't nagging, Ange."

She muttered something as she went out the door, causing Cole to sigh.

Tess was already at the clinic, sitting at the computer, when they finally made it to work. Cole had called her earlier to let her know about Grace so that he wouldn't have to talk to her about it in front of the kids.

"Good morning!" Tess seemed to be armed with her usual cheerfulness. But upon seeing Sophie, her eyebrows shot up. "Sophie, girl, come here for a second."

Dutifully, Sophie went over to stand in front of her. Tess grasped her shoulders and turned her side to side, then once around, inspecting the little girl's hairdo. "Did you do your own hair this morning, honey?"

"My daddy did it."

A smile tweaked the corner of Tess's mouth. "Lovely," she said, sending Cole a look with eyes that twinkled.

"Is it all right if I adjust these braids a little bit for you?" Tess reached to take off one rubber band and undo the braid without waiting for an answer. "Here, I have a comb in my purse. Let me get it."

"I told you, Dad," Angela muttered as she flopped down in a chair in the waiting room.

Not used to feeling inadequate in his environment, Cole leaned over the counter to grab his schedule book and then withdrew into the treatment room to organize supplies for the day. He could hear Tess and Sophie talking.

"Why don't I make some nice French braids? Would you like that?"

"Yes, I would. Mommy does those for me a lot."

"Good. You have lovely hair, Sophie. Is it naturally curly?"

"I guess so."

There was silence for a few moments, but Cole winced at Sophie's next words.

"My mom and dad got a divorce."

He listened while the conversation skipped a beat. Although sure that Tess must have heard the town gossip, he'd never told her about his family problems.

"Are you feeling okay about that?"

Cole thought Tess probably knew that he could hear them talking. He felt himself flush like a kid caught spying.

"No," Sophie said, her voice thin and strained. "I'm sad."

"It's okay to feel sad, Sophie. You have a lot to feel sad about right now. Here, let me give you a hug." There was a long pause. "Now, we're all done with your hair, and it's sooo pretty. Sometimes when we're sad, it's good to stay busy. Why don't I show you how to wash those syringes over there with that teensy brush? Won't that be fun?"

"Okay."

"And, Angie, I want to teach you how to work this computer program to check in patients. That would help us out a bunch."

Cole felt relieved to have Tess take on his children for the morning. Hearing the front door open for the first customer of the day, old Mrs. Holly and her sick cat, he moved toward the lobby to greet her and get started with the day's schedule.

Once involved with his clients, and with Tess to keep his daughters occupied, the rest of the morning went much more smoothly. He was wrapping things up around noon when Tess told him he had a call from a Tiffany Markley. He picked up the extension in the exam room, tucking the phone onto his shoulder with his chin while he started to clean up after his last patient.

But when the woman said, "I'm calling about some Bernese mountain dogs owned by Mike Chadron," she had his full attention.

"Yes?"

"I own a boarding kennel just south of Denver, and Mike left his dogs with me Saturday morning. I see that you've signed off on his health records."

"Yes, how many dogs did he leave with you?"

"Ten."

That matched the number he'd found in his records when Mattie had asked for it. "Are his dogs still with you?"

"Yes, they are. That's why I'm calling. Mike said he'd call me back yesterday and arrange a time to pick them up this morning, but I haven't heard from him. He doesn't answer the phone number he left with me. I wondered if you might help me get in touch with him."

That might be difficult. "I hate to break the news so suddenly, but Mike died last Saturday night."

"Oh my goodness, that's terrible. What happened?"

"It looks like a suicide. But the police have been looking for his dog trailer and his dogs."

"His trailer is parked behind my kennel. I told him he could leave it there. Oh my word!"

"Yes, it's a shock. I need to get your name and number so that I can pass it on to my contact at the sheriff's office here. Her name is Deputy Mattie Cobb. I'm sure she'll be calling you soon."

Cole wrote down the information. "Tell me, have the dogs been sick?"

"Well, that was odd, too. Mike said he'd tried a new diet for the dogs, a raw chicken diet, and it gave them diarrhea. He said he didn't want them to be stressed by transporting them while he went back home to pack. He said he planned to move to Canada." She paused to take a breath. "My goodness, what am I going to do with these dogs?"

"Talk that over with Deputy Cobb. The sheriff's office may want to come get them. I have another question before I let you go. Have the dogs' feces been normal?"

"Yes, they seemed to be recovered by the time he brought them to me."

"They've all been eating and drinking?"

"Yes, I haven't had any problems with them."

"Have there been any foreign objects in their feces?"

"Good gracious, no. Why do you ask that?"

The dogs must have expelled the cocaine on Friday night, just like Belle. "It's not important. Do they appear to be healthy now?"

"As far as I can tell."

"That's good. I'm going to call Deputy Cobb right now, so please stay by the phone. I'm sure she'll want to speak with you immediately."

As he was saying good-bye, Angela poked her head through the door, looking much less grumpy than she'd been earlier. The morning's activity must have been good for her. "Dad, we're hungry," she said.

"Why don't you guys walk Belle to the house and fix yourselves some sandwiches? I've got to make one more call and then I'll come, too."

"Don't take forever, okay?" She gave him a stern look.

"I won't, Angel."

After she left, Cole swiped to his contact list and called Mattie. She answered after the first ring.

"Hello, this is Mattie."

"Have I got good news for you," he said.

"I could use some about now."

"Just got a call from a kennel owner near Denver. She's got Mike's dogs."

"You're kidding!"

"I kid you not." Cole relayed the information he'd just learned, including the woman's name and phone number. "I told her to stay by the phone."

"I'll call her right now. Stella's here at the station. We'll talk to her together." Sounding in a hurry, she said good-bye but spoke again before he could disconnect. "And Cole?"

"Yeah?"

"Thanks. You've made my day."

"It's my pleasure. I thought I might."

Smiling, he disconnected the call. Tess came into the room to help him finish cleaning up. Instead of her usual pleasant countenance, she wore a look of concern. While squirting disinfectant on his exam table, he decided to preempt a lecture and start the conversation himself. "I heard Sophie tell you about the divorce."

She nodded, and he thought she looked relieved that he'd brought it up. He'd been right to suspect that she meant to do it herself if he didn't beat her to it.

"I wanted to tell you that if you need help with the kids or anything, just call," she said. "Tom and I would be glad to step in and take care of the girls if you need us. What's two more with our crew?"

Cole felt a wave of relief that took him by surprise. Though things really hadn't changed, just knowing that someone was willing to help with his burden eased the weight on his shoulders. And knowing that Tess knew something about raising kids and was actually *good* with his children presented an extra bonus.

"I may have to take you up on that. This afternoon, I have Angela watching Sophie at the house while I run ambulatory."

"I'll check in about midafternoon and make sure they're doing all right. And have Angela call me if she has a question or needs help with anything. Sophie's a little sad today."

Cole sighed. "I can't tell you how much it means just knowing you're willing to help out."

Tess gave him a scolding look. "If you'd told me you needed it, I'd have offered sooner."

"You're a lifesaver." Feeling somewhat more lighthearted than he'd been in days, he went out to his truck to join his girls for lunch.

Chapter 24

Stella called another meeting to summarize new findings for the case. Mattie hoped to finagle a seat behind Brody so she could observe him, but when she and Robo entered the room, she saw that he'd taken a seat toward the back. It would be awkward to sit even farther behind him, so she grabbed a chair and pulled it toward the side of the room where she could look at him now and then without having to turn around in her seat. She directed Robo to lie down near the wall beside her.

Once Sheriff McCoy had taken his seat near the front, Stella began. "Nice you could all make it," she said, looking pointedly around the room at Brody and Mattie, as if to indicate how odd it was that they'd chosen to distance themselves. "We have some new developments and additions to the case, so I wanted us all to be on the same page."

Picking up her marker, she went to the dry-erase board and wrote the word "Diary" on the grid under "Victim 1: Grace Hartman." "Now that we've found the girl's car, we can add more information. You all know about the diary. The important items gleaned here are the presence of another vehicle at the crime scene, a 'gray SUV kinda like' a Honda CR-V, and I'm using the girl's words here," she said, writing it down.

Instantly, it dawned on Mattie how she could get at least one of her suspicions out in the open. "There's a gray Ford Escape I saw out at the hot springs yesterday morning. It's got a similar shape." She glanced at Brody, as if including him in the conversation, and observed his face had taken on the color of a rich burgundy.

"There's about a thousand gray SUVs with that shape around the region. Are we gonna try to track down all of them?" Brody asked in a sarcastic tone.

Mattie spread her hands and shrugged. "We've got the hot springs crowd as people of interest. Maybe a coincidence, maybe not."

"You didn't happen to take down the plate, did you?" McCoy asked.

"Well, actually, I did. No reason to, really, but I knew we should be on the lookout, and it was the only car where I parked. Ran the plate, too. Belongs to Adrienne Howard, no priors, not even a speeding ticket. Met her while I was there. Pleasant woman. Massage therapist."

It wouldn't take a poker pro to read the anger on Brody's face now. *Interesting.*

Stella added the woman's name to the list of people to investigate.

"We can answer the questions regarding Grace Hartman's involvement with drugs and using her dog as a mule with a *no* to both, in my opinion." After an eye sweep around the room to see if there were any objections, Stella turned to write "Missing Cell Phone" under the word "Diary." "The Hartmans called and said that they've realized there's no cell phone among the belongings we've found. They can't find it at home either, and calling it goes directly to voice mail. I believe the killer took the phone and removed the battery so it couldn't be located. Maybe disposed of it, maybe kept it."

Stella moved her pen to under "Victim 2: Mike Chadron" and wrote "Dogs Found Near Denver." "As you also know by now, the dogs have been located, and Deputy Johnson is on his way to get them and bring them back in Chadron's trailer. From hearsay reports, it appears they've been used as mules, like Belle. In the interest of being thorough, we should have them examined to make sure they're clean. Sheriff, can we do that?"

"Yes, the department can spring for it. Deputy Cobb, will you make the arrangements?"

"Yes, sir."

"To update our list of persons of interest," Stella said, moving her pen, "I can clear Justin McClelland, our local attorney. He was more than delighted to have me visit him at his office and thought it hilarious that he might be a suspect. He has a solid alibi for Friday morning, verified by his secretary and a list of three clients he met with. Also, he seemed happy to tell me how he got the money for his new caddy. He got a settlement from his ex-wife, an independently wealthy heiress whom he sued for psychological damages. Says he represented himself, too."

Mattie glanced at Brody, wondering if he'd added the man to the list the day before as a diversion for the detective. His complexion had toned down, but he immediately met her gaze as if aware of hers. Not wanting to stir up his belligerence, Mattie looked away and back at Stella, who had resumed talking.

"Brody, did you find out anything about the tournament or the people in it?"

"I was in Phoenix the same weekend the gun went missing, but I was at a different tournament. There were four tournaments there that weekend. I never crossed paths with Brinkman or his buddies. I also reached Brinkman by phone, and he answered my questions the right way. His stolen gun report appears to be legit."

Stella stared at Brody for a few moments, seemingly thinking. "You know which one of these tournaments Brinkman was in?"

"Yep."

"I'll follow up from here then. I want to talk with the pro at the golf course he played at, see if I can discover anything there. Moving on, I think you all know my update on Dean Hornsby. I plan to continue to focus on him and now Ms. Adrienne Howard, so we'll keep an eye on the hot springs. Mattie, do you have anything to add on the O'Malleys?"

"I talked with the son Tommy and his mother yesterday. He told me he and his dad have new jobs and have been hired to work at the mine in Rigby. I spoke with the payroll manger there this morning, and neither one of them is employed at the mine. Tommy seems to be feeding me a line to divert suspicion over an increase in cash flow to the family.

"In addition, a social worker visited the family this morning. There are signs of domestic abuse—bruises on Mrs. O'Malley's face. She denies being hit by her husband. She also denies that her children are at risk and states that they now have money for groceries. The worker plans to revisit tomorrow, but there's not much she can do if the woman won't cooperate.

"I'm not liking either one of the O'Malleys for the homicides at this point, but I do think that at least young Tommy knows something about our drug traffic problem. We might be able to get something out of him that leads to our killer."

Stella nodded, her face serious. "It's time we questioned them together."

"I agree," Mattie said.

"Will you go over there with me after this meeting, Mattie?"

"I planned to stop by on patrol this afternoon anyway."

"This investigation takes priority," Sheriff McCoy said, "so manage your patrol duties around it, Deputy."

"Yes, sir." Out of the corner of her eye, Mattie could see Brody cross his arms over his chest, but he remained silent.

Stella turned back to the board. "Looking at the case here, is there anything that comes to mind? Any additions? Leads? Ideas?"

"You're wasting your time looking at Adrienne Howard," Brody said, his voice a growl. "I know her. She has nothing to do with this."

Stella took on a trace of her sweet smile. "Then I'll find that out when I talk to her. She's only a person of interest. No harm, no foul."

The group sat in silence, staring at the grid. Mattie could feel Brody steaming in the back of the room while she searched the board. There was something there that bothered her, but she couldn't quite put her finger on it.

Her cell phone vibrated in her pocket. When she pulled it out, she saw that Cole was calling. She realized Stella was watching her. "This is the vet," she told Stella as she tapped the screen to take the call. "Hello. Mattie Cobb here."

"Mattie. Thank God I reached you." His voice held an edge she hadn't heard in it before. "The kids are alone at the house. They heard someone trying to break in. Belle barked and they think he ran, but they don't know. I'm thirty minutes away, and I need someone there now to make sure they're safe."

Mattie's chair screeched as she stood abruptly and started toward the door. Robo followed without prompting. "I'm on my way. Hold on a moment."

All the others were watching her now. "Intruder at the Walker house," she said to McCoy.

"Do you need backup?"

"They think he ran already. I'll call in if I do."

"Go, Deputy."

"I can be at your house in two minutes," she said to Cole. She hit the station door at a run, Robo on her heels, and headed for the cruiser. Within seconds, he bounded into his compartment. She secured his cage, belted herself into the driver's seat, and headed toward the highway, talking to Cole at the same time. "Call the kids and stay on the line with them until I get there. All the doors are locked, right?"

"Yes. I'll call them now."

"And Cole, drive safely. These kids need their dad. I'll be there in about one more minute."

"Okay." She could hear the fear in his voice.

She felt terrible. Just last night she'd told him that citizens were safe in their homes. Tightness gripped her throat.

When she pulled into the Walkers' yard, she saw the two girls come to the living room window, Angela with a phone to her ear. She'd seen no one fleeing the place as she'd approached. She opened Robo's cage as she exited the cruiser. "Robo, come."

He jumped into the front seat and followed her.

Angela stepped out on the porch with Sophie beside her like a shadow, fear clearly evident on their faces. Belle trailed behind. "She's here now, Dad," Angela was saying as Mattie hurried to join them. "Yeah, yeah, okay. I'll give her the phone."

"If this is the man who killed Grace, you're all in danger," Cole said as soon as she picked up the phone. "I want you to load up the kids and leave."

"We're together now, Cole. Let me check something with Angela. Are you sure no one came into the house?" she said to the teen.

"I don't think so. We closed all the windows."

"The kids and I are going into the house, Cole. Robo, heel." She made sure Robo knew he was on duty so there would be no playfulness with Belle. She gestured for the kids to follow her, talking to Cole while they went. "We're all inside the house with doors locked. I'm going to do a walk-through with Robo to make sure the house is clear and secure. Here, I'm giving the phone to Angela so I can make sure." She handed over the phone before he could protest. "Angela, you guys stay by the front door with Belle."

With Mattie opening closet doors, it took only a little over a minute for Robo to sweep the lower level of the home. She felt certain there was no need to check the upper level, but it only took another minute or two for them to do it anyway. She returned to the girls and held out her hand for the phone.

"I'm giving you back to Mattie now," Angela told her dad.

"All clear," Mattie told him.

"You're sure it's safe to be there?"

"Yes. I'll stay with the girls until you get here, and then Robo and I will take a look outside."

"I'm about fifteen minutes away now."

"Uh-huh. You might want to slow it down a little."

"Advice from a cop."

"Yeah, buddy." Mattie ended the call and gave the girls a small smile, the tightness easing from her shoulders somewhat. Though their frightful time alone had passed, the aftermath was still apparent in their faces. "Let's go into the living room while we wait for your dad."

She and Robo followed the girls, and they all settled into seats, the girls together on the sofa. Mattie took a moment to check in at the station, asking Rainbow to give the others news that things were all clear, no backup needed. Then she focused on Angela. "Tell me what happened."

"We were watching TV in here, and then Belle got up and started growling. I followed her to the back door and she sort of rushed at it, you know, as much as she could with her limp. That's when she started barking, and she kind of lunged at the door and hit it with her front paws."

"Did you hear or see anything?"

"Yeah, the door knob was rattling, like someone was trying to get it open, you know. It was locked, so they couldn't, but they were still trying."

Mattie noticed that Sophie sat with big eyes and her arms wrapped around herself. She'd not seen her be so still in past visits. "Are you okay, Sophie?"

The girl nodded, putting a thumb in her mouth, and leaned into her sister. Angela put an arm around her and went on. "I looked out the window, you know, sort of staying behind the curtain."

"What did you see?"

"A man. I'm sure it was a man, but he had on a black ski mask so I don't know what he looked like." Angela's eyes widened as she spoke.

"That was scary," Mattie said.

"Yeah." Angela sniffed. "He turned and ran as soon as Belle hit the door."

"Good! Hooray for Belle, right Sophie?" Mattie wanted to see if she could animate the child a little bit.

Sophie smiled slightly around the thumb. "Right."

"How could you tell it was a man?" Mattie asked.

Angela thought. "Well, he was thick, you know, not built like a woman or skinny like a boy. And he was big, not as big as Dad, but not little either."

"So not skinny. Average build or heavy?"

"Average. But he ran like he wasn't too old—I mean, he didn't run like an old person."

"That's a good observation. Can you describe his clothing?"

"Well, I'm not sure. Jeans, a dark-colored sweatshirt, maybe navy blue."

"Did anything stand out? Anything unusual you could pick up on?"

Angela frowned, clearly trying to do her best. "Oh. He wore black gloves, shiny, like leather."

The sound of a truck driving up to the yard interrupted further discussion. "Daddy," Sophie whispered, and both girls hurried to meet him at the front door. Mattie and Robo followed, standing back as she watched Cole embrace his daughters and hold them for a long moment.

He looked over the top of Angela's head at Mattie. "Thank you," he said, his voice hushed.

She merely nodded. "I'm going outside to look around."

He made a movement as if to follow, but she stopped him. "Let me see what Robo can pick up before we all go out there and mix up the scent trail."

Taking Robo with her, she went to the back door and eased outside. Cement patio, lawn but no fencing, a few flower beds and shrubs. Without her needing to direct him, Robo sniffed at the door, his hackles rose, and he followed an invisible trail out into the yard.

He must know which scent doesn't belong.

Mattie went with him, breaking into a jog as he trotted toward the lane, nose to the ground. At the top of the lane, he stopped, circled a few times to sniff the area, and then he sat and looked up at her. Clearly he'd lost the scent trail.

Here's where the guy parked.

No neighbors to question, hard to say if anyone drove past and noticed a parked car. They probably thought nothing of it even if they did see one.

Mattie and Robo returned to the house. The Walkers met them out on the front porch, and she told Cole what little she'd discovered. "I wish I had more," she said.

"Maybe this is unrelated," he said, and Mattie understood that he meant unrelated to Grace's killing. "Maybe it was just an interrupted burglary."

"Maybe." But doubt made her probe her mind for that niggling thought she'd had back at the station during briefing.

"You girls can ride ambulatory with me this afternoon."

"Can Belle come, too?" Sophie asked.

"Sure. Go inside and pack a backpack with some books and snacks. Make sure you take a few water bottles." As the girls went inside, Cole called, "Angela, grab your cell phone."

It was enough to help her make the connection. "The cell phone."

"What?"

Her heartbeat quickened. "Grace's cell phone is missing. Her killer probably took it to see who she'd been calling lately. Maybe it was him. Maybe he was looking for something or evidence that Angela might know something."

"But she doesn't."

"He doesn't know that."

Cole looked stricken.

"There could be other kids in danger," she said. "Hold on a minute. Let me make a call." She swiped to her contact list and pressed a button. Cole went into the house, leaving Mattie alone on the porch.

"Yes, Mattie?" Stella answered.

Mattie explained her concern. "We need to check Grace's cell phone records and notify some parents."

"I've already ordered the records. I'll put a STAT on it," Stella said.

"Sounds good. I'll be back at the station soon." She disconnected the call.

Cole came out of the house; determination had replaced the distress on his face. "I asked Angie to write down a list of Grace's friends, anyone she might have been talking to on her phone."

"That's a good idea. It takes a while to get the phone records."

His eyes narrowed. "Let's find this monster."

"We will. We're making progress. And we're having Mike's dogs brought back to Timber Creek. Will you examine them for us and make sure they're healthy?"

"Sure. But you realize I can't tell if they were used as mules, right?"

"Yes. We want to be thorough and not overlook the dogs' needs if any of them were damaged in any way."

"All right. I'll put it on the schedule for tomorrow."

He extended his hand, confusing Mattie. She hadn't said anything about leaving. But she extended her own as if to shake hands.

"I owe you a debt of gratitude," he said, clasping her hand between both of his.

"You owe me nothing."

His dark eyes held onto hers, and she felt a sinking sensation. Warmth spread from her chest into her face. His hands felt calloused and strong, and that surprised her. She would have expected softer hands for a doctor. But then some of his patients were much larger and tougher than humans. Embarrassed beyond words, Mattie tried to pull away, but he held fast.

"These kids are all I have," he said. "I appreciate your concern for their safety. And I appreciate what you're doing to preserve this community and our way of life. I hope we can all get back to normal again soon."

The front door opened, and he released her hand. She took a step back. The kids came through the door, carrying their things, and Angela handed her the list.

Mattie cleared her throat and tried for normalcy. "Thanks, Angie. I'd better get back to the station with this. We have some phone calls to make."

"Thanks for coming so fast," Angela said.

Sophie came close and reached up to give her a hug. As Mattie bent to accept it, she caught the sweet scent of the girl's shampoo. She took in a breath as she held the child close for a moment.

"You girls keep my cell phone number handy," Mattie said after the hug. "I want you to call me directly anytime you're afraid, day or night. Okay?"

They agreed.

"Thanks again, Mattie," Cole said as she turned to leave. Sophie echoed his words in a soft voice.

Robo followed her, and it felt good to have the routine of loading him into the cruiser and getting into her own seat. She still felt flustered by Cole's warm demonstration of gratitude. Not wanting to dwell on it, she turned her mind to her main purpose.

"Robo, we've got to find this guy before he hurts anyone else, right?"

He looked into her eyes and panted.

She'd take that as a yes.

Chapter 25

Mattie and Stella were heading toward the O'Malley trailer, but after driving a few blocks, Mattie pulled over and parked at the curb. Her concerns about Brody kept gnawing at her. True, he wasn't the one who tried to break into the Walkers' home, but still, there were some indications that he could be involved with this crime in some way. It was time to speak up about her suspicions and let the chips fall where they may.

"I need to talk to you about something in private," she said, "before we interview the O'Malleys."

Stella turned to her, curiosity on her face. "What's that?"

"Yesterday, when I asked Tommy O'Malley if he knew anything about drug running through town, he said I needed to talk to Deputy Brody about that. When I asked why he'd say such a thing, he told me that Brody spent time in the park with Mike Chadron and his dogs this summer. This causes concern about two things: one, that Tommy knows something about Mike being involved with drug running, and two, that he suspects Deputy Brody is mixed up in it."

Stella pursed her lips.

"Tommy also told me that he saw Brody hanging out with kids at the end of the school year. He thought Brody might know Grace."

"Did Brody identify the body when she was found?"

"No. None of us appeared to know who she was at that time."

"This is serious shit, Mattie."

"Tell me about it." She paused. "There's more."

"Damn, girl. Give it to me."

"Yesterday, when you briefed us on the case at noon, I was sitting behind Brody. When you reviewed the evidence, I noticed him getting more and more agitated, his neck got red, and he acted like he couldn't wait to get out of the room."

"Maybe he just had gas."

Mattie appreciated the detective's attempt at levity, but she shook her head. "It all started when I mentioned the hot springs crowd as possible suspects."

Stella pursed her lips again and shrugged. Mattie could tell she was as yet unconvinced.

"Last night I couldn't sleep, so I took Robo for a jog along the highway. I happened to go past Brody's house and the car I mentioned was parked there, the one that belongs to Adrienne Howard. As you heard in our meeting today, Brody vehemently denies that neither she nor any of the hot springs crowd is involved in our case."

"Maybe they're not. They are only persons of interest at this point."

"Yeah, I know. But what if they're involved with drug running? And I also saw Brody flush when the sheriff asked him if he was in Phoenix at the time the murder weapon was stolen from the dentist's car."

"I saw it too, but that's natural. Anyone might get embarrassed if that connection was brought up in a group. Especially in a group of cops."

This wasn't going as Mattie planned. "I think we should confirm that Brody really wasn't near Brinkman that weekend."

Stella turned in her seat so that she could face Mattie. "All right. It's sticky, but I can do that when I contact the golf pro. I respect your observations, but most of them don't hold water. Now this bit from Tommy O'Malley? It bears checking out. Carefully, very carefully. We've got to tiptoe through this shit like we're going barefoot in a pig sty."

At least Stella agreed with her on the most important points. "That's why I wanted to talk to you before we got to them. I need some help on follow-up questions with Tommy, and I want to find out if Patrick knows anything."

"I like the sound of that. Let's go."

Driving up to the O'Malley trailer, Mattie spotted Sean sitting on the rough board steps at the front. He jumped up and beat it inside.

"That's odd," she told Stella. "I'm surprised he didn't come out to see Robo."

Patrick O'Malley stepped out onto the porch, and she put two and two together. She would bet her next paycheck that Sean had been told to stay away from her.

"There's the man we're looking for," she said as she parked the cruiser and rolled down the windows.

Patrick stayed on the steps while they approached. Mattie introduced the detective, who offered a handshake that he ignored. Stella ended up smiling and placing her hand in her pocket.

"Nice to meet you, Mr. O'Malley," Stella said. "We're visiting with parents who have kids in high school. I understand you have two of that age."

He acknowledged her with a slight nod.

"You've heard about Grace Hartman's death, I suppose."

"Yes."

"Did you know Grace, sir?"

"No, I did not."

"Were your kids friends with her?"

"How the hell should I know?"

Stella stayed friendly. "We're advising parents to talk with their teens about being extra cautious, especially those kids who were friends with Grace. Ask them to go out only when accompanied by a parent or have them stay in groups. That sort of thing."

Patrick stared and offered nothing.

"Could we have Tommy join us? We'd actually like to ask you both a few questions."

"Tommy ain't here."

"Can you tell us where he is?"

"Nope, I have no frickin' idea. Tommy's hard to pin down."

"I hear ya. Most teenagers are. That's why we decided to talk with families. No need for panic, but it wouldn't hurt to keep a closer eye. Are you aware of the antidrug campaign we've started in town?"

"Nope."

"There's been some drug traffic through town this past year. Have you been aware of that?"

"Nope."

"Well, we're making sure people know that we won't stand still for it. We have zero tolerance for illegal drugs in this community."

"Doesn't affect me."

"I'm glad to hear it." Stella paused. "We've also lost another citizen lately. Mike Chadron. Have you heard about that?"

"Nope."

"Do you know Mike?"

"I do not."

"Okay." Stella took a different turn. "I understand you're going to start work at the mine in Rigby."

A trace of confusion crossed his face. "Where'd you hear that?"

Stella turned to Mattie. "Deputy Cobb? Didn't Mr. O'Malley's son Tommy say that's where they were going to work?"

"Yes, ma'am, he did."

Patrick snorted. "Tommy's a liar. Don't listen to him."

"So where are you working then?" Stella asked.

"I'm a handyman. I work all over."

"And where are you working currently?"

"At the school. I'm doing a job for the principal."

"Have you worked there for long?"

"A couple weeks."

"So you were working there last week? Did you work on Friday?"

"Yeah, I did. What does that have to do with anything?"

Stella pressed on. "Did anyone see you working there Friday morning?"

Patrick gave her a suspicious look, not oblivious to the turn in her line of questioning. "Yeah. Friday was payday. The secretary gave me a check that morning."

That gave him an alibi for Grace's death, but Mattie wondered why he hadn't used the money then to buy groceries for his family. She wanted to ask but didn't want to interrupt Stella's momentum. It was a detail she could check later.

"The police are planning to have more of a presence at the school this fall," Stella said. "In fact, they started last spring before school ended. Have you noticed our patrols while you've been working there?"

"That big cop drives by a lot. He spends a lot of time at the school."

Stella smiled. "The biggest cop we've got is Deputy Brody. You might be talking about him. Do you know if he's the one?"

"I don't know the guy's name."

"Were you working at the school last spring?"

"Yeah. That's when I first saw him. Always hanging out in the parking lot before and after school. Seemed to be talking with the kids a lot."

"Did you see him with anyone in particular?"

"I didn't pay attention to that. Saw him talk to the principal a few times. He's stopped in to talk to the principal this summer, too."

"Oh, yeah?"

Patrick shrugged and didn't offer anything else.

Geez. Like pulling an elephant's teeth. Mattie wondered why Brody was stopping in to talk with Brennaman. What business did he have at the school during the summer?

Finally, Patrick went on. "He showed a lot of interest in those old buildings I tore down. Went in and out of 'em, carried some things out and put 'em in his car."

"Like what kind of things?" Stella asked.

"Hell if I know. I didn't stop working to look."

"Were you around during any of these meetings Deputy Brody had with the principal?"

"Oh, yeah. He wants my opinion on a lot of things," Patrick said with sarcasm. "I fix things, I tear things down, I clear things out. I don't sit in meetings. You want to know what's going on? Ask your cop friend. Why are you asking me anyway?"

Stella smiled her sweet smile. "I thought if you knew I'd save myself some time. Oh, yes. One more thing."

"What's that?"

The smile fell from Stella's face. "I hear your wife looks like someone might have hit her."

His face reddened. His eyes darted from Stella to Mattie. "Did she tell you someone hit her?"

Mattie cut in. "No, Mr. O'Malley, she didn't. It's something I noticed earlier."

"Did you hit her?" Stella asked.

"No! I don't beat my wife."

The silence lengthened while they all stared at each other.

"Good to know," Stella said, breaking the lengthy silence. "But you need to remember that we'll be keeping an eye on her now."

More silence while Patrick glowered.

"Well, sir, thank you for your time. We want to talk with Tommy again later, so we'll come by this evening," Stella said.

He frowned. "I don't know if he'll be home."

"We'll take our chances. It's not far to drive. But if he's not here, we'll need to find him and bring both of you to the station so we can question him." Stella turned to leave but stopped when Mattie stayed.

"Mr. O'Malley," Mattie said, "Sean got caught shoplifting food on Saturday. I was just wondering, if you got paid on Friday, why didn't you get groceries for your family then?"

He took on a mean look. "I didn't have time to get the damn check cashed when I got off work. The bank was closed."

"There's an ATM on the side of the bank."

"Shit, I don't use those things. Don't even have an account there. We pay cash for everything."

Mattie paused. This was truly a family who lived from paycheck to paycheck. "I see. A social worker will be stopping by again with services to offer your family. I wish you'd consider taking advantage of what she has to offer. It could ease some of the pressure you have when your cash falls short."

His face tightened. "And I'll warn you to mind your own business when it comes to my money and my family."

Mattie felt a flare of anger but held it back. "It's my duty to make sure you and your family have the means to be safe and secure. It's what we do."

Stella smiled her sweet smile. "And we stay at it until we're satisfied. Thanks again for your time, Mr. O'Malley."

This time Mattie followed her to the car. "What do you think?" she asked Stella once they'd driven away.

"I'll verify Brody's account of the two tournaments, and we'll keep an eye on him. We need to find out what he was taking out of those buildings."

"And why he's been going by the school this summer," Mattie said.

"Maybe he's been planning an antidrug program with the principal or something."

"That's my job."

Stella pursed her lips, looking thoughtful.

"I'm dropping off some information at the school for the principal this afternoon. I'll see if I can get some answers from him," Mattie said.

"Be careful, Mattie."

"I will." She intended to be careful, but she also intended to get to the bottom of it.

Stella stared out the passenger window, lips pursed. "This is some serious shit," she muttered under her breath.

Chapter 26

Leaving Robo in the car in front of the high school, Mattie entered the building, a manila envelope containing information about the antidrug program in hand. She was relieved to find Brennaman standing at the front counter, apparently filling out some forms. He tilted his head to look at her over the top of reading glasses perched partway down his nose. He gave her a teasing smile.

"Deputy Mattie Lu, you came to see me."

"Yes, sir, I wanted to bring by the materials I mentioned. I'm glad you're here."

"If you could just put them down here on the counter, I'll get to them when I can."

Mattie laid the packet down next to him. "I have a quick question for you. You know Patrick O'Malley, right?"

"Why, yes. Patrick does work for me around here."

"Did he work for you the past couple weeks?"

"Hmm . . ." He leaned on the countertop and peered at her over his glasses again. "Yes, he tore down and cleared out some old sheds out back. You know the ones, Mattie. You kids used to hang out there when you were up to no good."

Mattie decided to let that slide. "Can you vouch for him being here last Friday morning?"

"I was at a meeting, so I don't believe I can."

"Perhaps your secretary?"

"Oh, yes. Betty may have seen him." He walked toward the back and called down the hallway. "Betty? Could you come out front for a moment?"

Looking as harried as she had before, Betty came down the hallway. "Yes?" she said.

"Betty, can you tell us if Mr. O'Malley was here at work on Friday morning?"

"Of course. I gave him his paycheck like I always do on Fridays."

"Thank you." Brennaman raised a brow at Mattie. "Is that all you need?"

"Yes, thank you, Betty. That's all I need from you right now," Mattie said, as the woman hurried to leave. "Just another quick question for you, Mr. Brennaman."

"I have work I should be doing, Mattie."

"This won't take but a moment." She took a second to organize her words. "Deputy Brody initiated patrol and established a police presence here before and after school last May."

She paused, hoping he'd jump in. She wasn't disappointed.

"Yes, he did. We talked about that before he started. I think it helped keep down the roughhousing and carrying-on we get, especially at the end of the day when energies are high."

"So he was able to mingle with the kids then?"

"Yes, he did a great job. Spent time with the various groups, seemed to get to know them."

This was all news to her. She decided to take a chance. "That might be when he met Grace."

Brennaman appeared to be thinking back. "Yes, I believe so. He used to visit with her group now and then, although they aren't the troublemakers. I'm pretty sure I remember him talking to Grace sometime in the spring."

Mattie controlled the electric jolt that shot through her and remained calm.

"And has he had some discussions with you this summer about continuing that police presence in the fall?"

Brennaman frowned slightly. "No, not really. He stopped in before we tore down those buildings and asked if he could nose around out there. Said he remembered some things back there from his high school days and wanted to take another look. I told him it was all trash and he was welcome to anything he might want. It would save Patrick some time and me some money." He smiled.

Mattie covered her tracks. "Oh, I'll have to talk with him. He must be waiting for me to follow up with you about next year. So you haven't been having regular meetings this summer?"

"No, he just stops in now and then." He glanced toward the back room and then kept his voice low as he went on. "I think he likes to visit Betty. He likes to flirt and tell her jokes."

Mattie smiled and nodded as if she found the gossip entertaining. What she really felt was exhilaration; she'd been able to get the information she sought and apparently without arousing suspicion. She reached to shake his hand. "Thank you for your time, Mr. Brennaman. I'll leave you alone so you can get back to work now."

He held onto her hand as if keeping her from leaving and then released it as he started speaking. "So tell me, Mattie, why were you selected to manage this big dog?"

"I passed a fitness test. It's important that a dog's handler can keep up with him."

"Do you have experience with dog training?"

"A little bit, with pets growing up, but Robo was fully trained when I got him."

Brennaman frowned. "I wouldn't guess you'd had experience with pets growing up, with your childhood background."

Mattie's cheeks warmed. "Some of my foster families had pets."

"Even so."

She wasn't sure what he was getting at. Was he doubting her ability to handle Robo or trying to undermine her confidence? "Robo and I had three months of training at K-9 Academy this summer. We know what we're doing."

He studied her over the tops of his readers. "I certainly hope so, Mattie, if we let you bring him into school like you're proposing."

"I can vouch for Robo's good behavior, sir. I'm confident we can handle the program."

Brennaman gave her a dismissive smile and a short wave. "I won't keep you. Thanks for stopping by, Mattie. I look forward to seeing more of you around here."

Once outside, she realized she'd broken into a sweat. *Geez!* He could still get to her. She hoped she could get over that when she started spending more time with him. When it came to confidence, she could talk the talk, but could she walk the walk? She hoped so. She needed to put her past behind her and move on.

Unsettled, Mattie hurried to the cruiser. As usual, Robo's greeting lightened her mood.

"We'll just have to show him, won't we, Robo."

She headed to the station, thinking about what she'd learned. Both Tommy and Brennaman thought they'd seen Brody talking with Grace. It sounded like he was a real flirt when it came to women, though she'd never experienced it, and Grace had been an attractive girl. She realized she could ask Angela Walker what she knew about Brody and Grace.

She reached for her cell phone and dialed Cole Walker.

"Hello, Mattie," he answered.

"Hello. I was hoping I could catch Angela with you. I have a quick question for her."

"Sure. She's right here."

Angela took the phone, and they exchanged greetings.

"I hear that Deputy Brody spent some time at school last spring," Mattie said, "running patrol and meeting some of the kids. Did you ever meet him?"

"No, but I know who you're talking about. He mostly spent time with the kids who get in trouble."

"Do you know if Grace met him?"

"Not that I know of, but she could've."

"Think back for a minute and see if you can ever remember him hanging out with a group of kids she might've been with."

Angela paused, apparently following instruction. "Grace and I were usually together after school. I don't ever remember him coming over to our crowd."

Her answer didn't fit with the picture Mattie had created, and she felt disappointed. Although it didn't eliminate the possibility that Brody had met Grace, it would have been nice to confirm Tommy and John Brennaman's observations.

"Thanks for talking, Angie," she said. "I'll say good-bye for now."

She disconnected and put her cell phone in its slot on the dashboard. Maybe this last call confused the picture somewhat, but Brody was far from being in the clear. Where had he been on Friday morning? And what had he removed from the sheds before they were destroyed?

★

Mattie returned to the station to finish up paperwork and check out. She felt tired but planned to go home for some food and then set up a stakeout on Brody's house. Stella was still out conducting interviews, and Sheriff McCoy was in his office with the door closed. Robo followed Mattie back to her desk in the staff office, circled a couple times on his dog bed, and then lay down to wait for her.

She was finishing up when Brody came in, apparently looking for her.

"There you are, Cobb."

He walked over to her desk, sat casually with one hip on the edge, and crossed his arms. "Did you get any information out of the O'Malleys when you and Detective LoSasso talked to them?"

Mattie leaned back in her chair and studied him. What was his angle? "Some. Not much."

He gave her a look. They seemed to be sizing each other up. "Well, what did you get?"

Mattie hesitated. Should she keep things safe and not mention anything she'd learned about his recent activities? Or should she stir things up a little and give him something to worry about, something that might even force him to make a move tonight while she was watching?

"We didn't get to talk to the O'Malleys together," she said. "I talked to Tommy yesterday, but he wasn't home today, so we talked with Patrick alone."

"And?"

"We were able to get an alibi for Patrick O'Malley for Friday morning, and I confirmed it with John Brennaman. Patrick was working at the school that morning."

Brody nodded, looking thoughtful.

"Patrick denies knowing anything about either murder," she said. "He also denies even hearing about our local drug traffic problem, which I find hard to believe."

"That's true. Everyone's been talking about the new dog."

"The strangest thing happened, though. Patrick seemed to try to point me toward you."

Brody shifted, twisted slightly to face her directly, and raised one brow.

"He said you spent a lot of time with the kids around school, might have taken things out of one of the storage sheds out back."

He lowered his brow with a perplexed expression and shook his head slightly. "Old car parts from the industrial arts shop? Hub caps?"

Mattie acted amused. "So that's what you took from back there."

"I remembered how we used to store things out there when I was in school."

Mattie hung on to her smile, trying to keep it light. "What use do you have for that junk?"

"It's not junk, Cobb. I work on old cars. They're spare parts."

It sounded believable, but she didn't know enough about Brody's hobbies to verify it. "So I hear from John Brennaman that you increased patrol around the school last spring."

"You were at the academy. We thought I'd better get started sorting out some of the kids."

"Sorting them out?"

"Yeah, you know, sorting out the bad seeds."

Mattie nodded acknowledgment. "What did you find out?"

"Your Tommy O'Malley is one of 'em. I think it's time we cracked down on him. He and his crowd can be a real nuisance at the park, but he's also quick to avoid getting caught."

"I've talked to him there a few times. He may be trying to clean up his act."

Brody snorted. "I doubt that. He's the kind of kid that needs more than just talking to. We'll have to charge him with something sooner or later."

Mattie hadn't seen Brody this forthcoming in ages, especially not since they'd become competitors for Robo. She decided to try to get more out of him.

"You know, Tommy mentioned that Mike Chadron used to hang out at the park with his dogs. Did you ever see him there when you were driving by?"

"Yeah, Mike took his dogs there to train. I used to watch him. Helped him set up a track for one of the dogs he was training for American Kennel Club tracking certification."

This news surprised her, but again she tried to keep the emotion out of her words, tried to keep a conversational tone. "I didn't know that. I realized you must have known Mike, but I didn't know you'd helped him with his dog training."

"What do you think? That you're the only one around here interested in dogs?"

Mattie raised her hands slightly, fingers spread. "No, Brody, I didn't think that. That kind of training sounds interesting. So where did you and Mike work with the dogs? And what did you do?"

"At the park, up around the rocks and bushes on T-hill. I set up a scent trail, hid behind some brush, and then Mike had the dog track me and find me. He taught me some things about showing them, too. How to set them up to stand, trot them around the ring."

Mattie was beginning to get a different picture about Brody. "Oh, yeah? I didn't know that Mike taught his dogs tracking skills. I mean, I guess I knew that Bernese mountain dogs have been used in search and rescue, but I didn't think about it with Mike. I wonder if Belle had that training."

"I don't know what dog he was training last summer, but it was a male. He seemed to know his stuff. Told me about scent memory, how a dog like that can catalog the scents of different people in his brain and remember it forever. Like a human has memory for faces. And that a dog doesn't pay attention to what he sees as much as to what he smells."

All that Brody was saying matched what Mattie knew on the subject, and she didn't doubt that he must've learned it from Mike. Suddenly, she started to see the bits and pieces she'd picked up in a different light, and she wanted to get more from him. It may not have always been pleasant, but she'd worked with this guy for seven years and had always known him to be a competent cop. That counted for something.

Brody stood and stretched. "It's time to check out and go home. I've put in some long hours lately."

She saw her chance. "You have. You even worked Friday when you were supposed to be off."

He yawned. "Yeah. Sheriff called me. Said he had a hunch about this one and didn't want Johnson to cover it on his own. So I came in."

"Where were you when he called?"

He gave her a smug look. "Getting kind of personal, huh, Cobb?"

Mattie smiled and shook her head. "Just wondering if you were close or if you were out of town and had to travel a ways."

"Just having breakfast at home with my new lady. We had plans for a hike, but I went to work instead."

"I'm glad you weren't out of cell phone range. Sheriff McCoy's hunch was a good one, I'd say. We needed you." Mattie paused, thinking while Brody turned away. "Hey, Brody?"

He stopped at the door and looked back at her. "Yeah?"

"Did you ever talk to Grace Hartman when you were at the school?"

"Nah . . . I must've sorted her out in the good kids. I didn't pay too much attention to them. Didn't even remember her face that much when we found her. She just looked sorta familiar, you know?"

Brody paused, his eyes losing focus, evidently conjuring the memory of finding Grace because he shuddered in a small way. Then he gave her a devilish grin. "Okay, time to check out. I've got a purty little gal coming over tonight, and I need to get some rest before she gets there. I'm not getting much sleep these days, but I sure am getting a lot of exercise, if you know what I mean."

And with that, he turned back into the macho asshole she was more familiar with. She forced herself to remain neutral and ask one more question. "Is she anyone I know?"

He stared a moment, and Mattie could see him considering his answer. He leaned against the doorframe. "You said you met her out at the hot springs. Adrienne Howard."

Mattie decided to meet him where he'd brought the discussion, out in the open. "Geez, Brody. Why didn't you say so earlier? No wonder you think she's in the clear. Have you known her very long?"

Mattie noticed a dull red flush creeping up his neck. He glanced down and then straightened to stand away from the door. She'd never seen him uncomfortable like this before. Usually he was all swagger and bluff.

With his voice taking on its familiar hard tone, he said, "Yeah, I've known her a couple months. Spent some time out at the hot springs. That's why I know you and the detective are on the wrong track with them."

"They seem worth taking a look at. Maybe not Adrienne so much as the others."

"The only thing those people are addicted to is tofu. They aren't involved with drugs or drug running. They're complete health nuts. And I never observed a connection between them and Mike."

"Sounds like you've spent some time out there."

"Hey, I hurt my back this summer, okay? I decided to try them out."

By this time, Brody looked really embarrassed, and she could tell his discomfort was genuine. It was killing him to speak so openly. "I'm glad you're telling me this now," she said.

"I've been sayin' it all along. No one seems to want to believe it."

She could tell he was frustrated. "Okay, I get it. The hot springs is probably a dead end."

"So that's settled then."

"As far as I'm concerned. We'll see if Detective LoSasso agrees."

He gave Mattie one of his mean looks and turned to go.

"Hey, Brody," she called. "Were they able to help you with your back pain?"

He threw a wicked smile over his shoulder on his way out the door. "Sure did. No problemo."

Mattie leaned back in her chair to consider what she'd just learned. In hindsight, she realized the times she'd noticed Brody blushing was probably because he was embarrassed about his affiliation with the "hot springs idiots," as he'd once called them, and his new lady love, which he'd found among them. Sure, he and Adrienne would be each other's alibis for Friday morning, but she didn't doubt he'd been close when called to work. And the killer had way too much to do that morning, burying the body and then hiding the car, to be down in Timber Creek at that time.

She was beginning to feel a little embarrassed herself about her earlier suspicion. It seemed like he was telling the truth when he said he didn't know Grace. Strange how Tommy and Brennaman had thought he did. And it wasn't so much Patrick who'd pointed the finger at Brody; it had been Tommy, who also appeared to know something about Mike using his dogs to transport drugs.

Tommy's the one we need to sweat. We need to bring him in so that Stella can interrogate him as soon as she can.

Who would've thought Brody would help Mike train his dogs? She realized his interest had been sparked by Robo's addition to the force. While she'd been away at the academy, Brody had pursued learning what he could from Mike. And that information about scent memory? That was good stuff.

Mattie gathered up her paperwork, placed it in the out basket, and turned to Robo. He'd slept through the entire conversation with Brody, something he didn't do with just everyone. He must've been comfortable enough and not felt threatened.

She remembered how Robo had bristled when he'd first met Brennaman. She paused, standing still. The room fell away as a rush of adrenalin hit her system.

Oh my God. Robo's scent memory!

Robo had sensed danger the moment John Brennaman entered the room. She'd been too ignorant to read what he'd tried to tell her. Another click of her memory, and she remembered Belle barking furiously out the window when Brennaman came by the Walker house.

Had he come to the house to see what Angela knew? She probed her mind to recall the conversation. Yes! He'd asked Angie if she and Grace spent much time together during the summer, if they'd talked the past week. *Christ!* He had some ego to question Angie with a police officer standing by. Her ears grew warm as she realized that he'd gotten away with it, too. Except for the dogs. They'd tried to tell the humans that the killer was standing right in front of them.

And when she'd taken Robo out through the back door, he'd picked up Brennaman's scent immediately, as evidenced by the hackles raised on his back. Hell, she'd wasted time suspecting Brody, and she was sorry she'd ever mentioned her suspicion to Stella. She reached for her cell phone to give Stella a call, but it wasn't in her pocket. She must have left it out in the cruiser.

"Come on, Robo. We need to go," she said, heading out the door with her partner at her heels.

Chapter 27

She found her cell phone where she'd left it: in its slot on the dashboard of her cruiser. In the waning light of dusk, she could tell that she had two missed calls, one from Stella and one from an unknown number. Stella's message was first in the queue.

"Hey, Mattie. I wanted you to know that the details from Phoenix were confirmed as originally stated. But I turned up an interesting thing. When I talked to the golf pro in charge of the tournament Brinkman played in, I asked if they had any registrants in their tourney from Timber Creek. The answer was yes. A Mr. John Brennaman. I think I've heard you and the sheriff mention him. He's the high school principal, isn't he? I plan to talk with him first thing tomorrow. I have one more interview now and then let's go see Tommy O'Malley. I'll call you when I'm done."

So Brennaman had been at the tournament where the gun went missing. Even though it seemed unbelievable, Mattie grew more and more confident that he was their guy for both murders.

She saved Stella's message and listened to the next one. After a long pause filled with shouting in the background, a child's voice spoke in a near whisper. "Mrs. Cobb? This is Sean. I need help."

Mattie's heart sank as a sense of déjà vu almost overwhelmed her. She checked the time on the child's call. Twenty minutes ago. She started the cruiser's engine and headed straight to the O'Malley trailer, calling the dispatcher and telling him to send the night shift deputy, Cy Garcia, for backup. She told him it was a potential domestic disturbance and gave the trailer's exact address and location.

Following up on Brennaman would have to wait until she took care of this crisis. She sped the few blocks it took to get to Sean's home, chastising herself for leaving her cell phone in the car.

The first to arrive, she parked out front and switched on the rotary lights. Red and blue created a cyclical flash against the trailer wall. The trailer itself was dark; there was no sign of anyone inside or out.

Mattie opened the front of Robo's cage and then tested the door popper button she wore on her belt to open her vehicle door by remote. When she pushed the button to send the electronic signal, her door swung wide. Confident that her equipment worked like it was supposed to, Mattie knew she could call Robo out for backup if she needed him.

"Stay here," she told him, shutting the door again. She lifted her Glock in its holster while she strode to the trailer, assuring herself she could clear it quickly if necessary.

Standing off to the side, she pounded the tinny door, making it rattle. "Open up. Sheriff's Department."

Mattie could feel her heart beat as she waited. No response from the trailer.

She pounded the door again. "Fran O'Malley! Open the door!"

After what seemed like eons but was probably only a few seconds, the door opened a crack. Without lights on inside, Mattie couldn't see anything beyond the door. She strained to hear, but her ears weren't giving her much either.

Mattie took her flashlight from her utility belt and switched it on. Training the beam into the crack in the doorway, Mattie could see Fran peeking through from the other side. She squinted in the light, and it was obvious she'd been crying.

"Are you all right, Fran?"

"I thought maybe I should call you," she responded in a hushed voice. "But I couldn't."

That's right. Your child had to do it.

Mattie lowered the light so it wouldn't shine directly in Fran's eyes. "Step outside, please."

Fran did as she was told, at first clutching her arms across her chest and then wiping her nose with the back of her hand.

Sweeping Fran with the flashlight beam, Mattie couldn't see any new bruises. "Where's Sean, Fran?"

"I don't know." Fran's voice caught in a sob, and she covered her mouth with both hands.

Mattie had a bad feeling. "What do you mean you don't know?"

"Tommy took him."

"Tommy?"

"Yes."

They must have been running from their father. "Where did he take him? Somewhere safe?"

Fran covered her face with her hands and cried, shaking her head.

With a sense of urgency, she took hold of Fran's wrist to pull her hands away from her face. "Tell me what's going on, Fran. Is Sean all right?"

The front door banged open, and Mattie jumped to the side of the porch to keep from getting hit. She heard someone say, "You need to get in the house, woman."

She recognized Patrick O'Malley's voice. Where was her backup? She was afraid the situation might deteriorate rapidly. Also sensing the threat, Robo started to bark from his cage in the cruiser.

She stepped from the porch platform, off to the side where she could get some distance between her, the swinging door, and Patrick. "It's Deputy Cobb," Mattie shouted. "Step outside, Patrick O'Malley. Show me your hands."

Mattie trained her flashlight on Patrick as he stood at the threshold, his hands lowered where she couldn't tell if he was carrying a weapon or not. "Put your hands on your head!" she shouted, her voice gruff from the force behind it. "Do it now! Hands to your head."

"No, no," Fran cried. "You don't understand. He's not the one. He's not the one." Her voice dropped off in a low moan.

Patrick came off the porch in a rush, hands outstretched, headed for Fran. Mattie could see that he wasn't holding a weapon, but a jolt of energy shot through her as he grabbed Fran's wrist and started hauling her back into the trailer.

Mattie pressed the door button, and the cruiser door popped open. "Robo, come," she shouted. "Guard!"

Robo jumped out of the cruiser and loomed beside her in a crouch, toenails digging into the ground, flashing white teeth bared. A growl rumbled from his chest.

It was enough to make Patrick O'Malley pause so that Mattie could try to get him to stop. "Release her! Or I'll send the dog."

Patrick glanced at the open door behind him.

"You're not fast enough to beat this dog to that door. Let go of Fran!"

He dropped Fran's wrist and stepped back toward the door, hands halfway raised.

"Keep your hands there where I can see them." As she spoke, Mattie moved to the porch. "Fran, step off the porch."

Fran moved away from her husband.

"You got no right to treat a man this way in his own home," Patrick growled. "I'm gonna sue you and this town for all you're worth."

Moving her flashlight over his face, she could see that it showed signs of a recent beating—a fat lip, bruises, and an eye that was starting to darken. He was a big man, and he stood at the trailer door. In an instant, he could be inside with the door shut; if he had a weapon inside, their lives could be in danger. Where the hell was Cy Garcia? Mattie knew she had to get Patrick under control without his backup.

"Sit down on the porch steps," she told him.

Patrick's eyes widened slightly. "Not with that dog there."

Robo had stopped growling, but his silent crouch threatened more than sound.

Mattie kept her voice level and authoritative. "He won't move unless I tell him to. Sit down. We need to talk."

"You keep that son of a bitch away from me."

"Step off the porch."

He took two steps away from the door, eyes on Robo.

Mattie felt she'd won a major victory, getting him farther from the trailer door. Now she needed to neutralize him. "Sit down on the step please, sir."

From behind her, Mattie heard a siren chirp and then fall silent as Garcia drew his cruiser up beside hers to park, lights flashing on top. The baby started to wail inside the trailer.

"You can't arrest a man for no reason," Patrick said.

"You're not under arrest. Sit down on the step so we can talk."

Garcia parked so that his headlights lit the yard. He exited his car and stood at the perimeter, sizing things up. Since she was first officer at the scene, and as long as she had everything under control, it was Mattie's role to be in charge.

"Mr. O'Malley, I'm not going to ask you again. You need to sit down."

Mattie placed her hand on her service weapon, and Robo edged closer.

Patrick sat.

"Thank you. Now, keep your hands on your knees where I can see them," Mattie told him. "Fran, is there anyone else inside the house beside the baby?"

"Molly." Her voice came out in a moan.

"Molly, can you hear me?" Mattie called to her.

"Yes." The girl sounded frightened.

"Can you turn on a light inside?"

"Our power was shut off," Fran said.

"Molly, bring the baby and come outside," Mattie told her.

The baby had already quieted. With the child in her arms, Molly stepped onto the porch.

"Come down here beside your mother," she told her. Head down, the girl moved to comply.

Mattie decided to let Robo hang in his guard dog mode a bit longer. She needed some answers, and she wanted them fast. A little pressure on Patrick wouldn't hurt.

She looked from Patrick to Fran and back. "I need one of you to tell me where Sean is, and I need you to tell me that right now."

"We're not telling you anything," Patrick said.

Fists clenched against her mouth, Fran whimpered. "Tommy was mad when he left here. I'm scared he might hurt Sean."

"Shut up, woman."

"Where were they headed?" Mattie asked.

"I don't know, I don't know."

"How long ago did they leave?"

"Fifteen minutes, maybe a half hour."

"Who did this to your face?" Mattie asked Patrick.

With jaw set, he remained silent.

"Tommy did it." The information burst from Fran as if she could no longer contain it. "He hit me, too."

"Fran." Patrick's voice held a warning.

"I don't care," Fran shouted at him. "I don't care who knows. We need their help. I'm sick of being afraid."

Mattie realized that her own childhood experiences had colored her judgment, so she had not read this family's situation accurately. "Think, Fran. Where would Tommy go?"

Fran became utterly silent, and her eyes lost focus as she forced herself to look inward, trying to dredge up some memory that would tell her where her children might be.

Molly spoke up, her face blanched, eyes wide. "I think he might take him to the Powderhorn."

The Powderhorn mine had been abandoned decades ago, after a cave-in made it too dangerous to work anymore. "What makes you think that?"

"I heard Tommy tell someone that he'd been there a few days ago and how scary the place is. He said he wanted to scare Sean, teach him a lesson."

"Why?"

"For being friends with you. For calling you just now about the drugs."

Tommy must've caught Sean at it. She felt a sinking sensation as she realized how she'd failed the child.

"Did Tommy take your truck?" she asked Fran.

"No. It's broken down."

"What's he driving?"

"A dark-gray Jeep Cherokee."

"What's the license plate?"

"I don't know."

Mattie remembered the SUV that passed her when she was jogging last night. "Where'd he get the Jeep?"

Fran looked at Patrick. He glared up at Fran in silence as if warning her not to say anything more.

"Molly, do you know where he got the Jeep?" Mattie asked.

"No. He showed up driving it in the middle of the night."

Mattie decided she'd gleaned all the information she could for the moment, and she didn't want to waste time trying to get anything more out of the family. "Robo, out."

Robo gave her a look of doggie disappointment. He relaxed his position somewhat though he remained in a crouch.

"Deputy Garcia," Mattie called.

"Yes, Mattie?"

"Take this family into the department for questioning and for their own safety. I believe the son Tommy may be involved in drug running, and I think someone here knows more about it. Call the sheriff, and let him decide how to handle it."

Patrick's face darkened.

"Will you go peacefully, Mr. O'Malley, or do I need to put cuffs on you?"

"I'll go," he said. "But you're going to hear from my attorney on this."

Mattie held back a sarcastic smile. She knew a bluff when she heard one.

"Can you handle this while I go after the kids?" Mattie asked Garcia.

"Sure."

Mattie told Patrick to stand, and then she patted him down for weapons. Finding none, she let Robo escort him to Garcia's cruiser. She shut him and Fran into the back cage while directing Molly and the baby into the front seat.

Moving over to her own cruiser, she loaded Robo into his compartment through the front. She buckled into the driver's seat, reached for her radio transmitter, and keyed it on. She started her engine, pulling out into the street as she spoke into the microphone. "Dispatch, this is K-9 One. We've had a domestic dispute, and Officer Garcia is en route to the station with the family, including one adult male, one adult female, a teenage girl, and an infant. Notify Sheriff McCoy and tell him that any one of them, including the girl, may know something about our local drug traffic. I have not yet arrested nor Mirandized any of them. Got all that?"

"Sure, Mattie," Sam Corns, the night dispatcher, said.

By this time, Mattie was turning onto the highway. She hit the switch to turn on her overhead lights, but she didn't put on the siren. "I am en route code ten-forty to Powderhorn mine on a kidnapping in progress. Tell Sheriff McCoy that our teenage person of interest has kidnapped his younger brother for purposes unknown. Their mother fears for the child's safety. The suspect is driving a gray Jeep Cherokee, license plate unknown. Family suspects he's headed to the Powderhorn. Earlier this evening, the youngest child left a call for help on my cell phone."

Mattie almost choked as she added this last bit of information, and she paused for a moment to collect herself. "Advise the sheriff that I may need backup at the mine."

"Ten-four, Mattie. I'll set things up for you."

"I'll call in when I get to the mine."

By now, Mattie had accelerated to just under ninety miles per hour, and when she put down the transmitter, she nudged her speed up another notch. Her headlights pierced the darkness, and she hoped for clear highway up ahead without deer or antelope crossing her path. Her current speed wouldn't allow for much brake time.

Moonlight lit the landscape as it had the previous night. Her speed ate away the miles, and soon Mattie was able to turn off onto the dirt road that led to the mine. This road was maintained by the county and in fair shape, but as she rounded the first curve, her cruiser fishtailed, the rear end fanning out in the gravel. Mattie slowed. The last thing she needed was to end up in a ditch at the side of the road. She'd be of little help to Sean sitting with her vehicle high centered.

Though Mattie couldn't see farther than the beam of her headlights, she knew that this road ran straight for a while after the first few curves, and then it curved back and forth again as it climbed halfway up the first set of foothills in the mountain range. The opening to the mine was tucked deep inside a canyon formed by a creek bed, hidden from view until you drove right up to it. The mine's tunnels honeycombed the mountain.

Once as a teen, Mattie had tried to explore a part of the abandoned Powderhorn. But her fear of close, dark spaces had gotten the best of her. She'd barely made it past the first fork in the main tunnel. She knew from what friends told her that there were so many tunnels in the mountain that they feared getting lost. On top of that, some of the shafts were flooded with at least a foot of water from an unknown source, probably an underground spring.

"If they're up there, we're going to need your nose," she told Robo.

He stood, his eyes not wavering from the windshield. Mattie had never been so grateful to have a K-9 partner. If it meant going into a dark mine, she'd rather go in with Robo than any human partner.

It felt like it took forever, but barely twenty minutes had passed since she'd checked in with dispatch. She was approaching the tunnel entrance. As soon as she topped the last rise leading up to the mine, she spotted two vehicles, black shadows in the dark night. She reached for her radio transmitter and keyed it on.

"Dispatch, this is K-9 One."

There was no response except for static. The hillside must be blocking her signal.

"Dispatch, this is K-9 One at the Powderhorn mine. I have a visual on two vehicles and need backup. Do you copy?"

Nothing but static.

"Shit!"

For a split second, Mattie considered turning to drive a half mile back to try to make her transmission but decided against it. Sean was inside that mine with an older brother who meant him harm.

She drove up and parked close to the two vehicles. Getting out cautiously, she strained to see in the darkness. Taking her flashlight, she approached slowly, splaying the beam over the first vehicle, a gray Jeep Cherokee. As she directed her light toward the other vehicle, a chill flowed from her scalp down her spine.

The second vehicle was Brennaman's 4Runner.

Chapter 28

Two kids were in the mine with a killer. Mattie couldn't wait for backup; she needed to get to those kids now. She sprinted to her cruiser and started pulling her gear out of the trunk. Robo whined and shifted to the front of the cage, his weight causing the vehicle to bounce.

"Come, Robo," Mattie called, not bothering to open a door in back for him.

Robo bolted from his platform, over the front seat, and out the door. He sat at Mattie's feet while she put on his tracking harness. She poured a half cup of water into his bowl. This was not the time to get in a hurry and skip procedure. She needed Robo's nose to be as sharp as possible if they were going into the darkness to track those kids.

Finding Sean was her first priority, so she decided to get his scent from the passenger seat of the Jeep. From there, Robo might be able to trail him. After leading Robo to the vehicle, she opened the door on the passenger side. In a smooth transition, he sniffed the seat, moved his nose to the door panel, and dropped into a sit, telling Mattie he'd discovered the scent of some form of dope.

Oh, man! She remembered Robo acting so squirrely when the Jeep had driven past last night. Her own ignorance and inexperience had made her ignore her partner's signals. She didn't have time to moan over it now. She stepped to the back and took note of the license plate in case the vehicle was gone when she emerged from the mine.

She patted the seat and told him, "Scent this."

After sniffing the seat, Robo put his nose to the ground and moved to the mine's entrance. Mattie followed, pulling her flashlight from her utility belt, flipping it on when they entered the mine and the darkness consumed her.

The tunnel walls were constructed of hard rock. Wooden beams, spaced approximately every twenty feet, supported the sides and ceiling. The main tunnel quickly narrowed from a diameter of about ten feet at the opening to only six feet high by four feet wide. After fifty yards or so, they came to the tunnel's first branch. Without hesitation, Robo followed the left one, nose to the ground.

The darkness deepened, and Mattie felt claustrophobic. She fought the tight feeling in her chest as her flashlight illuminated the tunnel ahead, showing that it narrowed down even more, forcing her to crouch to make her way through. So far, the floor of this particular shaft was dry, and it angled upward, giving her hope that it would stay that way. Soon the tunnel took a slight turn to the right and started a steep descent, leveling out into what appeared to be an open room.

Robo showed no sign of pause, and Mattie didn't want to slow his momentum, so she quickly splayed her flashlight's beam around the cavern, taking stock while she tried to watch her footing. The ceiling was about thirty feet high and she guessed the space to be around fifty feet in diameter.

The air felt dense and dank, and she doubted there was another exit to this tunnel anywhere close. She battled her growing sense of suffocation as she turned her flashlight and her attention back to Robo.

Once the flashlight lit his glossy back, Mattie noticed that his hackles were raised, causing the same reaction on her own neck. What if Brennaman was ahead? What if he heard them coming and set up an ambush? She stayed close to Robo and continued to move forward.

After the space narrowed, it branched again. The tunnel that Robo chose took a steep angle downward to a smaller shaft. Here, the walls were rough, and rocky prominences poked out in several places forcing Mattie to duck to avoid bumping her head. Below, the footing grew damp and slippery. When it became muddy, it gave her a clear view of three different sets of footprints, two large and one small. The small ones looked so vulnerable, it made her chest ache.

The reassurance that they were on the right track gave Mattie a rush. She resisted the urge to praise Robo. She needed to proceed as quietly as possible. Sweat prickled her skin, and she trained her eyes on Robo, trying to read his body language. Their survival depended on it.

The tunnel walls looked less and less stable as they probed deeper inside the mine. Shale sloughed from the side when she brushed against it. She wondered why Brennaman and Tommy would come into an area of the mine so obviously at risk for collapse.

Her flashlight dimmed, and she fought a rising panic. When had she last changed the batteries? She couldn't recall.

Could Robo's nose carry them along in pitch darkness? Could she control her panic, or should she turn back and wait for backup and a fresh light?

While she considered what to do, Robo led them to another fork in the tunnel. Down the right branch, she spotted a light in the distance. She turned off her own. The other bobbed for a brief moment and then disappeared.

Mattie stopped in midtread, but Robo pulled against his lead, trying to tug her along behind him. She felt frozen in place, her eyes staring into the black void in front of her. Fear sucked the strength from her legs.

Her mind filled with questions. What was the footing like up ahead? Who was down there? Did Brennaman know she was coming? Should she turn her light back on or try to follow Robo without it?

Shortening Robo's lead, she took a few hesitant steps so that she could come up beside him. She placed her hand on his back and noted that his hair still bristled. Terror threatened to immobilize her.

Forcing herself to move, she kept her flashlight off and stayed in the dark. She whispered, "Search."

Crouching to protect her head from the low ceiling, Mattie inched her way down the tunnel, holding onto Robo's tracking harness. She kept him as close as possible, letting him lead her in the darkness. She focused on staying with Robo and finding Sean, and she tried to forget her fear of suffocating.

She lost all sense of direction and placed her trust in her dog. They crept down the tunnel for what seemed like hours.

Suddenly a light reappeared in the distance, and Mattie realized it was coming toward her now. Her adrenalin surged, and her muscles tightened. She started to draw her service weapon but realized she couldn't risk using it. A shot might bring the mine shaft down around them. She froze and held tightly to Robo's harness. "Wait," she whispered.

He took a step forward but stopped when she held him back.

She strained to see who was behind the light. It was directed at the tunnel floor, and she couldn't distinguish anything. She hoped that the person didn't know she and Robo were there. The element of surprise could make all the difference inside this close, dark place.

Crouching beside Robo, making herself as small as possible, Mattie waited until the light threatened to reveal them. Robo's muscles bunched, ready to spring.

With her heart pounding, Mattie shouted, "Police! Stop and put your hands on your head!"

The light whirled, and its bearer ran away. Mattie could see only one figure backlit by the light. And it wasn't small enough to be Sean.

Mattie unclipped Robo's leash. "Stop or I'll send the dog."

The person scrambled faster down the tunnel.

"Robo, take him."

This was the drill Robo had been waiting for since their run-in with Patrick O'Malley. His toenails scratched the rocky floor in the tunnel as he launched himself after the fugitive. In awe, Mattie watched him become a silent dark shadow.

Robo didn't bark a warning; he didn't growl. He hit the runner in silence, slammed his body into the runner's back, and clamped his jaws on the arm that held the flashlight. The force from Robo's momentum and his crushing bite brought the figure to the floor. His flashlight hit the ground and its beam went out, pitching them all into utter darkness.

The person screamed.

Flipping on her own weak light, Mattie rushed down the tunnel, pulling plastic tie cuffs from her utility belt while she ran. When she closed in, she could tell it was Tommy.

Robo was doing exactly what he'd been trained to do: bite and hold. Haunches in the air, he used his tremendous strength to pull on Tommy's arm, dragging him across the rough tunnel floor. There was no weapon in sight.

Tommy screamed the whole time.

In combat position, Mattie crouched near him, ready to use physical force herself if necessary. "Robo, out!"

Robo released Tommy's arm and backed off a few steps.

"Guard!"

Robo crouched, eager to attack again. His tail waved slightly and his teeth were bared in a scary grin. Mattie could tell he was having a great time.

"Put your hands on your head. Now! If you make one move toward me, this dog will attack."

Tommy put up his hands. "Keep that monster away from me! Son of a bitch!"

"Tommy, do you have any weapons?"

"What? No! What are you talking about?"

"Stand up and put your hands on your head. I'll warn you again, don't make a single move toward me. This dog can't wait to get another piece of you."

She flicked the light onto Robo, who had his eyes pinned on Tommy. The kid complied.

"Now, turn around and place your hands on the tunnel wall. I'm going to pat you down."

"Shit!"

"Do it!"

Tommy turned away from her, hands on his head. With his back toward her, he moved his hands to the wall and leaned on it.

Mattie asked, "Where's Sean?"

"I don't know."

"Where's Brennaman?"

"I don't know. He took him."

"He took Sean?"

"Yeah."

With her boot, Mattie tapped the inside of his feet. "Spread 'em."

After he assumed the correct position, Mattie started to search him. At the front pocket of his baggy pants, she felt a solid rectangular object. She slipped her hand inside and drew out a pocketknife. She said, "Tommy, I'm disappointed. You lied to me."

"What? That's just a pocketknife, man, not a weapon."

She slipped the knife into her own pocket and continued patting down his legs. At his right calf, she felt something hard and bulky. "What's this?" she asked, squatting down to pull up his pant leg.

The light glinted off a large knife strapped to his calf.

"I think we might agree that this would qualify as a weapon," Mattie said, reaching for it.

Tommy twisted, leaned over her, and grabbed her wrist in a viselike grip.

Robo needed no command. He snarled and leaped, snapping up Tommy's arm in his terrible jaws.

Tommy dropped Mattie's wrist and screamed. Robo weighed almost ninety pounds, and he used every ounce to pull Tommy down. The kid fell to his knees while Robo tugged harder, stretching him out. Mattie decided to let Robo hold him while she took the knife.

She crouched to reach for it. Suddenly, movement at the edge of the shadow made her look. Brennaman rushed out of the darkness, crouching, with a two-by-four raised as high as the tunnel would allow. In the moment it took to register that he meant to hit her with it, Mattie raised her arm to shield her head. The club smashed into her arm. The shock of the blow turned her forearm numb. Then pain ripped its way up her arm.

The only light in the tunnel went out as her flashlight hit the ground. Mattie's world tilted. She dropped to the floor to get her bearings. Her mind cracked open and memory flooded her senses. A child—quivering in the darkness. A creaking door—the sour smell of booze. Fear. Pain.

Robo's growls filled the darkness. Mattie heard a loud thud. Robo yelped. Silence.

Rage replaced her helplessness, infused her with power so raw it brought her to her feet. Brennaman had hurt Robo. Her partner needed her. She decided to use her baton instead of her Taser. No way would she risk a misfire in the darkness and hit Robo. She grabbed the baton, pressed the button, and heard the snick as it extended to its full length, automatically locking into place.

A click sounded from several feet away, and Brennaman's flashlight lit the tunnel. The light blinded her for a moment. She raised her injured arm to block it from her eyes and scanned the area. Tommy was still on the floor to her left, rising up on one elbow. And just beyond Brennaman . . . Robo. Her partner lay inert, the hair on his head wet and matted. Blood.

She crouched, lowering her right arm from her face, keeping her left low with the baton hidden beside her leg.

"Give it up, Mattie Lu," Brennaman said, his voice sounding like he was pleased with himself. He'd put down the club, and now he held a dark, snub-nosed revolver.

Tommy sat up, cradling the arm that Robo bit. "That black son of a bitch bit me," he said.

Mattie stared hard at Robo and saw his ribcage lift. He was still breathing. Not daring to look at him any longer and wanting to divert the other's attention from him, she asked the first thing that popped into her mind. "Where's Sean?"

Brennaman smiled. "Oh, he's still alive, if that's what you're wondering."

"Where is he?"

Brennaman used his head to gesture to the tunnel behind him. "I left him back there. We'll join him in a moment."

"You know that if you shoot me, you'll bring this mine down on yourself."

"I don't think I care about that. Better to die here than in prison. But if you cooperate, you might be able to save yourself and the kids. The kids seem important to you, Mattie, if I read you right."

"Of course they are," she said, hoping to keep him talking. "Are you one who killed Grace?"

"Oh, Mattie. You think you've figured things out."

"Did you?"

He dropped the smile and his expression turned fierce, the flashlight casting dark shadows across the planes and hollows of his face. "Grace should have never been there. Her death was on Mike Chadron."

"But you shot her."

"Quit trying to get a confession out of me," he said, his tone mocking. "You won't be able to; you're not that smart."

Tommy started to get to his feet.

"Stay there for a minute, Tommy," Brennaman told him. He directed his gaze back at Mattie. "Don't you want to hear my plan for how you can walk out of here with both of these kids?"

Out of the corner of her eye, she thought she saw Robo's ear twitch. She suppressed the joy that lifted her spirit and focused on trying to hold Brennaman's attention. "Sure. What's your plan?"

"Your vehicle's out front, right?"

"Yes."

"You come with me to the end of this tunnel where Sean is. I leave you and the kids tied up, leave your patrol car out front so the others know where to look for you, and have time to get way the hell out of Dodge."

Again, movement from Robo. She needed to keep Tommy's attention, too. "Tommy, why did you bring Sean to the mine?"

"He asked for it. He was going to tell you about the drugs. I had to scare him into keeping his mouth shut."

"Did you know Mr. Brennaman would be here?"

"Sure. We planned to meet up."

"Did you know that he's a killer? That you were bringing Sean into a dangerous situation?" she asked him. She flexed the hand on her injured arm, testing to see if she could grip. Though it set up shock waves of pain, she was relieved to find that she could make a fist.

Tommy shrugged. "I figured he killed Mike. Didn't know and don't care about Grace."

"Shut up, Tommy," Brennaman said with a sly smile on his lips. "Well, Mattie Lu, what do you think?"

"I think you're a murdering coward who gets his jollies from harming children, but that's probably not what you were asking about." She paused briefly. If she could get him to turn away, even for a moment, she could use her baton on him. "Yeah, I'll go with you to where you left Sean."

A scrabbling sound from Robo turned everyone's attention his way. He'd evidently pawed the floor of the mine in an attempt to stand. Even as they watched, he tried again, this time managing to rise up enough to lie chest down. He shook his head, spattering drops of blood on the rock around him.

Brennaman shouted at Tommy. "Take out that dog! Use your knife. Slit his throat."

Tommy tugged up his pants leg and reached for his knife. Mattie slammed the baton down on his arm, hearing the smack when it hit. He yelped and pulled his arm away. With her injured hand, she grabbed the knife and turned to take on Brennaman.

Robo launched himself off the floor, hitting Brennaman from the side. He buried his teeth into the arm that held the gun. The weapon flew, and Mattie heard the heavy clunk of metal skidding across the rock floor. Brennaman shouted in pain and lifted his flashlight to strike Robo. Eerie shadows flitted across the rock walls of the tunnel. Mattie sprang, drawing back her baton and slamming it onto Brennaman's wrist. The flashlight fell to the floor and rolled, stopping against the wall.

Brennaman fell to his knees, screaming at Tommy. "Get the gun!"

"Stay where you are, Tommy. I'll take out your other arm if you move."

Tommy stayed put, sheltering his injury, sobbing with pain.

By this time, Robo had pulled Brennaman down and was dragging him across the floor toward the gun. Mattie jumped into the middle of the man's back, stopping his momentum, feeling satisfied as the air went out of him. She straddled him, grabbed his injured left arm and pulled it to his back, causing him to scream out. Her own arm hurt like fury and seemed to have only half its strength, but she could still use it.

"Quit fighting and I'll call him off," she said, her voice gruff.

It was hard to tell with Robo still tugging at him, but Mattie thought she felt the fight go out of him. "Robo, out."

Robo dropped Brennaman's arm and the man lay still beneath her. "Guard."

Her dog loomed over Brennaman's head, saliva and blood dripping from his mouth. He couldn't have looked more terrifying.

"Stay still or he'll attack you again. That goes for you too, Tommy."

Tommy's sobs had subsided, but he sounded utterly defeated. "I ain't goin' no place."

She took the cuffs from her belt, tightening one on Brennaman's injured arm first, and making him groan. She grabbed the arm Robo had bitten, brought it around to the man's back, and put the other cuff on that one. Only then did she feel she could take a breath.

"Don't move," she told Brennaman. She stood on shaky legs and patted him down. He carried no other weapons, but she found a roll of duct tape in his jacket pocket. She picked up the gun and put it in a pocket on her belt. Then she picked up the flashlight. "Robo, out."

Brennaman lifted his head to watch.

She used her most authoritative voice. "I said don't move."
He put his head back down on the floor.

She called Robo to her. Shining the flashlight on his head, she could see that his wound was about an inch long and still bleeding. She stroked the fur at his throat and told him what a good boy he was. She moved the light away from his eyes and then flashed it into them quickly, feeling relief to see his pupils constrict evenly.

Many times, she'd cursed the weight of her K-9 utility belt, but now she was grateful to know that her supplies were complete. With fingers still trembling from pain and adrenalin, she took out her first aid kit. She placed a sterile gauze pad on Robo's wound and secured it with elastic tape around his head, forming a compression bandage. The white bandage contrasted with his black fur, making her give him a small smile. "There, that should fix you up until we can get you to a doctor."

"What about me?" Tommy said, sounding forlorn. "I think my arm's broken."

Mattie took a deep breath and stood. Pulling a set of plastic tie cuffs from her belt, she said, "Hold your hands together out front, Tommy."

He whimpered. "You're not going to put those on me, are you?"

"You can steady your arm with your other hand. That's why I'm not making you put them behind you. Now, do as I say and put them out front."

He complied, and she placed the cuffs, trying not to hurt him more than necessary in the process.

"Now I need to find Sean," she said.

"You lost your chance," Brennaman said from his place, face down on the ground.

"I don't need you, John Brennaman." Mattie took a short length of utility rope from her belt and bound his feet tightly. She made sure his cuffs were secure on his wrists. "I'll be back to get you later. Tommy, you're coming with me."

"I can't walk."

"There's nothing wrong with your feet. I need to keep an eye on you. Get up."

It took a few more precious moments, but Tommy managed to get to his feet.

Mattie hoped that Robo would remember the scent they were trailing before they were attacked. She didn't bother putting his leash on again; her arm was hurting too much to deal with it.

"Come with me," she said, taking Robo farther down the tunnel in the direction from which Tommy and Brennaman had come. "Tommy, follow me, but don't touch me. If you do, this dog will bite you again, do you understand?"

Tommy followed meekly, indicating that he did.

A few yards down the tunnel, Mattie said, "Robo, find Sean. Search."

Robo put his nose to the ground and moved forward. One more branch in the tunnel system, and he led them into a hollowed-out, open space containing railroad ties, chunks of wood, lumber of various lengths, and some barrels. Robo bounded over to one of the barrels, rising up to place his paws on top. Muffled cries came from inside the closed barrel.

"Sean," Mattie cried as she rushed to it and began tearing at the top. "Sean, it's Mattie. You're safe now. Robo found you."

Pain shot through her arm as she used both hands to work off the wire rim that bound the barrel shut. When she finally got the lid off, she shone the light inside. Sean peered up, blinking in the light, a strip of duct tape over his mouth, his face dirty and tear streaked. His hands and feet were also bound with duct tape. A chill passed through her as she realized this child was never meant to be found in the mine. She and Tommy wouldn't have been left alive to be found either.

Reaching into the barrel, she gently worked the tape off Sean's mouth. His nose was stuffy from crying, and she could tell his ability to breathe was compromised. He sobbed as she pulled off the tape. She wanted to pick him up but lacked the strength in her right arm to lift him. "I'm going to tip the barrel so we can get you out, okay, Sean?"

Glancing over at Tommy while she did it, she asked him, "Did you put him in here?"

Tommy had a frown on his face that seemed genuine. "Brennaman told me to leave, go back outside. Then I got lost and was trying to get back here when you found me. He must've put Sean in the barrel after I left."

Mattie was able to help Sean wiggle out of the barrel, and she quickly unbound his hands and feet. He placed his arms around Robo and clung to him. Robo looked proud to lend a crying shoulder. Mattie gently patted Sean's back.

After a few moments, Sean leaned away from Robo and studied him. "Why is Robo wearing a headband?"

Mattie almost chuckled with relief. "It's a bandage. He got a bump on the head, so be careful with him."

"Oh, poor Robo," the child said. Then he glared at Tommy. "Tommy's mean."

"Yes, he is. That's not a good way to be, is it?"

Then Mattie took the time to tidy up the business of arresting Tommy. She had a feeling that Tommy wanted to spill everything he had on Brennaman, and she wanted to be sure that what he had to say could be used against the principal—and even against himself if that's the way things turned out.

She stood and took a deep breath. "Tommy O'Malley, you're under arrest for kidnapping and the reckless endangerment of a child, threatening the life of a K-9, and transporting narcotics. Other charges may be added after our investigation."

"Oh, man, you don't want to do this. I've got information you can use."

She slipped her Miranda card from her pocket and read him his rights. Then she asked, "What information are you talking about, Tommy?"

"Like how Brennaman told me he killed Mike," Tommy said, with a nod toward the tunnel they'd come from. "He said Mike didn't want to use his dogs anymore and planned to rat him out. Brennaman threatened to kill me, too."

"So you felt frightened for your life?"

"Damn right I did."

"Be sure and mention your fear to the detective when she questions you. Maybe she'll go easy on you." She wanted to reassure him in hopes he'd keep answering her questions. "Did you call Brennaman?"

"I thought he'd know what to do."

"And the mine was his idea?"

Tommy hesitated, and for a moment, she thought he'd clam up, but he kept talking. "Brennaman thought it would scare Sean. Keep him quiet."

Mattie nodded. She'd learned enough for now; she'd leave his interrogation up to Stella. "Let's get out of here. Sean, you stay in front of me. We'll let Robo lead the way. You stay behind me, Tommy, and remember, no touching."

It didn't take long to get back to Brennaman. It seemed like he'd given up, and he said nothing when Mattie put him under arrest for the murders of Grace Hartman and Mike Chadron; the transportation of narcotics; and threatening the lives of a child, a police officer, and a K-9. She read him his rights and untied his feet. He managed to stand, and she took him by the arm to escort him out of the tunnel, Robo leading the way.

When they reached the open room inside the mine, they encountered her backup—Ken Brody and the rookie Johnson. Their flashlights shone brightly. She'd never been so glad to see these guys in her life. Even Brody.

Brody's flashlight moved over them all, pausing first on Robo and then on Mattie. "You okay, Cobb?"

"We've been better. Glad to see you guys. I have John Brennaman here under arrest for multiple charges, including two murders, and Tommy O'Malley under arrest for transporting narcotics, among other things."

Brody and Johnson took charge of the two captives. With Robo and Mattie leading the way, it took only a few minutes to travel through the rest of the mine.

Once outside, Brody spoke again. "Johnson, load these two in our vehicle."

"I'll take Sean with me," Mattie said.

Brody turned to Mattie. "How did you find these guys?"

"Robo tracked them."

"Shit." In the moonlight, Mattie could see he was looking at Robo with begrudging respect. Then he looked back at her. "I don't know how you could stand going into those old tunnels by yourself. That place gives me the creeps."

Finally, something they could agree on. "Me too, Brody. But I wasn't by myself; I had my partner with me."

Chapter 29

Cole flipped on the front light and unlocked his clinic door so that Mattie and Robo could come in when they arrived. It was after midnight, and her call had wakened him from a sound and much needed sleep. After apologizing for the late call, she'd told him that Robo had been hit on the head hard enough to knock him unconscious, and he had a gash on his head that needed stitching. A compression bandage she'd applied seemed to have stopped the bleeding, and Cole might have decided to wait until morning to suture it, but he was concerned enough about the head injury that he wanted to examine Robo tonight.

He went to the exam room to prepare but soon heard Mattie drive up to the clinic. He was shocked when he saw her. Pain and exhaustion pinched her face, and a ragged abrasion and deep purple bruise covered the top part of her forearm. Compared to Mattie, Robo looked jaunty as he trotted through the door beside her, compression bandage adorning his head, tail waving.

"Good God, Mattie. What happened to you?"

She tried to hide her pain and rearranged her facial expression to neutral. "Robo and I tangled with John Brennaman."

"What?"

"We arrested him for the murder of both Grace Hartman and Mike Chadron tonight. He's at the station being interrogated. This is still confidential, of course, but I wanted you to know."

Cole was flummoxed, but he felt pressed to help her rather than keep her standing here in the lobby asking her questions. "Come in here to the treatment room," he said, opening the door for her. "Have you done anything to take care of that arm yet?"

"No, I was in a hurry to bring Robo to you."

"You've done some good first aid for him. Let me do some for you before we get to Robo. Come over here to the sink. We need to wash that wound."

She followed him to the sink with Robo sticking close to her side. Cole hooked a rolling stool with his foot and brought it over. "Sit on this," he told her.

He turned on warm water, checked the temperature, and then extended a hand. She let him take her arm, sucking in her breath quietly when he gently palpated the bruised area. Robo pinned his eyes on Cole, looking worried.

"You need to see Dr. McGinnis in the morning," he told her.

"He's taking care of my prisoners right now."

"Your prisoners? More than one?"

"Yeah. I arrested two actually. Not both for murder, though. That was all Brennaman."

Cole bathed the abrasion on her arm, using an antiseptic wash and letting the warm water flow over it. As he worked, he realized what she meant. "Don't tell me you were fighting two people at once."

"Okay, I won't."

She was a great deal shorter than he, and as she sat huddled on the stool, she looked small and vulnerable. "Was there anyone else there to help you?"

She gazed up at him, a trace of amusement on her face. "Sure—Robo. We managed okay."

"Oh, yeah, you both look swell."

"You should see the other guys."

He imagined her being attacked by two men, and he didn't like her flippant answer. "Weren't there other officers who could have been there?"

"Sometimes you have to act alone."

He shook his head and focused on his task. At least it was something he could control. After patting her arm dry, he applied antibiotic ointment and some sterile gauze and wrapped her arm with several layers of paper towels. "Hold this while I get some ice. Did you take anything for pain yet?"

"No."

"I've got some Tylenol in my desk drawer. I'll get that, too."

After she took the pain reliever, he placed an ice pack over the bruised area and wrapped an elastic bandage over the whole thing to hold it. He hoped she felt better. "There. Now we'll look at Robo. Since he's been watching like he doesn't trust me one bit, I wonder if you'd be able to take that bandage off him so I can take a look."

"Sure."

Cole noticed that she could use her hand and move her arm, so he doubted it had a complete fracture. But it might have a greenstick fracture or a deep bone bruise, neither of which should be overlooked. She needed to take care of it. He hoped she'd take it seriously and not let her tough-girl attitude get in the way.

Once Robo's bandage came off, he could see a one-inch laceration with glistening white fascia underneath. The wound still seeped, but for the most part, Mattie's compression bandage had staunched the blood flow. He checked pupil dilation and was satisfied to see that Robo's pupils were equally responsive.

"Now, hold his head as still as you can while I check his visual tracking," he told Mattie. Using a dog treat, he watched Robo track it back and forth with no obvious problems. "Can I give this to him now?"

"Sure."

Robo took the treat from him with no suspicion or sulking. He was evidently more comfortable with Cole working on him than on Mattie. Protective of his owner—not unusual, but something to be aware of with a large, aggressive dog like this one.

"I can suture that laceration with some stainless steel surgical staples, and it will only take a few minutes. But first I need to block it with a local and clean it up. We need to muzzle him before I do all that."

"Sure," she said. "But let me put it on him, okay?"

"My thought exactly."

Mattie slipped on the red nylon muzzle with no hesitation or problem, and Cole could tell that she'd done it before. Robo didn't struggle, but his eyebrows puckered with worry. Cole watched Mattie soothe him with soft murmurs and stroking.

He drew a local numbing agent into a syringe and showed Mattie how to hold Robo still. "The first one feels like a hornet sting, but it works instantly, and he won't really feel the rest. I don't want to use any general anesthesia on him after that head injury, and we shouldn't need it anyway."

Robo flinched, but Mattie continued to reassure him. After Cole finished blocking the scalp area, she said, "We have to go back to work if you think it's safe for Robo."

Cole was surprised. "He's fit enough, but are you?"

"I won't have to do much. They're getting a search warrant for Brennaman's house. We want to search it tonight."

He began gently cleaning the scalp wound. "I'm blown away! I have all kinds of questions, but I hesitate to ask them. Maybe you could just tell me what you can."

"I started to suspect Brennaman when I remembered how Robo bristled when he first met him. Then I remembered how Belle carried on when he was here in your yard. We all thought she was greeting Mr. Hartman, but when I remembered it, I realized that wasn't exactly a friendly bark. I put that together with what we learned about scent memory in K-9 Academy. Robo would have picked up his scent at the crime scene. He knew who put Grace in that grave."

Cole shuddered but continued to work on Robo. "Good God. Belle was the only thing that kept him from my kids."

"A dog's the best deterrent to an intruder." She paused, apparently sorting through what she could say next. "Before we could do anything else, I got a call on a domestic disturbance and a child kidnapping that led me to the Powderhorn mine. When I got there, John Brennaman's vehicle was parked out front. I knew I had two kids in that mine with a suspected killer, so I had to go in."

That shocked him. "No, you didn't. You could have waited for them to come out."

"I was certain that he'd killed Grace. I couldn't stand by and wait for him to kill those kids and come out alone."

"He could have killed you and Robo."

Mattie shrugged. "It's our job. To protect and serve."

Cole wasn't sure how he felt about that. He'd come to respect and care about this woman during the stress-filled past few days, but he'd never stopped to think about how dangerous her job was. He remained silent while he assessed Robo's laceration, decided the margins were clean, and picked up the stapler. He clipped a neat row of staples along the wound and finished up quickly with a sterile gauze patch that he wrapped into place with an elastic bandage. Though the dog's brow remained puckered, he tolerated the procedure without flinching. He knew that Robo hadn't felt a thing.

He noticed that Mattie's face was filled with tension. "He's going to be fine. Scalp wounds heal fast since there's such a good blood supply. Let me know if he starts scratching at it or rubs the bandage off. We should take it off in a couple days anyway to check it. You could do that or you can bring him back in for me to take a look, whichever you're most comfortable with."

"I'm okay with taking the bandage off, but I'd rather you look at the wound to make sure it's healing right."

"Sounds like a plan. I want Robo to have a less stressful experience with me anyway. I really don't want him to take a disliking to me like he did Brennaman." He smiled at Mattie as he spoke.

She gave him a tired smile in return that made Cole glad to be able to lighten her seriousness. "I believe that was related to character judgment," she said, "and Brennaman brought that on himself."

Cole shook his head. "I still can hardly believe it. Wait 'til this gets out. Timber Creek won't stop talking about this for years."

Mattie's cell phone rang, and she answered it. After a brief exchange, she said, "We're ready to roll. I'll be right there." She looked at Cole. "So it's safe to take Robo back to work?"

Robo's tail thumped, causing Cole to glance his way. It was almost comical, the big black dog wearing a red muzzle and white bandage, wagging his tail eagerly when his handler mentioned work. No doubt about what made this dog happy.

"Yes, he can go back to work," he said, slipping off the muzzle. "How do you feel?"

"A lot better. This ice really helped."

"Leave it on. Keep the pack. You might need it again in your line of work." He helped her lift Robo off the table and opened the door for them to go while Mattie slipped off the muzzle.

"Thanks. I'll call tomorrow and make an appointment for you to see him the next day."

"Sounds good."

The shock from learning that Brennaman was a murderer had subsided, and Cole realized how he hadn't expressed his gratitude that Grace's killer would be brought to justice. He reached for Mattie's left hand and took it with both of his. She looked up at him, surprise evident.

"I haven't told you how much I appreciate you finding Grace's killer," he said. "I'm not sure that words can adequately say how that makes me feel. It's a real jumble right now. Nothing will bring Grace back to us, but at least her killer won't get away unpunished."

With that determination in her eyes that he'd become familiar with, she nodded. "And if we can get evidence from his house that will pin it on him in court, he'll pay big time—a child killer in prison doesn't usually fare too well."

Cole released her hand. "Then I'll let you get back to your job. To protect and serve. Thank you for that, Deputy Mattie Cobb. But be careful out there."

She smiled in a small way that touched her eyes and relaxed her face. She gave him a left-handed salute and went through his front door, saying, "Come, Robo. Let's go to work."

"And phone me after you've seen Dr. McGinnis," he called to her as she walked away.

She raised her injured arm in acknowledgement.

Cole stood and watched the black shadow gamboling at her side, white teeth visible as he grinned up at her, until she passed outside his entry light and got into her car. Although he wasn't a religious man in a traditional sense, he made a mental request for someone out there to watch over Mattie and to keep her and her dog safe.

★

Mattie could still feel the tingle in her left hand from when Cole had held it. She gave her head a slight shake, trying to dispel the fact that she was drawn to him more and more. His divorce had been finalized for only a few days; this was not a time that he'd be interested in a new relationship. And it was silly to think he might ever be interested in her anyway.

As she drove to the station, she couldn't help but think about the stuff that made up a family. She'd always craved a regular family life like Cole's. But his family had been flawed even when she believed it to be perfect. She decided that a perfect family didn't truly exist.

Then there was the O'Malley family, one she'd completely misread. Her own family background had colored her judgment, and that wasn't good in her line of work. She'd learned a lesson she needed to remember in the future: all families are different, and stay open so you can read the signs you're being given. That lesson would be second to the one she now truly understood: always listen to your dog.

At the station, she found the entire team. Stella had stayed to question the suspects. She still wore her tailored pantsuit, but she'd exchanged her dress shoes for black sneakers, and she was returning her service weapon to its holster under her jacket. Mattie could tell she meant to go with them to search Brennaman's house.

"Did you get anything out of Brennaman?" Mattie asked her.

"Nah," Stella said, clearly disgusted. She did a double take, looking from her to Robo and back again. "Mattie, what happened to you and your dog?"

"Brennaman."

"Let's get photos of your injuries before you go home tonight." With her head, she gestured back to the interrogation rooms. "Brennaman asked for a lawyer first thing. Won't say a word without one. He's in there with Justin McClelland. I told them both I'd be back in an hour. They can sit in there and cook. Let's go find something that gives me leverage."

Brennaman lived outside of town on a plot of land adjacent to the national forest. His log house sat at the back of the property near the trees. McCoy and Stella led the way, followed by Brody and Johnson. Mattie and Robo brought up the rear. Their caravan pulled to a stop in front of the house. The house was dark, and as far as they knew, the only person present inside was Mrs. Brennaman.

"Brody and Johnson, you cover the rear door," McCoy ordered. "I doubt this lady's involved, but we need to be prepared in case she tries to run. Detective LoSasso and I will serve the warrant. Deputy Cobb, you wait out here. I'll wait two minutes for you men to get into place. Then I'll knock on the door."

Robo stood when the men walked away. "Wait," she whispered to him. Her senses sharpened. She inhaled the scent of pine and heard a night bird take flight from a tree behind her.

After two minutes, McCoy stepped up on the porch and pounded the front door. Stella waited behind him, her service weapon held down at her side. After a long pause, the sheriff pounded the door again.

Lights came on inside the house and on the porch, but no one opened the door. A feminine voice called through it. "Who is it?"

"Mrs. Brennaman? It's Sheriff McCoy."

The door opened immediately, revealing a short woman of medium build dressed in a night robe. Her short, silver-gray hair was tousled. "Sheriff? What are you doing here?" She put her hand to her throat. "Something hasn't happened to John, has it?"

"Could we come inside, Mrs. Brennaman?"

"Surely." She held the door wide while McCoy and Stella moved inside. "Please tell me."

Mattie could see the woman's distress. While she waited by the cruiser, she imagined her shock when McCoy explained— that is, if she was truly innocent.

It didn't take long for Stella to signal her to come inside. With Robo beside her, Mattie passed through the front door into a living room filled with fussy furniture and knickknacks. Mrs. Brennaman was sitting on a couch, looking stunned, with Sheriff McCoy sitting beside her holding the warrant. He was still explaining the process to the woman in a gentle voice. Brody and Johnson had moved inside through the back door and stood by, Johnson shifting uncomfortably from one foot to the other and Brody standing solid with his thumbs hooked onto his utility belt.

Stella signaled for Mattie to follow her down a hallway to a room that looked like a home office. "This is a good place to start," Stella said.

With her right arm still throbbing, Mattie used her left hand to hold Robo's leash and guided him with her injured arm, starting at the desk and then working around the room. He paused at the closet door, sniffing its edges, and she opened it so he could move inside. A navy-blue sweatshirt hung amid coats and jackets; a black ski mask and a pair of leather gloves lay on the shelf above.

But Robo was busy sniffing the floor. Then he walked in and sat in the middle, looking up at her to tell her he'd found something.

Mattie praised him and asked him to come out. "We need to see what's under that carpet," she told Stella.

Together they started to move in, but Stella gently pushed Mattie aside. "Let me do it. You should be using that arm as little as possible."

She watched Stella work, pulling up carpeting that was barely tacked down and then lifting a hatch-like cover to reveal a hollowed-out space below the floor. "Do you have a flashlight?" Stella asked.

Mattie handed her one.

Stella lit the space where they could see two leather briefcases and numerous small parcels wrapped in plastic. Stella photographed and carefully opened a package of each type.

The leather case contained cash, and the plastic parcel contained cocaine.

They also found a small box that held a cell phone with its battery removed and a dainty ring, its thin gold band set with a ruby. Grace's ring—her last birthday gift from her parents. Tears filled Mattie's eyes, and she looked away.

"I think this should be enough to put him away forever," Stella said in a sober voice. "Let's have you sweep the rest of the house and then let the CSU finish up here. We'll take these things and the wife back to the station. Maybe all of it combined will be enough to make him come clean. Great job, Mattie."

Mattie shrugged. "It's all Robo," she said. Her body may have felt battered and bruised, but her spirit soared. She couldn't have been more proud.

Chapter 30

Tuesday

Sheriff McCoy had ordered Mattie to go home shortly after they finished up at the Brennaman house. He told her, in no uncertain terms, not to come back to the station until she'd seen Dr. McGinnis. The good doctor had agreed to open early so that he could x-ray her arm, and he'd given her a clean bill of health to return to work.

Well, not exactly squeaky clean. The bone in her forearm wasn't broken, but it was badly bruised, and he'd advised ice and elevation for forty-eight hours and then caution and rest to let it heal. Mattie figured she had reams of paperwork to do and a two-day break in her schedule starting tomorrow. That would be enough time to rest. There was no way she could stay away from the station today. She could hardly wait to hear the results of last night's interrogation.

As she drove, she wondered when Willie would call. She also wondered where her mother was and if Willie could give her any answers. She felt herself getting nervous even thinking about it. *Focus on work*, she told herself. *Take care of business.*

At the station, she pulled into a parking spot and let Robo out to follow her inside.

Rainbow sat at her desk out front, brightening when she spied Mattie. "Sheriff McCoy told me to let him know when you got in. He wants to see you in his office."

Mattie felt apprehensive when she was singled out to see the sheriff. Must be leftover emotions from her many trips to the principal's office in years past. "Okay."

Rainbow hesitated with her hand next to the phone, her smile deepening. "I'm so proud of you and Robo. You guys are a kick-ass team."

Mattie returned Rainbow's smile. It felt good to receive kudos from a colleague. "He's a kick-ass dog, isn't he?"

Rainbow raised the phone receiver to her ear but paused before paging the sheriff. "Do you want to have lunch together today?"

Mattie was surprised to realize she wanted to, but she feared she was too tired and painful. "I'd really like to, Rainbow, but I think I might go home during my lunch hour and put ice on my arm. Another time, okay?"

Concern knit Rainbow's brow. "Take care of yourself."

"Maybe Friday, after my days off. We could eat out at the picnic table."

Rainbow smiled. "Sounds fun. I hope your arm feels better." She finished buzzing the sheriff.

McCoy opened his office door and beckoned Mattie in. He gestured for her to sit in a chair in front of his desk.

"It took all night, but we got a confession from Brennaman for both homicides and drug traffic," McCoy said.

"What? That's great!"

"I want to congratulate you and your K-9 on the job you did last night. Your performance broke this case wide open, Deputy."

Mattie grinned and then ducked her head to glance down at Robo. He was watching her, reading her body language. She supposed he hadn't had much opportunity to observe her being happy. Well, now was his chance. This was her being happy.

"I don't think we need to worry about whether or not you need a probationary period for handling this dog anymore. As long as I'm in office, you can consider yourself his permanent handler. You behaved like a seasoned team out there, and anyone who decided to split you up should have his head examined."

Mattie nodded, not trusting herself to respond.

"I have some good news for you," he said.

"You already gave me some good news."

Sheriff McCoy's smile told her he was enjoying himself. "I suppose you studied asset forfeiture at the academy."

Asset forfeiture laws allowed local law enforcement agencies, along with federal and state jurisdictions, to share in seized monetary assets after a drug bust. "I did."

"I've already talked to some of the county commissioners this morning, and they're going to set up a K-9 team support fund with our share of the assets. I think we can begin to plan for things you need, like razor wire for Robo's enclosure and a four-wheel-drive vehicle. We need you to be as mobile as you can be in our mountain terrain."

Mattie couldn't believe it; she and Robo were going to pay their own way. "Thank you, sir."

"And I'm going to get approval for adding another deputy on staff. Although it's important for you to take patrol duty part of the time to keep in touch with the community, I want you to have the flexibility to fully launch the search program we've started for vehicles going through town."

"That would be great."

"The only loose end we have in this case is that there was too much cash involved for this drug ring to be contained in our small community. I'm afraid Brennaman may be just one link in a chain. We can't afford to let our guard down."

"Yes, sir."

"One more thing." McCoy paused, apparently searching for how to put into words what he wanted to say. "I watched you grow up, since that night I responded to your call for help. Do you remember that was me?"

"Yes, sir." Mattie's face started to feel hot.

"I worried about you but wasn't quite sure how I could help, until that opening came up in Mama T's home, and I got your social worker to transfer you there. I was on the sidelines every time I could be, cheering you on when you won a race. I'm proud of the person you've become, and I'm honored to have you as an officer in my department."

McCoy paused, the muscle in his jaw working. Unshed tears blurred Mattie's eyesight. She blinked but didn't look away from him.

McCoy stared at Mattie hard, his countenance stern. "Now, did Dr. McGinnis say you're fit to be here at work?"

Mattie cleared her throat. "Yes, sir."

"No broken bones?"

"No, sir."

"Then do what you have to do to wrap things up and take the rest of the day off. I've already arranged coverage for your shift." He picked up some papers from his desk and appeared to read them, though he was probably just giving

Mattie the privacy she needed to battle her emotions. "In the future, I'll stay out of your personal life, and we won't speak of this again."

Quickly, Mattie brushed the wetness from her eyes with the back of her hand and then stood. "Thank you," she said, glad to hear that her voice sounded like she was in complete control of herself. "Thank you for telling me that."

Outside the sheriff's office, Stella LoSasso waited. She took Mattie by the arm and steered her toward the front door. "I'm getting ready to go home and get some sleep. We've got Brennaman locked down tight, and we're gonna throw away the key. Come outside and talk to me for a few minutes."

Mattie let herself be led over to Stella's car, with Robo following along behind.

"Brennaman confessed," Stella said.

"Sheriff McCoy told me. That's great. I never thought he would fess up."

Stella made a gesture of dismissal. "He's small potatoes, a real amateur. Once his wife told us he spends every spring break down in Phoenix playing golf with the same dentist whose gun got stolen, we could tie him to the murder weapon. That and the fact that his prints match the print fragment on the casing Robo found. Whoo-hoo, Robo!"

Stella patted him, and he grinned up at her while waving his tail. "Then she told us they've been having financial concerns with his upcoming retirement. When he realized the wife was singing like Ella Fitzgerald, he cracked. The evidence you and Robo found at the house helped a ton. Hard to deny cash and coke!" Stella's grin slipped as she sobered. "And the kid's ring—that was the most damning of all."

She paused, head lowered for a moment as if out of respect for Grace. Then she resumed her story, and her satisfaction with its outcome showed. "They both claim the missus is innocent of everything, and she seems to want to cooperate. I've still got to sort that out, but it looks like we won't be bringing charges against her. At least for now."

"Did he say why he killed Grace?"

"We figured it right. She walked up to the cabin and confronted them. So he made an excuse, went out to his car to get the gun, and shot her while she was standing there on the porch."

"And Belle?"

"He wanted to add her to the mule train. Mike got her from the car and force-fed her. By that time, Brennaman had loaded Grace up in her own car and driven out to bury her. While he was gone, Belle bit Mike and got away. When Brennaman got back to the cabin, they searched for her and got close enough for him to shoot her. After that, she disappeared, and they were forced to leave her up there."

"What about Mike Chadron?"

"He says Mike didn't want to use the dogs as mules anymore. Wanted to quit. He thought Mike planned to turn on him."

Mattie remembered Belle's loyalty. "We owe it to Belle for giving us such a good start on this case."

"Yeah, we do."

"Did you ask him if he tried to poison Robo?"

"Yep. He's the one. Said he wished he'd been able to get the job done. I bet he does, too, since you and Robo are the ones who took him down."

"What's going to happen to Tommy O'Malley?"

"That kid's rotten, Mattie."

"Yeah, maybe. But he's still just a kid."

"He says he was starting to sell for Brennaman right before Mike Chadron got shot. Then he got pulled in to be a runner. They switched their meeting place from the cabin to the mine after Grace got killed, so he and Brennaman would meet up there to transfer the drugs. Must be why Brennaman suggested he bring Sean there." She shrugged. "For now, he's cooperating, and he'll be a witness against Brennaman. We'll try to keep him in the juvenile system, but it'll be up to the prosecutor in the end."

Mattie nodded. There really wasn't anything else she could do for Tommy, and maybe some juvenile jail time and a good "scared straight" program would do him some good. Just as likely, though, was the possibility of him hooking up with a kid who was bigger and badder than he who would take him in the other direction. Either way, it would be out of her hands.

"I need to get home." Stella extended her hand. "We couldn't have closed this case without you, Mattie Cobb. It's been a pleasure working with you. I hope we won't be strangers when this is over."

Mattie shook Stella's hand. "We could never be that. Thanks for everything you've done to help."

"I'll be around for a while to wrap things up."

"I have a couple days off. Back on Friday."

Stella got into her car. "I'll see you then."

"Good-bye for now. Get some sleep."

Stella seemed to be searching her face. "Appears I could say the same to you."

Mattie stood by the door as Stella closed it and then stepped back and lifted her hand while she pulled out of the parking space and drove off.

I wonder if Stella could help me find my mother. A shiver passed through her.

She looked down at Robo. He was sitting beside her, deep-brown eyes raised to meet hers, his bandage stark white against his black head. She bent to ruffle the fur on his chest. When he leaned into her legs, she hugged him close and patted him on his side.

Maybe this world wasn't such an awful place after all. With Robo's help, she'd overcome her fear in the mine; with Stella's encouragement, she might reconnect with Willie and maybe her mom; and with Rainbow's enthusiastic persistence, she might even learn how to make friends. Who knew?

And what about the vet and his family? She hoped they could at least become friends. She didn't dare wish for more.

One thing she knew for certain—her future could be filled with anger and guilt about her past or she could suck it up and move on. Like her track coach used to say, you have to decide what you want and then make it happen.

"Let's call your doctor and give him a progress report," she said to Robo. "And then let's get our work done so we can go home."

With him dancing beside her, she turned back toward the office.

Acknowledgments

It takes the support and efforts of many to take a book from concept to substance, and I'm grateful to everyone who has helped me along the way. I want to acknowledge those who played the largest role in the following paragraphs.

I extend my sincere appreciation to the professionals who assisted me with research; any misinterpretation or fictional enhancement of the information these experts provided is mine alone. Retired K-9 Officer/Trainer Beth Gaede of the Bellingham Police Department let me shadow her while she gave tracking lessons to dogs and their owners. She captivated me with stories about the K-9 work she did with her late partner, the real Robo, and she set my imagination on fire. I sensed that theirs was a special bond, and I'm grateful to Beth for allowing me to borrow his name. Owner and operator of Fort Collins Protection Dogs and police chief of Nunn, Colorado, Joe Clingan gave my husband and me a copy of the K-9 training book that he authored, a resource I've used repeatedly, and invited me to watch him work with patrol dogs and their handlers. He led an impromptu discussion with those present regarding mistakes a rookie handler might make, and I'm grateful to these officers for their input. Senior Deputy Head

K-9 Trainer for Arapahoe County Sheriff's Office Gordon Carroll answered long lists of questions during his valuable time off, giving me specific details to weave into my story. My husband, Charles Mizushima, DVM, assisted me with many aspects of this story, including helping me make Cole Walker know what to do.

I owe a huge debt of gratitude to my agent, Terrie Wolf, for countless hours of work on my behalf and for her encouragement and support; to my editor, Nike Power, for her brilliant editorial skills, guidance, and unwavering attention to detail; and to the staff at Crooked Lane Books, for bringing this mystery to print. I'm fortunate and honored to have these professionals on my team.

Special thanks to my writing group members, past and present, who helped keep my words flowing through easy times and hard: Leslie Patterson, Linda Richter, Cynthia Slosson, Catherine Cole, Saytchyn Maddux-Creech, Caroline Marwitz, and Brian Winstead, all wonderful writers.

I offer a warm thank-you and hugs to my daughters, Sarah and Beth, for reading several drafts of this manuscript, providing input, and for cheering me on and to my sister, Nancy Coleman, for always being in my corner. Their continuous support means so much to me.

And finally, I want to thank my husband Charlie a second time, for standing beside me no matter what I decide to undertake. From our first date when we missed dinner to care for a pony that survived a pit bull attack to brainstorming crime fiction together at our kitchen table, it's been an adventure. For everything he does, I give him my gratitude with all my heart.